THE
DEATHLESS

FRANCES JUNE

ISBN: 9798702829616

Any references to historical events, real people, or real places are used fictitiously. Names, characters, and places are products of the author's imagination.

Front cover image by Samantha Cummings.
Typesetting by Ines Monnet.

First printing edition 2021.

www.samantha-cummings.com
samwrites@hotmail.com

CONTENT WARNING

Please be aware that this book contains topics such as:
Abuse, alcoholism, death, depression, mild drug use, eating disorder,
mental illness, suicide and trauma.

CHAPTER 1

It's finally time. The tables are set, the decorations laid out perfectly, the cake is iced and the guests are starting to arrive, which is why I'm hiding out under the curtained branches of the old willow tree at the bottom of the garden. The party was beginning to start; far away in the huge house hidden by the green and gauzy leaves. Watching the shadows play across my skin, chased away by the sunlight as it found a gap to spill through, I can hear music playing in the distance but the house is just a figment of my imagination for now.

To have grown up here would have been great, but I didn't. That's not to say I didn't spend a lot of time running in these gardens and sliding around on the marble floors in the kitchen, but this house could probably eat my house about twenty times over. Oh the joys of my childhood. I'm trying not to think about it because there was one thing I promised myself I wouldn't do today and that was cry; although it's probably one of the only moments in my life where it might be appropriate to cry, I won't.

A hand appeared from the abyss, breaking into the cocoon I'd created. The warmth of his skin touched my shoulder seconds before Rob sat down next to me, the epitome of sophistication, decked out in a suit. I rested my head against his shoulder, prompting him to reach his arm around me in an old familiar pose. He sighed into my hair.

"Amelia, this is going to be a great party..." There was no trace of his usual sarcasm which made my stomach flip. I inwardly cringed, hating him for the fact that he could be so nonchalant on a day like this.

"You have a sick sense of humour, old man." I replied, nudging him in the ribs with a playfulness I didn't really feel. He gasped as though I'd mortally wounded him. I closed my eyes and leaned into his shoulder to savour the soon-to-crash-and-burn normalcy. "I don't know if I'm ready to face a crowd, how are you holding up?" I distracted myself by watching the long branches twitch in the afternoon breeze.

I didn't have to look at him to know he was frowning. It was funny. He was so carefree normally that a frown from him could change the temperature in the air, it was like something in the cosmos shifted. *A glitch in the matrix,* the overused quote from the movie we watched over and over again sprang into my mind and I involuntarily smiled.

"I'm OK, considering." He said and just like that I could feel the air warm again like the frown never happened. He was good at that whole thing of covering up serious thoughts with a smile or a joke.

"Y'know, I think turning older is having a good effect on me. Eighteen... I'm finally an adult, I can do anything I want, go anywhere I want, there are no limits," the laughter was an empty echo compared to the real deal. He exhaled and nudged me gently, "Come on, open your eyes!"

I did as he asked and looked up at his face, all angelic as the mid-afternoon sun was shining behind him. A halo of light flickered around him.

"It's not funny Rob." I squeezed my eyes closed again, irritated at his humour. Trying not to think about what was going to happen once we finally went up to the house took all my concentration. We'd all celebrate, chat, and laugh over memories of the birthday boy. We'd cut the cake and blow out the candles and then I'd have to make the speech I promised Rob and his mother I'd make. That was where the fun ended, because me and public speaking were not the best of friends, and this situation was just unfair.

Despite his knowledge of my predisposed fears Rob had made me commit to it. He played the guilt card well, saying it would make his mum so proud and *happy*, but all I could think was I was going to make her cry and I was going to make myself cry in the process. Rewind to the promise I'd made myself earlier.

Now I just had to decide which promise I was going to break. Of course, I knew the answer. Sometimes I think my niceness is my worst quality. All I really had to be thankful for was the small miracle that my parents hadn't shown up today.

"Look, today will be over and done with soon enough," Rob said softly, though a small smile played on the edges of his lips which undid any genuine compassion, "And it's not like it's *your* birthday, so don't go panicking that everyone will be looking at you - let's face it, they're going to be looking at me – and, boy, are they gonna have it good. I've seen the pictures mum has put up around the house, and if I do say so myself, I'm quite photogenic!"

I couldn't help but laugh as he pretended to toss his hair over his shoulder. Though his smile didn't quite light up his eyes like it used to, it was enough to make me relax a little bit.

The branches of the tree danced in a breeze that drifted over the garden like warm breath. The sounds of the garden always took me back to days where we'd race around the grounds, hiding and climbing until the sun got tired of keeping watch. The leaves rubbing together always sounded like there was a chorus of tiny creatures laughing, even now I felt the urge to search for the figments of my imagination.

Childhood seemed like a figment in itself. The past month felt like ten years. School was officially over and all that was left was the great beyond. I swallowed the urge to collapse into a heap of sobs. Rob was right, it wasn't like *I* was getting older. I still had a whole eight months before I turned eighteen and was free and able to do all the things Rob had said. I'd finally be able to get the hell away from here and my family and this life and I could start over. *If only*, I thought to myself.

"Mmm can you smell that?" Rob said, cutting me off in my voiceless dreaming. I pushed the panic of the future down, noticing the tree also seemed to quieten to the smallest of a whisper. I could smell the grass; the purest scent of summer, but nothing else through my summer allergies.

"Your bloodhound nose is truly a thing of wonder." I said, giving him a shove with my elbow. Rob ardently sniffed again trying to catch more of it, like it was tangible, something he could catch as it flew past us.

"That is the sweet scent of carrot cake. Oh my god, I love Mum's carrot cake..." He said with a sigh. I noticed a shadow pass over his features, his green eyes looked darker than usual and the sight of it sent a shiver racing down my spine. Before I could ask him what was wrong he did that thing he always managed to do, which was ignore it. Barely a second later his usual lopsided smile was back. I tried to smile back but he saw right through it. He always did; noticing the concern that hid behind my forced nonchalance.

"Not as much as I love pizza though!" He said dredging up an age-old memory of eating way too many slices on a day just like this several years ago. A trace of worry lingered in the air but he didn't mention anything. He knew not to test me today, which was strangely observant of him.

Standing, he held out his hands and pulled me to my feet. He yanked my hand so forcefully I left the ground in a shoulder ripping leap, having to grab onto him to stop from falling back down.

"Rob!"

My hands gripped his shoulders tightly. His face was pressed to the side of my head and I could feel his breathy laugh against my scalp.

Pulling myself away from him with a jerk I couldn't help but admire how handsome he looked in his smart clothes. His sandy blonde hair fell into his eyes which were wide with fake innocence.

"Well, look at you!" He said, like he hadn't seen me in years which was an ongoing charade of his. He spun me around on the spot like a dancer, only with little to no grace.

The dress I was wearing fluttered out around my legs like deep blue petals caught in the wind. The air on my legs made me feel self-conscious and I felt my cheeks warm. Even though it stopped just below the knee, classy if you asked me, I still felt exposed like when you left the house without your phone. The material clung to my top, flatteringly, which Rob wiggled his eyebrows at playfully.

Rob's mum, Florence, had bought it for me and it was probably the nicest thing I've ever owned. She owned more dresses than I could dream of owning in a lifetime because she wanted to wear them 'whilst she still could', which was plain crazy. She was barely 50 and looked like just like she did in the pictures she brought out when she was in one of her 'cataloguing' moods, minus the flared trousers and flowery 70's shirts. The fact that she'd had 3 kids and still looked so good was something most women bitched about, including *my* mother.

"Don't do that you pervert." I said at his expression, covering my chest with one hand as I bent to smooth out the skirt of the dress with the other. My heels were sinking into the soft grass, but I didn't mind so much; it was easier to stand up.

"Hey, I can't help it! Don't wear such things if you don't want that kind of reaction. Besides, don't you think it's a little inappropriate for such an event?" He raised his eyebrows again, a smile forming on his lips. It took a lot of self-control not to verbally accost him for perpetrating the idea that a girl is merely an object to be looked at. The fact that I knew he was trying to get to me meant he only got a quiet 'humph'.

"Like you said, it's a party," I said, side stepping his comments. "What? Did you want me to dig out my black veil?"

I pulled my heels out of the ground and carefully walked to the tree's trunk, trailing my fingers along the grain as I circled around to the swing that was tied to one of the thicker branches under the canopy. Rob's dad had made it for us when we were kids and though it was old, and slightly rotten, the rope was still strong and I sank onto the seat, feeling the branch dip a bit under my weight.

Rob followed, as ever. I felt his presence behind me as he pushed me gently, his hands soft as they pressed into my back as I returned to him again and again. I let my legs dangle and leaned back slightly to give myself momentum, auburn hair flying in loose curls behind me.

"You know I'm joking Melia, I like it," Rob said. When I didn't reply he laughed. "The dress. I like the dress."

"Oh, thanks." I said, glad he couldn't see my face and the reaction the comment had.

The conversation was taking a turn to the uncomfortable. We had always had a strange relationship according to our friends. We were friends, nothing more, but sometimes I wondered if he felt more. Sometimes I thought *I* did but I buried it down in the deep cavern in my mind where I kept all thoughts that I couldn't dwell on.

With nothing but the fear of the unknown churning in my mind again I continued to swing, before slowing and dragging my heels when I heard someone shouting across the garden.

"Mummy's calling!" he said in a sing-song voice. I tried to block out the sound of his mother's voice as it carried across the garden, putting up an invisible barrier between me and the outside world, but all that did was make me painfully aware of the sound of my heart pounding with anxiety. My stomach was in knots.

"She'll send backup if you don't answer her," Rob's voice whispered in my ear. I stopped swinging, letting my body twist side to side so the ropes above my head coiled and uncoiled.

Rob shrugged his shoulders and rested his back against the trunk of the tree. Little wood chips dusted the back of his suit jacket, but he didn't care.

"And here they come." Rob said. I glanced over my shoulder to see his brothers making their way towards us. Both were tall and athletically built, a stark contrast to Rob's wiry frame. Their mother had obviously sent them to retrieve us so this whole charade could begin. I inwardly cringed but didn't move, waiting for them to reach me.

"Getting closer... closer... It's not too late to run..." Rob said, smiling and apparently taking great pleasure in my agony.

After what seemed like an eternity the two brothers came to a stop about four meters away from me, as though they couldn't penetrate the invisible barrier I had built under this tree.

"Mum said you had to come in now." Mark said. He was the younger of the two by about 30 seconds. Rob's brothers were pretty much famous in town for being the 'hot identical twins', a lot of girls didn't even care that Mark wasn't really the nicest guy in the world. Even now, his tone was so automated that he sounded a little bit like a robot. A really grumpy robot.

As soon as he had delivered his clipped message he turned on his heel and sulked back up the garden. His shoulders slumped uncharacteristically as he shoved his hands in his pockets like Rob often did. The other twin, Dean, stayed. His eyes followed Mark as he walked away.

"Sorry about him," He said, chewing his bottom lip as he watched Mark disappear back into the house. "He's not doing so well today... Dad, y'know?" He said as he turned his attention to me. His face was ashen but he mustered a smile that made my lungs inflate like bubbles and churn like the sea before a storm.

"Getting nervous?" He asked. Rob laughed under his breath and I shot him a warning look which wiped the smile off his face.

"I'm... OK," I said, smoothing the skirt of my dress which had ridden up past my knees. "Trying to not to think about it. How about you?"

Dean took Rob's place, gently pushed me on the swing. He was probably just to keep his hands busy and his mind off other things but there was a feeling of purpose behind his movements. Though he used the ropes to swing me, rather than putting his hands on my back, the ocean inside my bubble-lungs roared to life, giving me goose bumps.

"Better than expected," He said, exhaling like he'd been holding his breath for too long. "Mark's a mess but won't admit it, Mum and Dad are powering through…"

"And you?" I asked, staring at a spot on the horizon but not really seeing it.

"I'm just trying to keep it together." He said quietly.

The silence engulfed us but it was comfortable, like we both needed it.

Rob coughed.

"I'm still here y'know?" He waved from where he was still leaning against the trunk. For the briefest of moments I'd actually forgotten he *was* there and my stomach twisted into the biggest knot imaginable.

I sighed and planted my feet on the ground, scuppering to a stop. Dean dropped his hands as soon as I'd regained control of my movements.

"Right, yeah, Mum said she wanted us inside in five minutes for the cake and everything, shall we?"

We walked up the garden towards the house. I imagined the bubbles I'd created shatter. The reflective fragments littered the grass and sparkled in the sunlight and as I treaded over them I imagined they were all my happy memories, left out here to melt.

"Too bad, Amelia, wish we could have played on the swing all day." Rob said from behind me. His voice sounded like a hollow echo like he was a million miles away, rather than just a few steps.

I found myself trailing a step behind Dean with Rob by my side. It didn't feel right to walk right next to him anyway but I could see him glance around a fraction just to check I was still there.

Rob was uncharacteristically quiet, his hands dug deep into his pockets. I frowned at him, not needing to use words to convey my concern. He was looking up towards the house, his eyebrows dipped deeply like lost in a memory. If it had been a different day, maybe even a few months ago, I would have laughed at him for looking so serious but not today.

The house appeared as we rounded a large flowery bush. The music and chatter from inside poured out from the open windows as though it couldn't contain the sounds.

If it were up to me we wouldn't go in there; we'd walk straight past the kitchen's French doors and we wouldn't stop until we hit unoccupied countryside. I was almost to the point where I had to make that decision but fate took it from me, wagging a finger at my petulance.

Florence opened the door as we approached and smiled broadly. She kissed Dean, just a quick peck on the cheek, and reached for his hands.

"Do me a favour and check on your father for me," She said quickly. I noticed her squeeze his hands before he nodded to do her bidding. "Before he drinks us dry," she said, and we both watched as he left to put out a small fire that had the potential to turn into a raging inferno.

Before I knew it she pulled me into a tight embrace. Her arms wrapped around my arms, pinning them to my sides.

"Amelia, you look so beautiful!" She said, releasing me to tuck some of my hair behind my ear. She smiled at me as she took in my appearance, wearing the dress she'd picked out. Though she smiled her eyes glistened with tears she tried to hold back.

"Thanks Mrs Wood." I said, looking to Rob for help. I was fully expecting the next few hours to be full of teary eyes and lingering looks but the reality of it was worse than anything I could have imagined.

Rob ignored his mother's emotional fragility, either that or he was simply unaware of it. He milled around the kitchen, poking at the different plates of food that were strewn on every surface like the backstage area of the Mad Hatters tea party.

"You don't have to tell me I look beautiful Mum, I already know it to be true."

He didn't look up from the food selection as he spoke. Florence tutted and shook her head gesturing to my feet and ignoring Rob's comment.

"Look at this, mud on your heels! See if you can knock it off at the door," She pushed me back towards the French doors gently and started to fuss over a giant cake on a cake platter. "I'll be back in a moment so don't run away, I'll need your help with this."

I watched helplessly as she left the room, clip clopping in her peach heels and matching peach skirt suit. Her light blonde curls bounced as she tottered out to tend to her guests like a professional hostess.

Don't run away, she'd said. Like she knew it was the only thought pressing on my mind like a bird trying to escape its cage.

"Look at all of this!" Rob waved his hand around grinning. "All my favourite foods in one place. Celery and peanut butter, mini pizzas with ham and pineapple, chocolate covered pretzels, onion bhaji, skittles. Best party ever, eh?" He winked at me and I cringed.

"A. don't do that, and 2. How can you think it's anything other than miserable?" I took my shoes off, tapping the mud off the heels. Rob continued to pick at the food though he didn't eat any of it. The room grew colder, or so it seemed to me. I half expected him to agree with me but the other half won out.

"All my friends and family in one place, all the best food in the same room, you wearing that dress... What's not to like? Plus, look how happy it's making Mum..." He picked up a celery stick and waved it at me like it was a wand.

"If you think your mum is happy you've lost your mind." I continued to knock my shoes together, even though I was pretty sure all the mud and grass was now off them.

"Trust me, she's happy, she's planning stuff and entertaining. She needed this to keep her mind off... other things. If she's not crying, she's pretty much as happy as she's gonna get right now." He bit his lip, hesitant to say more. I smiled meekly at him, still knocking my shoes together just for something to do.

I knew he was right. After recent events Mrs Wood had been a wreck, if she wasn't constantly crying it was because she'd exhausted herself and fallen asleep. The fact that she was now chatting to people in the living room and handing out skittles from a bowl was a good sign.

Still, this whole party ordeal seemed unnecessary to me. Nobody wanted it, least of all Rob no matter how much he feigned interest in it. I had been sensing his growing trepidation in the days leading up to this day. He didn't know how I watched him when he was distracted with something else. I could almost see the thoughts running through his mind like cartoon thought bubbles; he was praying for a miracle, a way out of this mess, but it never came. He wasn't as good at hiding his torment as he thought he was.

My stomach growled and I contemplated grabbing a mini pizza but I didn't have time. Florence whipped into the room with a bowl that was still mostly full with skittles. It looked like people didn't like to eat sweets whilst they were trying to dine on the most random selection of Rob's favourite foods. She placed the bowl on the worktop next to Rob who looked at them but didn't eat any either.

"The red ones are the best." He said to himself. The way it sounded like a reminder rather than an affirmation made me hate this day even more.

"I think we're ready for the cake Amelia..." Florence said sitting at the breakfast bar. For the first time in my life I thought she looked old. Or at least, older. Putting my arms around her I gave her a gentle squeeze.

"The cake looks amazing." I said. It was a distraction technique but it worked. She stood up, straightened herself out and smiled at me again, her show-face back on like a well painted mask.

"Doesn't it? Three-tiered double chocolate with raspberry sauce," She smiled as we regarded the dark chocolate monstrosity before us. The red sauce spiralled around the top like a spider's web and the side dripped with glossy red tears. "I don't know where Rob got his taste from, it certainly wasn't me. I almost picked out a lovely fruit cake with royal icing but Andrew thought it was too much like a wedding cake." She sighed, folding and un-folding a napkin. Rob snorted with laughter from where he sat.

"Even if I was getting married I would *never* have fruit cake!" He stuck his tongue out and grimaced. I couldn't help but laugh at his reaction.

"He's right, of course. Chocolate, chocolate, chocolate. Rob's entire world!" She offered me a genuine smile and I returned it. She *was* right, Rob was like a teenage girl when it came to chocolate, he couldn't get enough.

"I resent that Mother, chocolate is but one element of my world... OK, maybe a large part, but still..." Rob jumped down from the counter with the grace only a boy could muster. He whistled low as he peered into the living room. "Big turnout, Melia, you think you can handle this?"

He was pushing the door open slightly, peeking through like a naughty child spying on his parents on Christmas Eve. I ignored him as best I could.

"Well, what do you say we get this party started?" Mrs Wood asked, immediately frowning at her own words. "Oh, I don't think I can pull that sentence off, can I?" Her face lit up in faux embarrassment as she laughed.

"Of course you can, and yes, let's get this party started!" I picked up the cake and followed Florence and Rob out of the safety of the kitchen. My stomach dropped to the ground and remained on the floor behind me as I entered the packed living room.

Friends lined the outer edges of the room, huddled together protectively. No doubt feeling overwhelmed by the presence of the well-dressed; Rob's family. I was the only one who looked more like a family member but it was only because of Mrs Wood's love of charity work.

She was no snob but that didn't mean the rest of her family weren't just a little bit class-conscious. Money still leaked out from some old family crypt, paying dividends to those still living with the family name. Something to do with their great-grandfather inventing something that went into cars to make them more fuel efficient. She was probably trying to save me the embarrassment of having to stand up in front of them all dressed like some sort of pauper girl, or at least that's what I would have looked like had I worn something from my own closet.

I walked across the room keeping my gaze down. I pretended not to feel my friend's gazes on the back of my head. Since school had ended I hadn't been the greatest friend, I'd pulled back from them all and after a few weeks of missed phone calls they'd gotten the picture and backed off. Still, they were here today. I had thought seeing them would make me feel better, like things had gone back to normal, but I couldn't have been more wrong. Resentment pulled at my heart mercilessly.

With the cake to focus on I sailed through the room on Florence's heels. The chandelier that hung above rattled as I passed underneath and I momentarily flashed back to the day me and Rob planned on swinging on it. Of course, we never actually did it. Once we were tall enough to try we realised how much trouble it would cause; the story of our youth, really.

I mustered up a smile for the family members I recognised, quickly glancing at Dean who was leaning against the far wall. He smiled back and then nudged Mark who was sitting on a chair next to him. Mark didn't smile at me, his face resting in its permanent scowl as he said something to Dean before downing the drink in his hand.

It was then that I noticed Mr Wood sitting next to Mark. He also had a small tumbler glass which was filled with a dark brown liquid. Obviously booze. Unfortunately, he tended to drink when he was upset, something I hadn't witnessed many times, but of the times I had seen it I had worried. He was a big man, with a big temper. Not to be confused with violence, he was just loud and opinionated. His strong-willed parenting style had made it difficult for him and Rob to form the same closeness he had with the twins. Rob was too much of a fly-away; a joker with a lack of respect for *any* authority. Mr Wood had never hidden his annoyance at this.

In the blink of an eye Mrs Wood had roused her husband from his perch, they came and stood on either side of me, Florence clearing her throat and signalling the start of the horror that I had been dreading for a week.

The room, which had been buzzing at a soft level with people talking and quietly laughing suddenly became very silent and still. Mr Wood put his hand on my shoulder in his own quiet way of telling me he understood my hesitation. Mrs Wood, on the other hand, didn't bother trying to make me feel better, I think she wanted this out of the way as much as I did.

She began thanking everyone for coming but the rest of her words were drowned out by the loud thumping that filled my ears.

She lit candles on the cake and it was only then I realised she had stopped talking and everyone was now looking at me expectantly. From the corner of the room I could see Dean and Mark watching me, Dean's face was open and encouraging, whereas Mark was staring at me without any visible emotion.

And then there was Rob. Rob standing at the back of the room from where I was, back towards the kitchen sandwiched between some distant relatives. He grinned and gave me the thumbs up.

"Amelia?" Mrs Wood took my hand gently which brought me back. I tore my eyes away from Rob's smiling face. "Are you OK to give the speech?"

"Um, yeah, OK…" I tucked my hair behind my ears nervously and spoke to the crowd, making sure I kept my eyes away from Rob.

As I began to speak I could feel everyone's attention on me, feel their gazes burning my skin like drops of acid rain.

"It's kind of hard to talk about Rob getting older," I paused to take a breath. I could feel the colour warming on my cheeks but knowing I had no way of escape I pushed on whilst trying pretend I was just rehearsing. "Mostly because it means I have to think about getting older myself, and all of our friends getting older and the thought of us all being considered 'adults' is a terrifying concept." I made air quotes and heard a few sniggers from the outskirts of the room. My muscles relaxed just a little as Mr Wood let out an exhaled laugh as well.

"I remember last year we were talking about what we were going to do for our eighteenth birthdays. Rob really wanted to go skydiving…" I shook my head and looked over towards him, not able to stop the smile creeping onto my face. "I told him I wasn't doing it with him because it's just insane."

"I still think it would have been a great idea." Rob said, shrugging and tucking his hands into his pockets.

"He then told me," I continued, pretending he hadn't interrupted, "if I wasn't willing to live a little he wasn't willing to attend *my* party. Which was nice of him, so thanks for that understanding Rob." The room laughed again but it didn't make me feel that warmth that usually followed laughter. "Anyway, he'd planned on skydiving into a huge birthday party, which was outdoors. He said he wanted to land on an elephant's back - I don't know what he was thinking, I'm sure he came up with things like that just to wind us all up!"

Mr Wood snorted and sipped his drink, muttering something under his breath which Mrs Wood shushed him for.

"It's like he knew he'd never have to go through with it…" I said, the gravity of my words created a silence like a vacuum in space. I stopped for a moment, the words I'd written hit me hard, like I'd never even really considered what they'd meant.

"This is definitely the kind of thing he would have really liked…" I said, turning to Mrs Wood as a tear slid down her cheek. Mr Wood reached over to her to hold her hand and I looked away, to my shoes which were pinching my feet. I focused on the pain and closed my eyes, squeezing them shut as hard as I could. When I opened my eyes Rob had moved closer and was looking at me, a small frown creased the skin between his eyebrows.

"I've never known anyone like him," I forced a smile which instantly had Rob smiling again. He was easy to please like that, or maybe he was trying to please me. "Never felt so accepted by someone. He's one of those guys everyone wishes they knew and everyone who knew him loved. I mean, how couldn't you?" I heard a girl sniff in the back, without looking I knew it was Sara Weiss, a girl from school who'd always had a thing for Rob.

"He was my best friend," I carried on, a little louder, blocking out Sara's bid for attention, "and I'm glad you're all here to wish him Happy Birthday. So, Happy Birthday Rob."

Everyone raised their glasses and repeated the 'happy birthday', some were more enthusiastic than others.

I locked eyes with Rob and smiled, though I felt like it might have been the saddest smile in the world. A tear formed in the corner of my eye, which I quickly rubbed away.

"I miss you." I said, ending my speech for the birthday boy. My eulogy.

CHAPTER 2

Rob stood motionless, surrounded by friends and family yet I was the only one who was staring back at him. The room, which had seemed to be holding its breath, suddenly started to respire again. People started talking amongst themselves very quietly; probably judging my mishmash shambles of a speech.

Mrs Wood sniffed behind me and I turned to see her patting away silent tears whilst Mr Wood rubbed her back with the heavy-handed comfort of a man who was teetering on the edges of drunk.

I caught Dean looking at me, his face creased with concern. Just as he looked like he was about to say something, his mouth parting just slightly, he seemed to realise he was too far away so he turned to Mark, leaning into his brothers ear to say something. Whatever he'd said seemed to push Mark over his good-behaviour level though because he sank the drink he was holding and walked out of the room.

No one else seemed to notice his departure but I could feel the tendrils of torment and stress that he left in his wake. The mood in the room was already weighing me down like a cast iron anchor so I was happy when Mrs Wood broke through the wall of depression that was piling up around me.

"Right, who wants cake? Amelia?" I turned at the sound of Mrs Wood's voice. She offered me a slice of thick chocolate gloop which she expertly slid onto a paper plate.

"Thanks. Hope you don't mind, I might take this outside? I think I need some fresh air…" I took a deep breath and closed my eyes. I wasn't lying, the tension that had built up from the speech had faded and I was woozy with a strange sense of both relief and heartbreak.

Mrs Wood nodded at me and rubbed my arm delicately. I took the plate with the cake, the paper weighed down in the middle, and tried to make my way back to the kitchen with as little fuss as possible.

Rob was tucked right into the centre of the room, taking full advantage of his new ghostly form by listening in to everyone's conversations. His current target looks to be the tall stern looking man who is wearing a dark blue suit with a crisp white shirt. One of his estranged uncles.

I managed to reach the kitchen door with minimal fuss. It seemed people wanted to tell me I'd done a good job but they didn't want to engage in a full-blown conversation, thinking it kinder to leave the poor grieving best friend alone. At least, that's what I told myself. When I saw Sara weave through the crowd I ducked through the door as quickly as my cake bearing legs would carry me.

I pretty much ran the last few steps to the back door, kicking off my heels before my feet sank into the soft grass. I sighed audibly at the relief.

When I reached the sloping hill that led down to the rest of the garden and I sat down. I let my legs stretch out in front of me as I gulped in the fresh air, placing the plate of cake down next to me. Even looking at it made me feel sick.

I sat alone for a few minutes, letting my mind wander freely. I almost jumped out of my skin at the interruption that came from a voice behind me.

"Can I sit down?"

Squinting up I saw it was Dean holding a plate of party food. I nodded and he sank to the ground handing me the platter of assorted snacks.

"You haven't eaten anything, so I nabbed you some of the more edible food," He gestured to the plate casually as I took it and pretended I didn't notice how his eyebrows dipped at the sight of my untouched cake.

"I'm just not feeling very hungry right now…" I said, but I picked at some of the skittles that were scattered amid the food anyway, popping a couple of red ones into my mouth and sucking them. Dean picked one too and popped it into his mouth leaving a hanging silence between us for a couple of seconds that were both blissful and torturous.

"Shoes giving you a hard time?" He asked, smirking as he gestured towards my bare feet.

I immediately felt self-conscious and pulled my feet up towards me, puzzled he'd even noticed them at all.

"No!" I said, embarrassed at the thought of him thinking I couldn't walk in heels. I felt the blush creep across my cheeks but there was a numbness to it, like I was watching someone else blush. "I took them off so I could escape faster, but I guess I didn't get very far." I glanced around the garden, looking for signs of Rob. It wasn't usual for him to be out of my sight for so long, at least not recently, and his absence felt like a crushing weight on my chest.

"What are you doing out here anyway?" I asked whilst trying to breathe like a regular human being.

"I came looking for you - just wanted to check you were OK." He paused for a moment like he didn't want to break the illusion of the party but he did. "That was a good speech, Rob would have loved it." Five words and he'd turned this party into a wake again, like either of us needed reminding. Like either of us could stop dredging up memories of his brother that wouldn't be kept away today.

It was tough, ever since Rob had died, almost a month ago, the memories of him were all around the house, but people were avoiding looking at them in any detail. You could almost see them floating around like soapy bubbles; fuzzy and distorted images that his family were batting away, or walking through to get to the next room and away from anything that might make them think of him.

"Yeah, I'm sure he would have just *adored* the way I humiliated myself, I can just see him laughing and giving me the thumbs up..." I trailed off. It was hard being the only person who could see Rob as a ghost. Apart from the obvious drawbacks of people classing me as clinically insane and the white vans coming to take me away it would be great to be able to share a laugh with someone about how Rob was still a pain in the ass even in death, but I just couldn't take that risk. For now, I had to deal with the fact that to the others I was laughing on my own, and I just had to try to hide it.

"How's your mum doing?" I twisted my hair around and around until it was a tightly coiled bun at the back of my head before letting it loose and letting the curls fall back around my face. Dean sighed and stretched his legs out in front of him looking both relaxed and stressed all at once.

"Doing better than expected I guess. To be honest I thought she would be a mess today but she's not. I suppose it's kind of like closure, you know?" I nodded not wanting to interrupt. "Have you seen Mark by the way?" He wiped his hands on his trousers as he changed the subject, no longer trying to remain smart now the formalities were out of the way.

"No, not since he left the living room, why?" I tried to act like it was no big deal but I was more worried for Mark than I let on.

"Just worried about him," He said, standing up and looking out across the garden. He dug his hands into his pockets and shrugged in a very Rob-like manner. "He didn't want to go through with this whole party thing, but tried for mum and dad's sake. He's not good with dealing with his emotions which I'm sure you're well aware of..." He looked concerned and sad, which was understandable. Dean always took care of everyone else and make sure they were fine but to do that he often pushed his own problems to the back of his mind. Today was taking its toll on him but he seemed determined not to let anyone know it.

"Want me to help you find him?" I asked, knowing the answer before he gave it but I asked anyway, a strange yearning crept up my spine which I put down to restlessness and the need to escape.

"Nah, it's OK. I don't think you should be around him when he's like this, for your own sake."

"Yes, his hatred of me is quite potent today isn't it?" I quipped, trying to avoid his foot as he playfully nudged my hip.

"Don't be stupid, he doesn't hate you, he just sees you as an annoying little sister... I think he just finds it hard being around you at the moment. You and Rob are pretty much considered the same person and I don't think he can separate you."

I bit my lip and felt guilty for a million and one reasons, but none of which I could pinpoint. Dean and Mark were the closest thing I had to Rob, in this world anyway. If Mark couldn't stand to be around me I couldn't help but wonder if Dean would always see me as this shadow of his dead brother as well.

"Very insightful." I said quietly, trying to push down the rage that bubbled under the surface. I was thankful for the distraction of Rob finally re-appearing. He sat down next to me and started picking at the leftover food on the plate.

My chest felt light again, the closeness of Rob eased the anxiety; the tightly spun coil that now resided in my soul and wound even tighter with every passing day, but the guilt of Dean's grief rolled over me like a tidal wave. I was a liar, talking like I could ever understand how he and his family were feeling when I still had Rob.

I stood up suddenly, before I even knew what I was doing.

"I think I'm just going to go for a walk and clear my head," I was hesitant in my escape from Dean, torn between my enjoyment of his company and my need to find out why Rob was giving me *that* look from where he was still sat, looking between me and Dean like he was watching a tennis match. "If I see Mark I'll try to herd him back towards the house. Maybe I'll poke him with a stick... a really long stick." I feigned looking around for one. Dean laughed and put his arm around me gently.

"OK, but be back in before it gets dark. Mum's going to kick everyone out in the next hour or so and we're going to have some drinks without all the circus. You should stay over tonight - I know mum wouldn't mind." His face was full of genuine concern which only made me hate myself even more. I put my arm around his waist, something I hadn't done since we were much younger. In fact, I don't think Dean had hugged me in over five years except for at the funeral but that was different. Rob was now eyeing me gleefully, looking happier than I'd seen him in a very long time.

"No, it's OK, I should head home later, if I stay out of the house longer than a few days mum changes the locks..." I half joked, wishing I didn't have to fake the smile. "But I'll come in for drinks in a bit. I'll help clear things up."

He nodded, dark hair catching the rays of the dying sunlight, and left me to go looking for Mark. Before Rob could even say a word I walked away from him, down the slope and back towards the gardens.

"Amelia!" He called, voice raised loud as he trailed behind me. He didn't have to worry about being too loud and now that we were alone I didn't have to worry about looking like a crazy person.

A grin spread over my face a second before I started running. I ran past the willow tree we were sat under earlier and towards the small pond that lay hidden between strong smelling bushes that flowered pink buds; the smell of my childhood.

I stopped, gasping for breath, and threw myself onto the mossy ground in their shade. Rob merely walked over to where I was, not even a little bit breathless. It must have been some sort of ghostly power. Damn him.

He dropped to the ground and lay down next to me, reaching over and holding my hand, which I could feel. We didn't know what the rules were for his being here but I could certainly touch him but he couldn't walk through walls, though it wasn't for lack of trying. We were silent for a few minutes, just staring up at the darkening sky, inhaling the warm but damp summer air.

"Amelia?" He whispered. I turned my head to look at him, letting my hair fall around me in a tumble of curls.

"Yeah?"

He didn't look at me as he spoke so I looked away too. I had a feeling he was about to be serious and I didn't want to ruin the moment by accidentally laughing in his face.

He was quiet for a while again and when he spoke his voice was soft and delicate; something it had never been in life, once again reminding me of the situation we were in. It was strangely easy to forget your best friend was dead when he was haunting your every waking moment. Easy and comforting.

"I really liked your speech... you know, considering..." He turned to me finally and smiled such a small smile and my heart almost broke again. The first time being on the day I found out he had died.

I had been at work, serving tables at a big restaurant called Blue. We were pre-dominantly a seafood restaurant and I often went home stinking to high heaven of baked sea bass. I hate it there, but the tips are great.

It was vaguely busy that day, with people coming in droves and then leaving all at once – it was like they were coming in on the tide, eating all the fish they could and then leaving when the tide rolled back out. I was taking an order at a table and I remember looking out of the window and thinking it was such a beautiful day and I was wondered what Rob was doing whilst I was slaving away.

He didn't work because he didn't need the money. Well, that was a lie. He kind of worked as he took photographs for the local newspaper, but that was more because one of his dad's friends ran the newspaper and Mr. Wood thought he was doing Rob a favour by getting him the job – a bid in closing the gap between them. Rob took the job as a favour to his father – a bid to make him happy so he would stay off his back. It was a win-win situation bar the fact that neither of them was very happy. Mr Wood wanted his son to be less of an 'arty kid' and more of a serious athlete with an eye for finances. Rob hated the job because it 'cramped his style' – he liked wildlife photography and the more artistic views through the lens. His dad didn't really see the difference between National Geographic and Local News.

The call had come whilst I was thinking about Rob – I heard someone in the kitchen call me and I assumed it was him – not the first time for me to be thinking about him just when he called. I was planning on what I was going to say to him. I told him every time he called that he couldn't call me at work, but it had always been an emergency with him. There were some tickets on sale and he wanted to check I could go. Or there was a movie marathon on and he wanted me to pick up snacks on the way over. He drove me insane sometimes.

I could tell this time was different though, as I headed into the back to the wall where the phone was mounted. Tony, the manager, was holding the phone with one of his hands covering the mouthpiece. He looked pale and I was instantly worried. He handed me the phone and I felt the tiny stars burst into my view before I saw them. That moment of panic that numbs you before you know what it is you're panicking about. I put the phone up to my ear and Tony walked away to lean on the chopping table. I remember watching his elbows sink into the chopped parsley wondering what he was doing. About to wave at him to move. That's when I heard Mrs Wood's hollow voice on the phone.

CHAPTER 3

The memory of The Day was constant in my mind, but the more time Rob and I spent together the more it felt like a dream; the edges blurred with every passing day. We lay on the grass by the pond and stared up at the darkening sky, talking quietly when we had to, but not really making any other noise.

I knew this was hard for Rob, I'd seen his face when his mother had broken down in tears when she accidentally broke a vase on the day of the funeral. Seen his face when his dad had yelled at someone on the phone and then threw the handset across the room. It hurt him but, Rob being Rob, he looked on the bright side and pretended he didn't see the dark cloud that his ghost cast. In his mind he could help his parents get over this, or rather I could on his behalf.

It was a little bit stressful but then I was always stressed these days.

Rob's hand reached over and played with the hem of my dress. I knocked it away and scowled at the early evening sky. The brightest stars shimmered and sparkled in good humour. I wish they would tell me what was going on, but they were ever silent. His hand moved to my hem again and he placed his forefinger on my knee and drew circles. He sighed and looked over at me.

"I'm glad I can feel things." His voice floated towards me as it often did. His solitude was so apparent it hurt my heart to think about everything that was going on.

"Corporeal." I interjected, putting my hands behind my head and watching a plane pass over. I imagined I was actually looking down and it was really a ship sailing in a dark ocean, rich and blue. The ruby coloured lights that flashed remained in my vision even when I closed my eyes. Rob continued to trace circles and he hummed some tune but I couldn't tell what it was.

"It's getting late - think I should head in. You coming?" I sat up leaning back on my hands, forcing him to stop tickling my skin.

"Of course my darling, where you go, I go, remember?" He scrambled to his feet and helped me to mine.

That was true, or partly. We weren't really sure of the ghostly rules so we generally stuck together just in case he ceased to exist outside of my general vicinity. We didn't get a Handbook for the Recently Deceased like in the movie Beetlejuice.

The early evening was full of the sounds of summer. The birds had started their calls, possibly calling the younger ones back home before the cats started to prowl the garden. The trees all hummed and swished with the breeze. It was peaceful enough until one bush in particular sounded like it was caving in on itself.

"What was that?" Rob said, fear tinged his voice.

"Relax, you big baby, it's not like you can die again."

I couldn't stop the joke from coming out of my mouth and I cringed, thankful Rob just rolled his eyes. It was a good job his feelings couldn't get hurt. Or at least they couldn't anymore.

The bushes in question gave another shudder and I took a step in front of Rob, pointlessly shielding him from view. Something large and human shaped was wedged in the branches. It was a holly bush so unfortunately, for whomever it was, they were likely to be sore. Just on cue we heard the voice.

"Shit. Ow, shit!" It was a gruff voice we both knew well. Mark protruded from the bushes, bursting forth like a deer spooked by hunters, though more human shaped than Bambi, and built like a rugby player. He stumbled towards the pond and stopped himself just before he hit the shallow, murky, water. Staggering he stood and ambled towards us, or rather, me.

"Mark, what are you doing?" I caught him as he lurched forwards, my hands hitting his hard muscles and what felt like a hip flask in his jacket pocket. He was obviously very, very drunk, which was unlike him. He hardly ever drank, so this was new for all of us.

Mark saw himself as a serious athlete, despite the fact that he only played Rugby locally and had no actual intention of ever trying to go pro. His rules were no alcohol or junk food, yet he failed more on the second part of those rules than the first. I'd never seen him drink, so I was a little out of my depth.

"Taking a... walk..." He slurred at me, as I helped him steady himself. When I was sure he seemed firm on his feet I let go of him.

I looked over to the bushes he had fallen in and doubted he'd walked far after drinking. Farther up the garden was a tree with a tree-house type platform perched in its ancient knotted branches and I assumed that's where he had vanished to. I inwardly winced at the thought of him falling out to get back to the ground.

"Oh, Mark..." I watched him sway as he watched ripples scatter across the surface of the pond, transfixed. He wasn't totally out of it but he was quite far gone. Rob could only stare.

"I've never seen him drunk, this is hilarious, if not a little sad. Honestly, I'm touched. My death caused him to break his rituals...who knew he cared so much?"

"Of course he cares." I said, but Rob either didn't hear me or pretended not to. Anger welled up inside me but with nowhere to put it I shoved it down and did what I did best; managed.

Rob has begun poking poor drunken Mark, causing him to sway more than perhaps he would have done in this state. I couldn't tell him to stop so I tried to discreetly push Rob's tormenting hands away.

"Damn wasps!" I said, trying to cover my actions even though Mark didn't notice anything out of the ordinary.

I stared meaningfully at the younger brother of this hulking wreck of a man which did the trick. Rob stopped knowing I'd only punish him later somehow. Mostly my punishments consisted of my ignoring him, which he hated.

"No, no, no, I think you've had enough of that," I said, grabbing the hip flask Mark had fished from his pocket out of his clammy hands. Thankfully his reactions were slow or I'd never have been able to grab anything off him; he was normally too fast. He grumbled and put his arm around me.

"You're like my sister Melia," Mark started but I shushed him immediately. A heart to heart was not what we needed right now.

"A little help here." I whispered to Rob who immediately slipped himself under Mark's other arm.

"Are we going inside?" Mark seemed to be getting sleepy as we stood and 'talked' and thankfully, due to his state, Rob was able to help without Mark even realising he was being grappled by the spirit of his younger brother.

"Yes, come on, let's get you to bed. But be quiet, OK? I don't want your parents to see you like this."

I had a feeling if they saw him they would be upset, but I knew for a fact that it would be Mark who would be the most upset tomorrow when the humiliation set in. I didn't want him to have to live through the shame of getting drunk like this. Alone and depressed. I blinked back the sting of unwanted tears.

Rob helped as we stumbled and dragged and pushed at the bulk we carried until we got him back to the house.

"We needed to get him inside before someone comes looking for us," I gasped, out of breath from directing the staggering man.

"The mud room?" Rob suggested as we made a bee line for the room with the washing machine. He wasn't out of breath at all, making it look all too easy like he did with everything.

They called it a 'mud room', which to me was ridiculous because you actually weren't allowed in there if you were covered in mud; something Rob and I had learned a long time ago.

"Here, hold him..." I pushed all of Mark's bulk onto Rob. It didn't even matter that Mark was now pretty much being held up by an invisible force because he wasn't listening to me anymore, but staring up at the sky and trying to whistle a song that sounded familiar but I couldn't place it, it was so out of tune.

"Shh," I lightly slapped him on the cheek whilst I jiggled the door knob as quietly as possible with my other hand. "Stay with me Markie!"

Rob, not even struggling with Mark's weight despite being half his size, started to laugh and sway his brother to the music.

I glared at him as I managed to open the side door. Finally, home safe. Almost.

Getting Mark up to his room was the next challenge and one I wasn't looking forward to. Luckily his room was right next to the stairs but unluckily *up* the stairs.

"How are we going to do this?" Rob asked, casually standing by the door as though his brother weighed as much as he did, which at this point was nothing.

My brain throbbed with stress.

"Quietly." I said pointedly, hoping prolonged eye contact with Mark would help the way people who stared at their dogs when they told them to sit hoped they were secretly mind-melding with their pet rather when really the animal only wanted food.

Mark took it upon himself to decide he was partaking in a mission of espionage once we broached the perimeter into the main house; crouched low and creeping along the wall behind me.

We had one shot; run past the kitchen, down the hall past the living room and up the stairs. It was a track I knew well, after all the times we'd attempted to sneak in and out of the house.

I was confident, to say the least, as the doors to all the rooms were always kept closed to keep the warmth in which had a tendency to sneak out and escape due to high ceilings.

I traced our old footsteps, careful not to trip up on the old coat rack which had a foot like an old ravaged lion's paw. I noticed Mark step over it deftly behind me, even in his state.

We passed the living room where I could hear the TV's muffled sounds and quiet chatter. The party had well and truly disbursed, thank God. We would never have made it through the house if people were still lingering around, snooping, as people in this town do.

When I reached the bottom of the stairs I turned to see Rob forcefully pushing Mark towards me, his body leaning back into Rob's super ghost strength arms.

"Do not drop him!" I hissed, but I could tell from Rob's face I didn't have to worry. He was grimacing, not from the effort of pushing Mark but something else.

"I think he's going to puke."

Rob pushed Mark towards the first step and the momentum did the rest. Mark fell forward onto his hands and knees, breathing deeply and intentionally. I'd been drunk only once, but I knew the signs.

"Oh no, hold it in, do *not* be sick here!" I whisper-shouted at Mark, but he didn't seem to hear me. He was now trying to climb up the stairs on his hands and knees like a toddler.

"He's a maniac. Let's get him drunk more often!" Rob said, as we watched Mark's great hulking frame slowly creep up the stairs. I pressed my hands into my face.

"Could this day get any worse?"

I let out an exasperated sigh and looked to see Rob's smiling face. A few months ago I might have seen the smile for what he wanted me to see it as; humour, but today I saw it for what it really was.

"Sorry…" Rob's smile faded in a moment of clarity between us. We'd been having these moments more and more over the past few days, where the illusion of life was shattered and reality lingered in the air like second hand smoke. "Super Rob to the rescue!"

Just like clockwork the illusion was back up, shining and bright like Rob's life used to be.

I looked to the top of the stairs just as Mark reached the plushly carpeted landing. He stopped right at Rob's shiny black dress shoes.

"How did you get up here so fast?" I asked once I'd caught up; stepping on the outer edges of the steps to avoid any creaking.

"What are you talking about? It took forever!" Mark groaned at my feet.

"Come on, Muscles!" I said using the nickname he loved to hate.

I grabbed him under his arm to help him to his feet and Rob took the other side. Thankfully Mark seemed to have gotten over the puking part of his drunkenness and was onto the next stage. The head-loll.

We pull-walked him into his room, which was right at the top of the stairs, and threw him face down onto his bed. His body dipped and bounced with the force which I couldn't help but laugh at.

"Ow…" Mark's face was pushed into his pillow and his muffled voice was so pathetic Rob could hardly contain himself.

"Do you think I have time to run up to my room and grab my camera?" He was leaning against the door as though he might actually do it.

"And how would I explain that to everyone?" I asked, silently praying he would behave for once in his life.

The idea of having proof of this, on Rob's camera no less, send waves of panic and light headedness over me.

He snorted in response which I hated but I bit my tongue. I rolled one of his dumbbells from the centre of the room back to the stack in the corner. The whole place was a shrine to Mark's sporting achievements. He had bookshelves around his room, which was probably the size of the entire downstairs of my house, but there were no books.

Trophies, pictures of him playing all kinds of sports, even bronzed sports shoes, littered the room.

Without warning Mark reached out his hand and grabbed me by the arm. "C'mere,"

He pulled me down to the bed and I sat perched on the edge with my small hand planted in his giant palm. I felt Rob lingering at the edge of my vision. Blurred around the edges and out of focus.

"I don't want to sleep on m'own." Mark mumbled, his eyes closed in alcohol induced exhaustion. He looked so sad as he lay there, and I reached over with my other hand to stroke the hair away from his head.

The intimacy of the moment hit me hard. If I closed my eyes Rob could have really been gone.

It was all a lie. Of course. I looked towards Rob and rolled my eyes.

Mark started snoring the second I took my hand away from his.

"I like him like this." Rob said, sliding his hand into mine. I didn't complain that his hands were freezing cold, I just squeezed it and mentally thanked whoever it was who had sent him back to me.

We peered down on Mark's snoring form, his mouth agape, like proud parents. Finally, our little boy had fallen off his pedestal.

If it had been Dean I have no doubt we would have laughed about this tomorrow. Of course, with Mark being the way he was, come morning he would no doubt forget all about it, or pretend to, or else tell me never to tell anyone and go back to ignoring me. I had a feeling it would be the latter.

Rob was outside the room before I'd even turned to leave. The question of how was on my lips but before I could form the sentence Dean came out of his room. I froze, not knowing what to do.

"H-Hi. I... um, I found Mark," I just about saved myself but dragging out the greeting, he still frowned at me like I was acting strangely, which I was, but I didn't want him to know that. "He was out in the garden, just walking around..." I pointed at the door behind me when Dean's eyebrow arched just like Rob's did when he suspected me of something. "We were just talking, he's going to bed now though. He said he's really tired..." I stepped away from the door and moved towards the stairs, trying to hide my blushing cheeks.

"Are you coming down?" I asked. Why was I talking? He looked at me strangely as though I'd spoken in another language. He looked at Marks door quizzically and then back at me.

"Yeah... I was just going to come and get you..." He said, drawing out his words as though trying to figure out why I was acting like a psychopath.

I nodded and mentally kicked myself as hard as I could. Rob was already at the bottom of the stairs so me and Dean descended in silence

I passed Rob at the bottom and ignored him as I walked to the living room. He had his famous up-to-no-good smirk painted on his face.

Mr and Mrs Wood were sat on the sofa eating some cake in silence. At our arrival Mrs Wood sprang to life, doting on me like she always did.

"Oh there you are Amelia - do you want some cake? There's quite a bit left, I suppose I forgot that the cake eater wouldn't be... well, you know..." I could tell she'd had a drink or two of her own this evening.

"Yeah, please!" I smiled at her as Dean brushed past me to sit with his dad. As I turned and left the room I heard him mention Mark being asleep. Ever since the funeral being in a room with the family, *his* family, felt wrong. Like I was trespassing.

I took my time getting cake in the kitchen, happy that Rob had stayed with his family. I would never voice my need for space out loud, who knew when God or whatever was going to take him back again.

Both Rob's mum and dad spent a good hour recounting stories from when we were younger, whilst I nodded and laughed at the appropriate places and they either didn't notice or pretended not to notice when my cake was set down without so much as a dent in the icing.

Every now and then Rob laughed and added to the story, like he was still a part of the world rather than a shadow left behind. It took a lot of self-control to ignore him each time he did it but what was worse was when he stopped doing it altogether. Though he still laughed and made faces, he kept his comments to himself. His silence was the loudest I'd heard him scream in a long time.

"I'll never forget how many pizza's the two of you ordered, Amelia. I'm still paying off the credit card." Mr Wood said. His eyes crinkled into a smile and he looked at me as though I was there with them all, in the same boat with the same pains but I was so much farther away than they could even realise, so I laughed even when I noticed Dean looking at me with the same concerned frown he'd had outside Mark's room.

"That wasn't me, I swear! It was all Rob…" I smiled in spite of the ache in my cheeks and the pain in my chest.

The room relaxed into a nostalgic silence as everyone picked at slices of cake and watched the TV. I couldn't tell what was on the screen because I was trying so hard not to look at Rob, meaning he was all I could see out of the corner of my eye.

"So unfair to blame the person who can't defend himself." Rob pretended to be angry but he couldn't stop himself from smiling.

"I have to go." I said, as suddenly as I'd seen Rob smile. As suddenly as the pain in my chest felt like a bubble which was about to burst.

I realised I was standing up when a wave of dizziness hit me but I pushed through it. Rob was at my side in an instant, and so was Dean.

"What's wrong?" They both managed to ask in unison, so I answered them both, lying to one and telling the truth to the other.

"I'm fine, just tired," I stepped away from both of them, their hands dropping from my waist. One cold spot and one warm lingered as a shiver went up my spine. "Today was perfect… I'll see you later in the week?"

I made my way to the door, careful not to look any of them in the eye directly.

"Amelia, thank you for today, you have no idea how much it meant to us." Mrs Wood brushed her hand past mine only to be pushed aside by Mr Wood, who took my hand in his.

The awkwardness was only outweighed by the importance of his action. Mr Wood wasn't a sentimental man. In all of my years of being friends with Rob I could count the times he'd consoled me on one hand. Once when I'd fallen from the treehouse and split my lip, once at the hospital and once at the funeral. This one was the one that meant the most, though. I could see it in his eyes; this wasn't duty or grief, this was purposeful and kind.

I looked into his face and felt a tear slide down my cheek.

"Don't be a stranger."

The hallway was welcomingly cool as I closed the door behind me.

"That will probably be his kindness quota for the year, then."

Rob was leaning against the front door, one leg propped up behind him like some bad boy from a movie.

"Don't do that today." I reached around him to pull open the front door but he knocked his weight back into it and it clicked closed again. "Rob!"

A hand reached past me to pull the door open again and I jumped back and into Dean's chest.

"I do that too, sometimes."

I scooted out of the way as Dean pulled open the front door, letting the warm fragrant air sweep past us. I hadn't even heard him follow me out to the hallway, I was so wrapped up in Rob, as usual.

I stared at him blankly.

"Talk to Rob, pretend he's still here." Dean nodded his head towards the door and shrugged his shoulders like he'd admitted something embarrassing.

I blushed involuntarily which he took as admittance. "It's OK, I won't tell anyone if you don't."

"It's not that…" The urge to protest was a gut reaction, it was only Rob's cough from the front steps that made me snap out of it. "I guess it *is* that."

"I can drive you home if you want?"

Dean was leaning into the open door now, his hand resting on the handle like he was inviting me in rather than letting me leave.

"No, it's OK. I don't mind walking. I need some time alone." The moment I said it I felt that feeling of shame and acidic hatred wash over me. I was saying all the right lines, going through the motions like they were but the truth was I wasn't. Not really.

When Dean nodded, his expression one of understanding and compassion, I could have screamed but I didn't. I hadn't let myself really scream or cry since the funeral and that was almost two weeks ago now. Two weeks of lying to everyone I knew. If Rob ever got into Heaven I sure as hell wasn't going to.

CHAPTER 4

I left Dean at the house, watching me from the doorway whilst I forced myself not to look back. He'd made me promise I'd come back, like he was scared I would disappear once I left his sight.

The whole family had been like that since the accident and at first I'd found it comforting but now it smothered me like summer heat.

I hadn't lied when I said my parents would change the locks. Well, OK, it was an exaggeration, but they wouldn't be happy at how late it was when I traipsed through the front door.

Their pride was even stronger than their ability to be utter morons.

They said it was embarrassing the way I sponged off the Wood family, and that we McHale's '*might not have much money but we at least knew that it didn't buy happiness*'. To them anyone with money was unhappy.

Rob had laughed to himself the entire walk home making a short twenty-minute walk feel like twenty hours.

"What's so funny?" I asked him as we walked up the garden path. Our small terraced house loomed ahead; the red brick glossy and dark in the night, with only the street lamp picking up the white of the door and window frames.

It was a small two-story home, sandwiched between identical houses which were joined like twins who had to dye their hair different colours to be told apart.

The one to the left had a green door and yellow window frames because our neighbours, Mr and Mrs Davies, thought it was cute and countryesque. Everyone else on the street agreed that it was oddly revolting.

The other side had pure white trims on the doors and windows, the actual door itself was bright red with a very old looking, antique brass knocker.

I hated even looking at the red lacquered paint because of how much I detested the mother and her daughter who lived there. They were the kind of show off snobs who liked to park their matching red Mini Coopers in front of *our* house, because they *just didn't have enough room for two cars outside*.

It was unjust snobbery. They lived identically to us, yet somehow acted like they were better.

A strong dislike for them was the only thing me and my parents actually agreed on.

I stuck my key into the keyhole in our door; sky blue and set with a bog-standard brass knocker. Nothing fancy, just something cheap I'd picked up to try to make our house seem like a home. From the outside, anyway.

I softly closed the door behind me.

"Isn't that supposed to be on the outside?" Rob asked, looking at the welcome mat my mother refused to keep outside. I didn't answer him as payment for not explaining what had kept a smile on his face the whole way home.

"Hello?" I called out quietly, for courtesy more than anything.

I didn't really want to let my parents know I was home but I didn't want to surprise them either. Surprising them usually led to arguments about coming and going as I please or some other ridiculous argument that was unnecessary. These days I argued with my parents a lot.

My mother materialised from the darkness, the hallway lights off as usual. She was framed by the flickering lights from the TV.

"Amelia? Where have you been?" She melted back to the darkness and I followed her into the living room. Rob, my constant shadow, bowed and gestured towards the opening.

"M'lady" He said, sweeping his arm across his chest.

"Thanks," I replied under my breath, careful to make my face as blank as possible for when I faced my parents.

I had mostly managed to keep my distance from them over the last couple of week. They didn't appreciate how I was coping, or they couldn't understand. Either way, it was too hard to pretend to grieve so I avoided them altogether. It wasn't just them, I'd been avoiding almost everyone recently.

Rob and I had the same friends, the same lives. When his ended I had wanted to continue with mine but when he came back it became nearly impossible for obvious reasons.

My parents had yelled at me for pulling back from life; which is how they saw it, but to me it was the only way to keep living. I knew it was screwed up and to be honest, I was pretty impressed they even had any ounce of interest in my emotional state.

You can't choose your family. That's something they had told me often as a child, and something I fully understood seventeen years later.

I walked into the living room, which was small, with an electric fire implanted in the wall like a glowing tic on a dog's back. It was a relatively nice room but that was because I had purchased most of the furniture myself. The room, in fact the whole house, was devoid of any kind of picture of us as a family. I didn't even think they had baby pictures of me, the only pictures I had seen of me as a kid were in Rob's mum's photo albums, of which she kept many.

My mum, Pam, was sat curled up on the sofa. I wasn't stubborn enough to deny we looked alike, my reflection confirmed it every single day.

Her slim arms and legs were wrapped up in her dressing gown, her youthful face was free of makeup; something she would never do in public or with company here. I almost felt bad for her that Rob was seeing her this way.

I sat on the arm of the chair as her eyes glued themselves to the TV, watching some sort of soap opera that I had learnt to mentally tune out since I was around six years old.

"So, it's a Sunday, you weren't at work were you? Didn't think you worked Sundays."

She was right about that, I didn't work on Sundays, and I was utterly perplexed that she would even remember that.

"No, Mum, I was at Rob's birthday-remembrance-party-thing, remember? I told you about it the other day..." I stared at the TV, not really seeing what was going on. It was small and chunky, not one of those cool flat screens they had at the Wood's house, and the picture seemed fuzzier still through unfocused eyes. She dragged her gaze from the TV, something that seemed almost painful for her to do.

"What? When was this? Today? AMELIA!" She untangled her hands from her dressing gown and pounded them onto the cushion on either side of her. I looked at her, shocked at the outburst.

"What? I told you about it a million times, what was I supposed to do? Dress you and drag you there?" Her face turned a speckled shade of red and she gave me the angry look she usually saved for when I didn't pay the rent on time or mentioned the neighbours.

"Do you know how embarrassing this is? They probably think we didn't even care..." She looked appalled and I felt another wave of guilt hit me like a sack of bricks. "They probably just think we couldn't be bothered, when really we didn't know about it. You've certainly done a good job of painting us in a bad light, Amelia, you've spent your entire life sponging off them..."

At this point in her Broken Record Rant I got up and left the room, not even bothering to reply. I knew the tune too well. I was halfway up the stairs when I heard her voice again, and even though I had expected her to say it my stomach still sank at the sound of it.

"...Just because they have a spare place in the family now doesn't mean they'll adopt you, we're your family and that's all there is to it!"

I raced up the last few steps and slammed the door as hard as I could, I winced as the wood slammed into the frame.

Typical Pam. It was all about how she looked in the Wood's eyes. All about her mothering skills. Always about money. I let my back slide down the door and focused on breathing white light in and red light out. The one time I'd been to see a therapist after Rob's death and that was all they could suggest for my anxiety. I had no idea why they were surprised I didn't go back.

When I looked up Rob was sitting on my bed, I hadn't even noticed him follow me up the stairs.

"Wow... that was... nice. She really doesn't let up, does she?" Rob's face was full of sympathy. I buried my face in my hands.

"You have no idea." I said miserably, muffled voice slipping out from between my fingers. I exhaled loudly and Rob jumped up, crossing the space between us in two steps.

"UP!" He instructed grabbing my hands and pulling me to my feet. He led me to the bed and I sank into the soft sheets, letting my head hit the pillow.

"She's just… I'm sorry you had to hear that." I closed my eyes, feeling Rob's breath on my cheek as his head settled into the pillow next to me. I didn't feel the bed dip under his weight though and for a few seconds my brain imagined what it would be like if I opened my eyes and he wasn't there.

"Don't be stupid, you have met my family have you?"

I let the illusion disperse into the air like a forgotten dream, biting the inside of my cheek to remind myself I was… What? Alive? Awake? To blame? I don't even know anymore.

I opened my eyes to let him know I wasn't amused.

"Not my lovable homies. My less immediate, more ass-holey family!" He sneered, rolling onto his back so we were both looking up at the white cracked ceiling. "Come on, you saw my Uncle Roy didn't you?" I tried to picture which one he could have been, but there were too many people in his family who looked like they could have been called Roy.

"I overheard him talking to my Aunt Juliette about how the death of a son would 'increase the value of the shares' in dad's business." He used air quotes and adopted a snobby accent and suddenly I could picture which uncle he meant.

"He's such a loser!" I said. I couldn't believe how awful some people could be and I made a mental note to smack Roy in the face if I ever had the misfortune of meeting him again.

Rob reached to the bedside table and switched on the fake Tiffany lamp I got from a charity shop. It cast warm light through the room, comforting me with the familiarity. Rob nodded and laughed a little at my proclamation.

"Pretty much, yeah…" He trailed off, the only sound I could hear was the TV downstairs, which is how I knew Rob was planning on saying something serious. He never normally let silences linger that long.

"How come I didn't know your mum was this horrible before?"

"Before what?" I asked, buying myself time. I don't know why I said it. At first I was trying to be cute but there was something lurking under my own words that felt bitter.

"You know..." Rob couldn't bring himself to say it. It wasn't often he could and sometimes I wondered if he even remembered he was gone.

I turned to him and shrugged. Words ceased to exist at that moment.

"I'm good at keeping secrets," I said, frowning. I felt a familiar numbness in my mind and I tried to quietly breathe the white air in again. "They've both gotten worse over the past couple of years. I feel like I'm not even their child anymore, y'know? Just an annoying tenant who doesn't pay enough rent."

"Pay? You pay rent?" He looked at me, eyes wide and utterly flabbergasted. "How do I not know anything about this?" He buried his head in his hands, like this was the worst crime my parents had committed.

"Not everyone gets to live at home for free. In their opinion if I'm making enough money to save, I'm making enough to pay for my keep... and theirs." I added, thinking back to what my money actually gets spent on.

I cursed his life after death for the millionth time and the millionth reason.

It's not that I didn't share things with him, but I had never wanted him to feel *sorry* for me. Ever since I could remember I'd always made sure we'd hang out at his house, and if he *did* come over, I'd do my best to make sure my mum and dad were either on their best behaviour, or else just not here.

Sure, it was probably a bad thing to keep things like that from your best friend, but facing up to the truth that my family would never be his... I learnt how to hide lots of things from an early age.

Keeping up the pretence was never the plan but the lie started to take on a life of its own. Now it feels like it's more alive than me.

Ever since I could get a job I was working. Waitressing wasn't my life plan but it was a plan nonetheless.

I had it all worked out, it would be next year on my eighteenth birthday. I'd be out of there, in the world, living somewhere amazing on my own terms.

I'd been secretly planning it for as long as I could remember, always assuming Rob would be there with me. Not that he needed to escape.

There's no point in lying; living in Rob's shoes would be great. Would have been. But he was too comfortable. Living at home wasn't the best thing for him. His parents loved having the boys in the house still and they had all the space in the world to roam and no curfew, but if I was starting over, I'd always assumed Rob would be starting over with me. In a living capacity.

Now my plans were scuppered I had to start rethinking my plan.

"I know not everyone lives for free but, I dunno, I just assumed… and you're only on a waitress's wage, and you never told me, so I never knew, OK?" Rob actually looked hurt as he sat on the edge of my bed. Every reality of my life was on the verge of breakdown. "Why didn't you tell me?" He said, his shoulders slumped.

"I didn't mean to *not* tell you," I hesitated, caught on the edge of the lie. It pressed against my heart like a broken rib. "I didn't want to whinge about my parents. I knew you'd probably speak to your parents and I don't need help. I'm doing fine on my own."

Rob didn't say anything for a while. He got up and walked to my window. I could only watch. After a minute of dead silence I rolled onto my back, head lolled back so my hair dangled over the edge of the bed instead of my legs.

He was upside down, as was the rest of my room, the bookshelves fixed onto the wall looking like they might spill the books onto the ceiling.

"What ya thinkin'?" I asked in a sing song voice, the blood was rushing to my head quickly but I ignored the thumping in my ears.

The only way I knew to break the tension was to act silly, it always made Rob smile.

He turned to look at me, hands still deep in pockets but his face softened.

"Stop being cute… do you think I'm a bad friend?" He asked. A shadow I'd hoped to never see again clouded his eyes, making them seem dull and lifeless. He stared past me, past the room and into a void.

"What?!" I rolled onto my front, hoping it was just the blood rushing to my head making me hear things. "Don't be so stupid, that's not what I meant. I just meant…" I didn't know what I meant, really. Thinking about it made me realise how stupid I'd been but it was way too late to do anything about it. I sighed and buried my face in my hands. "I just meant that I didn't need help with money, I didn't mean anything else, honest!"

He sat down next to me on the bed, the mattress dipped, pushing me towards him and reminding me he was real; in the loosest term possible.

"I wouldn't have told anyone if you didn't want me to, and if you didn't want money I wouldn't have given it to you. Sure, I might have forced you to move in with me, but isn't that what good friends do?" The cloud passed and he wrapped his arm around me and squeezed us together. I feigned thought-fulness as I tried to pry myself away from him. He was cold to the touch.

"Hmmm, no. Probably not. I mean, moving me into your parent's house just screams Jerry Springer, doesn't it?"

He made a noncommittal noise and shrugged. I knew I wasn't out of the woods but I didn't feel like talking about it so I pushed myself off the bed and decided to do something about it.

"Wait here," I said, grabbing my pyjamas and heading for the door, "I'll be right back, don't go anywhere." I had been getting ready in the bathroom across the small hallway ever since Rob had started to 'haunt' me. At first I would sneak into the small green tiled room with my things, so I didn't raise suspicion, but it soon became obvious to me that my parents didn't notice what I was doing, so I no longer hid the fact that I was getting changed in another room

"Where would I go?" Rob asked. His voice was light but there was that crackle of darkness behind the words that I'd just started to notice since his death but probably should have noticed sooner.

I sat on the closed toilet seat and wiped the makeup off my face with one of those never-damp-enough face wipes. I smudged the day away as best as I could, used to the stray tears that flowed when I was alone.

I moved to the sink to brush my teeth, probably taking too long as I deliberated on what I was going to tell Rob, how much of myself I was going to give away. After all the years of friendship it was hard breaking down the walls I'd unknowingly built up. I peeled my dress off and stepped out of it, watching as it pooled around my feet. Despite being alone I always felt like I was being watched so I quickly changed into my PJ's, throwing my clothes in the washing basket on my way past. I sighed, knowing I'd have to sort it all out tomorrow anyway. The sound of the TV downstairs sent a familiar shiver of rage up my spine.

I crept back into my room, quietly. Rob didn't turn around and in the dim light he looked semi-transparent, as though he was an underdeveloped picture with the light of the computer screen glowing through him.

He was sat at my cluttered desk surfing around the Internet. As I walked up behind him I saw he was partaking in his new favourite past-time; spying on our friends on different social networking sites.

He liked to do this even in life, even though he'd never had any account of his own. His argument was that he didn't know why other people would want to know his every move but that never stopped him from using my accounts to check on everyone else. Morbid curiosity is what he called it, which at the moment had never felt so apt.

"Look at this, 5 hours ago 'Johnny James is still reeling and missing Rob like crazy!'... and then..." He scrolled up a little bit, "3 minutes ago 'Johnny James can't wait to see the wolf pack later and cause some trouble. Hashtag YOLO!'"

Rob laughed lightly and shook his head, spinning the chair to face me.

"Literally 5 hours after the first post. Am I that easy to get over?!" He asked. I shrugged my shoulders and leant over him to close the window, making a mental note to delete James from my friends list in the morning. I was annoyed people were so flippant with their online 'voices' - nothing was sacred, even someone dying was just a passing comment on a web based social group.

"YOLO?" I cringed, wishing I could punch James in the face.

"You only live once… insightful." Rob scratched his chin, Freudian-like.

"I know what it means, doofus." I messed up his hair, rubbing my hand through it. Not that it mattered, he had the un-done look going for him anyway but I did it just to make sure. "And to answer your previous question, I would find getting over you easier if I couldn't still see you, talk to you, or even escape you…"

"Oh har-har" Rob batted me away and flattered his hair down, not that it looked any different. Not like he'd changed an iota since he left.

"OK, sit on the bed!" I grabbed him by the arm and hauled him to his feet, pushing him towards it. Now was the time to really embrace the whole notion of 'YOLO', without the embarrassing or insulting connotations.

"OK, but if this is a sex thing I might have to draw the line," Rob sat down and put his hands up like I was going to throw myself on top of him. "I won't have your first time be with a ghost, that's just too desperate!" I cringed and felt my cheeks burn.

"Don't say the 'G' word, besides, who says it would be my first time?"

He smiled that smile, the one that said he knew me too well.

"Oh, really? And who was it with? Anyone I know? Perhaps Dean? No. You would have told me... although after tonight I'm not so sure about that anymore..."

He was teasing but I was still embarrassed at the other lettered word I didn't want to talk about. I had never had a boyfriend, not with both the world's best deterrent and the world's worst wing-man.

"Just sit and stay, I'm going to show you something...magical!" I said, oohing and aahing and waving my arms around as I walked to the wardrobe. I heard Rob mutter something sarcastic under his breathe but I ignored him, trying to get as far away from reality-crashing subjects as possible.

The bottom of my wardrobe was where I dumped most of my clothes because I knew my parents would never think to snoop where they may also have to clean.

After a lot of tangled shoe laces I managed to pull out an empty shoe box which was held closed with a red elastic bands.

"OK, what I'm about to show you is really, really personal. I'm talking Open Heart Surgery personal... I never told you about it because I never wanted you to laugh at my stupid-ness, and I guess I never wanted to show you because I worried it would never happen... this doesn't make sense. OK. Hold on." I sat down and stopped talking, conscious my rambling voice might draw the attention of my parents if I carried on.

He was patient, but I could see the curiosity in the way his mouth had set into a straight line, holding back on what he'd usually do, which is rip whatever I was holding out of my hands.

I eventually opened the top of the box and pulled out the contents. Wads of cash, hundreds of pounds worth, all banded together tightly.

Rob continued to watch as I stacked it up on the bed carefully, along with other things; pictures of houses and faraway places where the beach and sea and sun all blurred and ran into each other in luxury.

"Oh my god! What did you do? Rob a bank?" Rob picked up the top pile of notes and flicked his fingers through them.

"Not quite..." I watched as he leafed through the rest of the contents, carefully touching each of them as though they were breakable rather than pictures and pages ripped from books and magazines. "It's all mine. From work, well, from my tips. I never put it in the bank, I bring it home and hide it. It's my secret fund, for when I run away..." I stared him dead in the eye, and waiting for his reaction.

"You're going to run away? Didn't we try that when we were 11, how far did we get?"

The pictures of all the places I would dream of going to, moving to, getting lost in their cultures and starting a new life were laid out in front of us. Places where my parents weren't able to torture me with their negligence, and I wasn't the best friend of one of the richest families in a ten-mile radius.

"We got to the tree house, but that was different, back then the tree house was its own world," It really was, it felt like we'd trekked through the garden for hours, time and distance distorted by youth. "I plan on getting a little further this time. Somewhere different..." He cut me off with a droll stare.

"Running away doesn't solve problems, Amelia." He said, imitating his father's voice to a tee, "What do you have to run away from? What's *that* bad?"

He winced as though he had actually forgotten his recent trip to Deathville.

"You've been planning this for a long time, there must be thousands of pounds here... I don't know what to say..." He looked down and his hands, his expression pinched my heart.

"It's not like *that*," I tried to explain, seeing the familiar look of abandonment I'd seen in the mirror recently mirrored in Rob's eyes felt like a slap in the face. "I wasn't ever running away from you - it's just... this place, this town, the people are all the same and my parents are the worst. My dad drinks, he's mean... My mum, God... do you know how long it's been since they told me they loved me? I can't even remember. Even after you..." I trailed off because if I carried on I'd end up crying and I was still working on keeping that promise. "It was never about running away, it was about starting a new life."

Rob didn't seem overly happy but he put his hand on my pyjama clad knee and squeezed it.

"I get it, I do, but... would you have..." He looked back at all the pictures and the money and let out a long breath which seemed to make the air colder.

"Rob, I was going to take you with me, you idiot. You didn't need the money but I did so I saved it up. I was going to tell you," I grabbed his hand, cold like a shadow. "I was. I don't know what to do now, everything's change."

"Sorry for ruining your plans." He said, bitterly. The tension between us was electric. Like a thunderstorm was brewing in in the space between.

"It's not like that, Rob. I just always assumed we'd be together, forever..." I bit my lip and closed my eyes. I felt my cheeks burn red, as my admittance fell out of my mouth. When I looked at him again he was smiling sadly just like when I was giving the speech at his 'party'. It was a smile I had a feeling I was going to have to get used to.

"Forever, hey?" He lifted his hand and stroked my hair.

"I just always assumed we'd, I don't know, end up married on some desert island, taking photographs and making movies!" I smacked his hand away when his fingers reached to tickle my ear.

"Hubba-hubba!" He laughed, pulling me into his arms so we were awkwardly hugging between my carefully constructed dreams.

"Not like that, pervert!" I pulled away and started putting everything back in the box. His reversion back to his playful-self annoyed me as much as it worried me.

"I know what you meant Amelia. You're my best friend. I guess I'd never thought about our future-"

"That's fine," I cut him off, "I don't think it's wise either of us say anything more on the matter, things have changed, what was going to be or not going to be is neither here nor there now. I just wanted to let you know. I wasn't running away from you..." I let the unsaid disappear into the void, the place where neither Rob nor I could go. Or the place we were both stuck.

I got up to put the box back in its hiding place and when I returned I shoved him out of the way and climbed into my bed, it wasn't a single, but it certainly wasn't a double, it was one of those in between breeds. I pulled the purple covers up and over my head, Rob stayed on the outside of the covers, he didn't sleep, or at least it seemed that way.

The truth was I hadn't really gotten a straight answer out of him about it. He was awake when I went to bed and awake when I woke up, always perched near my bed, waiting for me.

"None of it matters now, anyway. I don't want to run away on my own - how boring would that be?" I said, voice muffled in my quilted cocoon, hot breathe circulating and making me feel sticky.

I felt Rob shuffle around on the covers and realised as he spoke he had rolled onto his side so his face was right next to mine, only separated by the duvet.

"What do you mean, it doesn't matter? You've got the money what more of a push do you need? You have to do this, if this is your dream please don't let my circumstance get in the way. You're going, OK? I'll help you plan it..." I frowned and pulled the covers back so I could face him.

"Well, that's all fine and dandy, but what about you? You're going to come with me and be my invisible companion through life? Or you'll stay here? What if you can't?" I didn't know why I was trying to talk myself out of it, but now all of a sudden everything seemed muddy, and unclear.

"We'll figure it out baby," he winked, rolling back onto his back, "Besides, there has to be someone out there who knows what's going on with me and with you, someone will know - all we have to do is find them."

I frowned again and snuggled up to Rob, even though he was cold to touch the familiarity of him soon made me drowsy.

"OK, we'll find someone..." I yawned. He pulled the covers up to my chin.

"Yes, that will be Step One in the Free Amelia campaign."

I could only nod as sleep took over me but I was sure I heard him mutter something like 'maybe that's why I'm here'. I thought about asking him to repeat it but sleep took my words.

"Amelia? Honey, are you there?" her voice was thick with what I now know was grief, she spoke with a shaky voice. I put my hand on the wall and leaned into the phone. In an instant I thought Mr Wood had been in an accident, but that split second thought ebbed away into a dull throb in my chest when I realised she wouldn't be calling me to tell me, Rob would be, and then my knees buckled and I slid to the ground.

"I'm here... what's wrong?" Secret tears spilled from my eyes, I clenched my teeth in anticipation for her next words. I knew already. I knew.

"Oh, Amelia, something awful has happened..." She sobbed. "It's Rob..." That's all I heard because there was a scuffle on the phone. I didn't realise I was pressing the phone right into my head until my ear started to ache from the pressure. My earring was digging into the skin behind my ear.

"Hello?" I couldn't hear what was going on, just mumbling voices and sobbing. My heart was thudding so much I started to gasp for breath. I could see Tony in my peripheral vision talking to someone. They looked over at me. I ignored them, they didn't mean anything.

"What's going on?" I forced out, urging my voice to reach someone's ears at the other end.

"Amelia?" It was Mr Wood, "it's Andrew..." He was talking to me but it didn't register. I had never spoken to him on the phone before and the strangeness of the situation was jarring. He never answered the phone at their house, always Mrs Wood.

"Mr Wood, what's going on? Where's Rob?" His next words were just muffled noise. Like someone was talking into an electric fan; the words all chopped up and backwards. My ears rejected the sounds.

"What? I don't understand?" My throat was closing up – I knew. I knew but I didn't want to hear.

CHAPTER

The next morning I woke to the sun streaming in through the window; I swore as I rolled over.

"What time is it?"

The room was quiet. Too quiet. Over the past few weeks I'd grown accustom to the constant noises Rob created. When I woke up it was usually to the sound of typing or pages of a book being turned.

Right now the room was eerily quiet which made my heart leap into my throat. Gasping I threw back my covers and sat upright. I searched the room frantically, my eyes darting to every corner, every shadow. Empty.

I looked at the clock that perched on my desk as it flashed 7:30 am at me in luminous green. My heart thumped erratically. I hadn't woken up to an empty room since Rob came back. I drew my legs up to my chest and hugged them tightly, not sure what to do. Thoughts raced through my mind faster than I could even think them.

The silence was starting to press against me as though the walls were closing in. I had to close my eyes to stop the world from being there. I had to think about what this meant.

"Morning grump, want some toast?"

I looked up to see him stood with his back to my closed bedroom door like he'd just walked through it carrying a plate of what looked to be a whole loaf of toast, which was impossible because he couldn't walk through walls. We'd tried. We'd been disappointed.

"Where have you been?" I was wrapping my arms around him before he even had a chance to react. His suit was clean and pressed like it was straight off the rack.

"Careful!" He pulled away, "What's gotten into you?"

He sat on the edge of the bed sniffing the buttery toast like he could savour the taste without actually tasting it.

"You weren't here when I woke up…" He offered the plate of toast to me but I waved it away. "I was worried… how come you're carrying all my bread?"

He frowned when I said I was worried so I shook the fear from my mind. It was much healthier to focus on the now. It was important.

"You need to eat something." Rob said, flatly.

My stomach growled in protest to my stubbornness. I felt empty but I was starting to get used to it.

"I'm really not hungry."

I watched his face, seeing him internally debate whether he could be bothered to argue. After a moment I could tell he'd decided to drop it and he took another slice for himself.

"So? The bread?" I sat next to him and tried not to breathe through my nose. The smell of the butter making me nauseous.

"Patience, grasshopper." He licked his fingers and put the plate on the bed between us. "Today comes to you in two parts. First, the toast. I heard your mum get up earlier to have a shower and I heard her say she wanted toast... so I went and made all the bread into toast so she couldn't have any... I'm sorry." He wasn't sorry at all though, I could tell by the way his face lit up at the thought of it. "I couldn't help it. Besides, what's a ghost to do?"

"She'll blame me, you know?!" I said, already pre-empting the fallout. A chuckle rose in his throat which he turned into a little cough at my glare.

"Don't worry about it!" He said, drumming his fingers on his knees, although I couldn't not worry about it and his nonchalance was irritating me. I was the one who was going to take the rap for it later.

"So, what's the second thing you mentioned?" I asked which caused a bright smile to light up his face. It was moments like this that made everything else seem OK.

Reaching over to my desk he pulled a pad towards him and flipped the pages open. It was covered in his boyish scribbled writing.

"I have been planning and plotting your escape into the wild, Miss McHale!" His face creased in concentration as he flipped pages over looking for something in particular.

"OK..?" I couldn't make out his hand writing, it was like when you started at something for too long and it stopped making sense. I'd never had a problem before but now it was like looking at writing through one of those carnival mirrors. Backwards and contorted. He didn't seem to have an issue with it though, I could see his lips moving as he skimmed the information.

Finally his eyes stopped flicking from side to side and he looked back at me. My stomach did that little flippy thing it does when a rollercoaster hits the highest point and starts to drop you.

"I counted all your money so far, and saw you had £3800 in cash," I nodded, wondering how he'd managed to do all of this without waking me up in the night. "Now, considering you get about, what? £30 a week in tips? Give or take anyway, you could be in the position to save about £800 more if we give ourselves the deadline of your birthday?" I nodded again and pressed my lips together, trying to calculate where he might be going with this. My birthday was in March; a whole eight months away.

"Right… but, you know this whole running away thing doesn't actually have to go ahead now." I started to protest but he ignored me.

"All you have to do now is decide where you actually want to go. I took the liberty of looking at flight prices, seeing as they are usually the same all the time. If you, say, decided you wanted to go to America, you'd have to put aside enough for the flight, and then have enough to pay for a hostel or hotel or whatever until you found a job and then a place to stay. Of course, you'd need a visa for that…" His words flowed out of him in one breath, making me dizzy from the information overload.

He handed me the note pad and I flipped the pages over and over, looking at all the work he had done in. From what I could tell there were lists of places I could go along with places I could stay in different price ranges. I assumed there was a page of job prospects as well as I could see a few doodles of a cartoon version of me in different job-situations.

"Cute." I said, pointing to a drawing of me wearing the typical office workers uniform. From the mind of a teenage boy.

He smirked and took the pad back from me.

"Rob, this is… I don't know…amazing…" I stammered quietly, pushing the feelings of trepidation and negativity away.

I wrapped my arms around him and squeezed him tightly, not wanting to let him go.

The notebook dropped to the floor with a thud, the plate of toast fell shortly after.

"Oh crap."

I slid from the bed and began picking up the toast, stacking it back on the plate whilst leasing buttery crumbs all over the carpet.

When I had the last slice of toast back on the plate I heard the tell-tale sounds of anger stomping up the stairs.

My dad's heavy footfall stopped outside my room right before he rapped on it hard with his knuckles. I was surprised the door didn't just fall off the hinges there and then.

I stood up to open the door, my face reddening, but I didn't need to bother.

"What the hell are you doing?" His face was red and creased from his sleep and he loomed over me, his large slightly laze-induced rotund frame blocked the doorway.

He'd once worked at the local construction company but, after an accident, he'd thrown his back out and was unable to continue working. He got his money from benefits, which his piggish pride hated but it was something he liked to remind me every day. The way he saw it he was like a war hero whose life had been taken away.

In his opinion I was never going to amount to anything because I wasn't 'willing to put any effort into it'. He didn't see how hard I worked for the money I got. To him waitressing wasn't a career it was servitude, which he sneered at. Both my parents were the very essence of contradictory. They were both as much a snob as the people they deemed snobs.

He looked down on me, his sleepy eyes narrowed and his face contorted into a cruel grimace.

"Sorry if I woke you," I said. My eyes shot to the carpet where crumbs from the toast disaster still glistened.

"Just for once I wish you'd consider the other people in this house," He said, louder than necessary. "And don't get me started on what you did to your mother this morning. Eating all the bread so she couldn't have her breakfast." He glared at me and I glared back, inwardly screaming at Rob.

"No, I-" I said, about to defend myself before I realised I had no excuse. Nothing I said could make the situation any better so I bit my lip, trying to keep my emotions and my voice under control. "I didn't do it on purpose." Was all I could muster. I felt pathetic and even worse was the look on Rob's face as he watched me get trodden down.

He didn't look like he believed me but his face did soften slightly when he saw my crumpled dress on the top of my washing pile.

"Just clean this up, Amelia."

And with those final words he left my room. It was funny how I could hate him so much one minute and then see myself in his eyes the next.

I slumped into the bed and buried my face in my hands, biting back tears. Rob sat next to me quietly and rubbed my back.

"Are you sure you don't want to celebrate your birthday a few months early?"

He was joking but I could hear the sincerity in his voice.

It was moments like this where reality crept into the cracks of this alternate reality I found myself living in.

Back when Rob was alive I used him to distract myself with.

I'd never thought those words before but there they were. I'd used him.

I'd go to his house and forget all about this hell hole I called home. Now Rob was dead, I could confide in him like I couldn't before, but there were no distractions. When he was alive, though, he'd never confided in me at all and it took his death to make me see the real him. No secrets, or, I guess, less and less with each passing day. How much more I had to give was anyone's guess.

Right at this moment I didn't know which situation was better.

"No," I sighed, "March is March. Unfortunately. But as long as we wait it out I'll have enough money to move further away right? So how are we going to decide where I go?"

I straightened up and forced myself to smile. My eyes flickered to the dress on my washing pile but I mentally shook myself and sat back on the bed with Rob.

"Why, my dear, this is the best part!" he said, grinning. He grabbed a few sheets of paper from the printer under my desk, waving it around in the air as it were burning his fingertips.

I tried to reach for whatever it was but he pulled away and was standing by the wall in an instant, leaving me feeling dizzy and light headed.

"Hey, how'd you do that?"

I opened my mouth to say more but all the words in my head got caught in my throat as I watched him grab some Blu-Tac and stick the paper onto the wall.

His whole body was cast in a strange glow, like he looked more solid which was strange because he'd never looked un-solid to me before.

When he turned around the glow was gone but the air in the room was electrified, giving me goose bumps.

I squinted at the paper, swallowing the lump in my throat. My heart hammered in my chest, thinking about what was going on with Rob. What was going on with me. I focused all of my attention on the here and now and refused to think about what this meant, like I had been doing since it happened.

"Well?" Rob stood to the side like the weather man from the TV, hovering next to the country like some omniscient being.

It was faint because my printer was so old. The picture Rob had stuck together looked like it had been printed several years ago and had been bleached in some desert sun in the middle of nowhere.

It was a crappy print out of a map. The world, in all its black and white glory, spreading its self out on the A4 piece of paper like the universe had suddenly turned to something small and fragile.

What ensued for the next 15 minutes consisted of us taking it in turns to throw small bits of Blu-Tac at the paper to try to determine where my new life would start.

If the sticky bits of blue rubber didn't bounce off the wall and land on the floor they were hitting the ocean. Although I didn't mind the idea of living on a boat we decided early on that it wouldn't be practical without proper training so Rob ruled it out.

Eventually the Blu-Tac stuck onto landmass and Rob rushed to the wall to determine the results.

"Seattle..." Rob said as he peeled the Blu-Tac off the map. "Well, I suppose if you had to go anywhere it might as well be as far away from here as possible!"

He was too cheery for my liking but I made my smile as big as his anyway.

I got up and pushed my finger onto the little dot on the map. It was small and so the Blu-Tac hadn't landed on Seattle itself but on the whole state of Washington. Seattle was on my wish-list, though, with its towering space needle set in front of a brilliant blue sky.

So, Seattle it was. I shrugged and smiled at Rob, my face starting to ache.

"What's up? Too far? Not far enough?" His face creased into a frown, the sadness that had often hidden in the depth of his eyes seemed darker. I had to look away to hide the shiver that went up my spine.

I sat back on the bed trying to squash the swirling thoughts back into the box I tried to hide them in.

"It's perfect... at least I know where I'm aiming for now. It's all real... it's just..." The words stuck in my throat again, this time I couldn't swallow the lump that was blocking my airway. "What's going to happen with us... with you?"

Rob inhaled, a long deep breath that he never seemed to breath out.

His face was serious for a moment before a sly smile caused his lips to curve up.

"What?" I watched as he grabbed another piece of paper from the printer. The way he moved, full of excitement, made me smile and my heart fluttered like it skipped a beat.

My mind was filled with memories of all the times me and Rob had planned trips with our friends or weekend movie marathons. "What if I told you I'd already figured that out?" He said, waving the paper at me for the second time today.

"What d'you mean?" I grabbed the paper from him and skimmed the page quickly.

There, in faded grey print, were names and addresses; all local.

There were several listed but the top four were scribbled out in black ink.

"What is it?" I asked, reading aloud, "Who's Claire Voyant?" I asked, raising an eyebrow at the awful pun. I looked at the address and noticed it was about 15 minutes away from my house in a car.

"Well-" He began but was cut off when my mobile phone rang, I jumped up and grabbed it, with its flashing lights and annoying buzzing sound annoying me more than usual.

"Hello?" I answered as though I didn't know it was my boss.

"Hi Amelia, it's Tony, you OK?" He didn't wait for a reply. "Can you come into work early today? Jess has called in sick so I need someone to cover her shift this morning."

I looked at Rob and saw the excitement all over his face at what he was about to tell me.

"Um…" I stalled. Rob frowned and cocked his head to the side like a confused puppy.

"I know the party was last night and I wanted to give you some time in bed or whatever, but no-one else can do it..." He trailed off and I let him sit and panic for a few seconds before I answered.

"No, it's OK, I can make it. What time does Jess's shift usually start?" I asked, looking at the clock. It was 9:57 now.

Rob looked at the clock too and then his face dropped. It was like he zoned out completely, his face went slack and lifeless. I kicked him with lightly in the shin and he shook himself out of it, staring out the window like nothing had happened. I bit my lip hard as Tony talked at me on the phone.

"Eleven - If that's OK? We shouldn't be too busy, Monday lunch is usually slow."

I didn't usually work until six on a Monday so I'd be pulling a really long day. Staring out of the window to where Rob was looking I sank into a darkness inside my mind in an instant. I got this sudden urge to run a bath and just submerge myself under the water.

"That's fine, as it so happens, the extra money will come in *very* handy."

Rob turned to look at me, his face was back to normal and he was giving me his most impatient look, the one where his eyebrows dipped and his mouth set into a straight line. It was serious which had always had the opposite effect because he was hardly ever serious. Hardly ever.

"I'll see you soon." I finished the conversation and hung up.

"You're going to work *now?*" Rob walked towards the wardrobe and leaned on it casually.

"Yeah, I need the money, remember?" I didn't mean to snap at him but I couldn't help it for some reason.

I smiled at him as I silently picked up clothes and left to get ready. Sometimes it really sucked that I couldn't even get changed in my own room anymore.

Dressed, I managed to sneak out of the house with Rob trailing behind me. He didn't say a word as he watched me put my makeup on.

I bit my tongue. I wanted to remind him that it was his plan that had inspired me but his sunken shoulders warned me against it. Plus, I would look like a crazy person if I started having an argument with thin air. That was exactly what I'd been trying to avoid since he came back.

As I started my shift, setting tables and re-filling the salt shakers, I re-played Rob's excited face over in my mind and pausing at the moment his expression changed when I said I was going to work. There was something in the downturn of his mouth that scared me.

As I moved around the restaurant, in and out of the kitchen, Rob sat at an empty table. Sometimes I caught him watching me but at other times he just stared out of the windows and watched people walk by.

I had the urge to sit with him, talk to him to try to make him smile again but even though the restaurant wasn't *that* busy there was still plenty of staff and enough customers to keep me from actually doing it.

The name Claire Voyant filled me with dread and amusement at the same time. I concocted an image of an overly dressed woman, shawls and beads hanging from her skinny frame. Every time I tried to catch Rob's attention to ask him about her someone walked past and I had to act normal.

I didn't take a break all day. I tried to pretend it was because I was actually enjoying the bustle of the work but my self-aware brain kept on reminding me it was because I didn't have time to think about anything else in the world.

Rob kept himself busy too; walking from table to table and listening in on people's conversations. I kept trying to catch his eye but he never looked over at me. He watched the customer's faces intently, like he was trying to figure them out.

When I finally finished work later I got a ride back home with Dan; one of the chef's. He was stern during working hours, not really one who would chat idly like me and the other waiters, but when we clocked out he was actually one of the nicest guys I knew.

Getting Rob into the car was tricky. We'd been caught in this situation before but still had yet to perfect it without it looking awkward.

It didn't help that Rob wasn't talking to me so when I opened the back door and pretended to Dan that I was going to sit in the back like he was a taxi driver I didn't even have Rob's sarcastic comments to laugh at and hide my embarrassment at the bad joke.

I forced myself to laugh as Rob climbed in instead, hearing his voice in my head instead as I imagined him making a 'back seat' joke at my expense.

As we drove Dan managed to stir up all of the emotions I had ever felt about Rob and I was forced to lie to his face, as usual.

"You know, I've been there. Losing loved ones is never easy and it doesn't get any better, it just gets further away." Dan said, repeating the sentiment I'd heard a million times since it happened. "You'll always miss him...you seem to be doing really well."

His hand slid from the steering wheel and grasped mine for a second. His clammy skin felt so different to Rob's ice cold touch.

"I am. I think." I lied. "Sometimes I feel like he's just in the next room, y'know?"

Dan said something else but I didn't hear him. I watched Rob in the back seat, seeing his reflection in the side mirror. His eyes were glassy as he stared at the passing scenery.

"…I mean, that's totally normal but you have to remember he's not."

I blinked a few times and looked over at Dan. We'd stopped driving and I noticed we were already at my house.

"He's not what?"

Dan's eyebrows raised in that way parent's ones did when they wanted you to tell them the answer instead.

"Oh, yeah, I know. It just helps…" My brain finally caught up but not before I felt that tug in my stomach. The sting of lying mixed with the bitterness of grief for something I didn't understand.

"Moving on takes time."

I nodded, letting Dan's words hang in the air. They were stale to me. Useless in every way.

I nodded and slowly got out of the car, trying to make as much movement as possible when I gathered my things so that he didn't feel the car rock as the back door opened a crack so Rob could slip out.

"See you later." I waved as he drove away.

I stood on the curb under the orange glow of the street light. An overwhelming sadness reared up suddenly. Moving on was the most important part, everyone said it like it was a decision you made, like it was something you could control. No one said it to the Wood's, it was just me. As though I'd chosen to love Rob so I could choose to stop thinking about him.

It made me angry. I wasn't able to laugh it off like Rob did. He found the clichés amusing because he didn't have to pretend to believe them.

He didn't have to deal with the fact that I couldn't move on, and I felt guilty that the smallest part of me wished I could.

CHAPTER 6

Before heading to my room I snuck into the kitchen and put a fresh loaf of bread I'd taken from work in the bread bin for my mum in the morning. I knew I wouldn't get a thank you, but the lack of appreciation was better than a shouting match.

Upstairs I wordlessly undressed in the dark and went to sleep, not caring if Rob saw me. It had been a long day and exhaustion wasn't just a feeling but a state of being.

When I woke up the next morning Rob was awake, as usual, but this time he was sat on the floor with my phone in his lap and my note pad open in front of him.

"What y'doin'?" my voice was thick with sleep. Yesterday's freeze-out was over, I could feel it in the air. It was replaced with another kind of freeze though.

"Why is the window open?" I pulled the covers up to my eyes as the chill from the window sent shivers across my exposed skin.

Rob's head jerked up, surprised, and he smiled and pointed to the note pad.

"This, Grumpy Sleeperson, is the beginning of the start of the last conversation we actually had." He continued to watch me, his forever boyish face, turned towards me. His lips turned up with excited charm. I frowned trying to pull the details together in my mind.

"Close the window!" I yanked the covers over my head and snuggled in the warmth my body had created in the night. It was dark and purple under here and I felt like a kid who'd built a fort out of sheets.

I only pulled the covers down once I'd heard the window close with a soft thump, though I never heard Rob move to do it.

"Start again, what is that?" I reached a hand out and pointed at the pad. He waved it at me.

"Come and see…" He said, and with a little chuckle he got up and ran out of my room.

I willed myself out of bed in my t-shirt and pyjama bottoms. As I poked my head out of the door, looking down the hall, I saw Rob disappear down the stairs.

He'd done this to me when he was alive too; sparking my interest in something and then running away, forcing me to stop what I was doing and follow him. I hated that it always worked.

I dressed as quickly as I could, throwing on a pair of jeans and a t-shirt with a light cardigan over the top. The day had looked and felt cool, but after the week of glorious weather we were having this August I knew it would soon perk up.

I checked my face in the mirror and tucked my hair behind my ears out of habit. The warm weather was to blame for the millions of freckles that had appeared on my arms and face. Every time I looked in the mirror I could swear a few hundred more had appeared.

I starred at my reflection for a moment, looking into the mirror-world where Rob never appeared. For a second we were exactly alike. No Rob, just our identical faces. I had to tear my gaze away.

I quietly crept down the stairs and poked my head in the living room, my mum and dad were sat watching TV and eating breakfast. Toast from the loaf I had brought in last night. Neither of them commented on its appearance.

"I'm just going out..." I said, expecting them to question where. They didn't, they just nodded in agreements not even blinking.

As I left I heard my dad mention something about Rob. I couldn't listen to him speak Rob's name aloud. If felt wrong. I slammed the door closed as I left.

I walked down the smallest path in the world, barely 3 steps to the end of it, and pinched Rob on the arm.

He was still in his suit; however, he only wore his shirt and trousers, no jacket. He'd left that draped over the chair in my room. I didn't know if mum could see it though it would make sense if she couldn't, if anything made sense at all, so I didn't need to worry about it.

"I hate it when you do that." I said as he pulled his arm away and winced. Despite my annoyance at his success in getting me out of bed I did have to laugh, because it worked every time. The smile that spread across his face told me he knew it, too.

"Come on, let's go out, we never go out anymore." He pulled at my sleeve, sticking out his bottom lip like a child, yet his eyes held a smile. They always did.

"I go out." I said, immediately having to lower my voice and start walking when I noticed the postman was looking at me strangely as he cycled past. It was too late to avoid looking crazy now, so I just carried on walking making a mental note to watch myself more carefully.

The lie throbbed in my brain like it had its own pulse. My friends, our friends, had stopped calling me to check if I was free.

Rob refused to tell me what was so important to get me out of bed I stopped asking, just enjoying the sun and cool air as we rounded the corner and started to walk to the local coffee shop.

The people who worked here knew me well enough to start my drink order before I'd gotten to the counter. They knew why I was alone these days and they were kind with their words and they didn't stare for very long.

I paid for my coffee and cake automatically, thinking Rob would eat the chocolate slab that landed on my plate. As I sipped, the smell of fresh brewed coffee engulfing my senses, the cake didn't move.

Rob's inability to eat wasn't a surprise but it also didn't fit into any rules we'd figured out. He could touch things but when he had tried to eat after he reappeared it was like he just couldn't stomach the thought. Inches from his lips and his stomach would turn. It was the same for me, really, I just didn't have the luxury of being invisible, despite how much I tried.

Rob flung the pad onto the table in front of me causing my heart to thump too hard in my chest.

The clatter drew the attention of the waiter but I managed to cover it up by pretending I'd dropped it myself. I winced at him, feigning embarrassment and he smiled. I dropped my eyes to the pad and tried to take in the information in front of me.

Since I had last looked at it there were a few more names and addresses, all of which were kind of local.

I scanned the list of names that were scrawled in Rob's boyish writing. There was Claire Voyant, at the top of the list, the other two were named

Miss Mystic's Crystal Ball Services, and, less impressively, John Ruby psychic practitioner.

I read them a couple of times, mulling over what this was all about. It was taking longer than normal for my brain to put the pieces together but when they finally clicked into place I didn't want to actually believe it.

"What is this?" I asked, speaking low and trying not to move my mouth too much. I lifted my coffee cup to my lips just in case anyone was looking.

I must have looked confused because he laughed, always amused by my lack of understanding.

"This, Wednesday Addams, is a list of paranormal experts." He waved his fingers at me for emphasis.

"Paranormal experts?" I said, rubbing my temples in an attempt to stop the dull ache that had taken residence in my skull over the past few weeks. "What in the hell would make you think these people are in any way experts in the paranormal?" I asked in a whisper, careful not to look like I was talking to an empty chair.

"I don't think they're all experts," He sank back in his seat, defensively. "Look, I did a lot of research when you were asleep. Called them, even. Managed to speak to some of them..."

I almost choking on my coffee as I sipped it. I got a few looks from the serving staff, but I laughed it off.

"Hotter than I thought!" I said, awkwardly. Better to have them think I'm a klutz than a raving mentalist. I looked back at the pad, avoiding eye contact.

"You spoke to people? On the phone?" The shock of his secret experiments bruised my ego. I quashed the urge to ask him why he'd done these things without me, but that didn't mean I was happy about it.

"That's what I'm trying to tell you, dummy! I called a load of places, I even called my house to see what would happen-"

"Rob!" If we'd have been alone I would have shouted at him. His family were already falling apart, they didn't need prank phone calls on top of it.

"But, as it happens," He spoke over my chastising, "none of them could hear me, not even Mum." His eyes turned black like onyx and a chill ran over my skin, making my shiver. "They all hung up like all they could hear was static, but these three, they could hear me."

He pointed to the list again, looking smug. A few girls walked into the café, saw me sitting alone and so sat at the opposite end of the room, I recognised them from our school.

"You talked to them?" I asked, looking down at the pad rather than at Rob. I could feel the eyes of the girls on my skin like moths hitting a light bulb.

"Well, not very well, but enough that I could tell these were the best. Think about it," He said, his face full of renewed excitement, "someone might be able to help us. You know, tell us what's going on, if it's happened before. We need the rules and at least one of these people is going to help with that."

I frowned. This was something big, but also new and scary. I couldn't stand to get humiliated if these people couldn't see or hear Rob, or if they didn't believe me, or worse, tried to scam me. I was a sceptic, even though I had a dead best friend. Just call me Agent Scully.

"Right. Well, OK... What are we supposed to do? Make appointments? How much does it cost?" I didn't want to be worried about money but, in a selfish way, I was just starting to think my life might come first for once.

I was glad one of the tricks of Rob's condition wasn't telepathy. I pushed down the thoughts that made my head ache and put on my best friend face. Rob shook his head and patted my hand.

"*I'll* pay," he said, which I frowned at, "we'll get the money from my house." He explained as though that would help clear up my confusion. It didn't.

"Rob, unless you've forgotten in the past three seconds, you're not really in the place to be asking your parents for money, and I'm certainly not asking them. What would *my* parents think?"

I was only half joking about that last part. I didn't really care what my parents thought but the shame of asking for money, especially when I couldn't fully divulge what it was for, wasn't something I was willing to take on.

The last time I had taken money from them was when we had been kids and our school had gone on a trip to France for a weekend. My parents couldn't afford it, I knew, so I never asked for the money, but Rob had told his parents and they paid without even thinking.

I never told my parents, instead I lied and said the school was paying for it.

I still felt guilty for that, not lying to my parents, but taking the money. Going on the trip. I wouldn't put myself through that again anytime soon.

"Not my parents, my brothers!" He smiled at me, his annoying all know-ing smile. The one he used when he was thinking something he wouldn't say to me. I shook my head. No.

"Which one though?" He mused, "Dean has a soft spot for you, sure, but asking for money from him will no doubt fill you with guilt and have a dampening effect later..." I didn't know what he was talking about and didn't have time to ask as he ploughed on, "Mark... probably best to ask Mark. We haven't seen him since his drunken decline and you could blackmail it out of him." He seemed to like this idea very much.

"I'm not blackmailing Mark, Robert!" I never meant to scold him like a parent, but at that moment I really did feel like the adult in this conversation despite Rob being seven months older than me.

He continued to try to argue his case as we left the coffee shop, and walked home. I had refused to discuss the matter further and sat quietly whilst I finished my coffee. The looks from the girls finally got to me and I left the shop with my head hung low.

I had hoped Rob would drop the idea of blackmail but as soon as we got out into the open he started with his ideas again. I point-in-fact told him that I wouldn't, under any circumstances, stoop to such a thing. Especially after me and Mark had had a moment of actual closeness.

I once again stopped talking to him and managed to continue the silent treatment all through my shift at work. He wasn't happy with me to say the least.

CHAPTER 7

The next morning I awoken to my phone buzzing on the pillow next to me. Rob was nowhere to be seen and I relished in the momentary privacy.

The phone continued to buzz as I stretched out under the quilt, feeling like I finally had room to breathe. When I looked at the screen to see who had decided to wake me up so rudely I was hit with both warmth and bitter coldness inside my heart.

Rob's mum's number glowed from the screen and dread made my heart beat a little heavier in my chest, making my breath catch.

"Hello?" I answered, talking quietly in comparison to the all-encompassing sound of panic my heart was making.

"Hi Amelia, it's Florence… Did I wake you?" Florence sounded farther away than just the distance of the phone line. Her voice was tinged with just shed tears.

"Hi! No, I was already awake." I lied.

The strangeness of her calling me was starting to make my skin crawl. My room was eerily silent and for once I had this feeling of clarity that Rob was actually…

"Amelia, did you hear me?" Florence's voice tuned back in, like I'd turned the volume of my life down somehow.

"Oh, sorry – I was miles away," The truth. "What did you say?"

Florence made a small sound of understanding. I had to squeeze my eyes closed, blocking out the morning light in my room that was too bright. Too quiet.

"I just wanted to see if you would like to come to dinner," She paused and I heard the voice of someone else in the background but couldn't make out what they were saying. "Tonight."

I hadn't seen her since the party and as much as it pained me to spend time with the family since Rob's death, I also craved it. The feeling of normalcy and some semblance of family unity.

"Tonight?" Even though the idea of doing something so sudden without it being planned first gave me palpitations I forced the correct answer to come out. "Yeah, of course!"

"Oh good, I was hoping you'd say yes," Florence did sound relived but there was something else in her tone that prompted me to check up on her, after all, I was sure that's what Rob would have wanted me to do.

"Is everything OK?" If felt strange asking an adult if *they* were OK, but recently I'd found myself doing it more and more.

"Oh yes, don't worry about me," She sounded light but it was fake. We hung in awkward silence for a moment.

"You didn't try to call me yesterday, did you?" She asked. Again, she tried to sound casual but there was something else under her words that I couldn't grasp. The sounds of pots and pans being moved around.

It took me several seconds to piece together what she had said and what must have actually happened.

"I must have pocket dialled..." I tried to sound aloof but I think I sounded more like I was avoiding something, luckily she was far too polite to push the matter any further.

There was a loud crash and I heard the sound of Mark laughing in the background.

"See you tonight at seven then," She said, obviously distracted by what was going on in her kitchen. "Do you want me to send one of the boys over to pick you up?" I heard another loud crash and Florence huffed.

"No!" I said. Almost shouted. The idea of either boys coming over to pick me up was unnerving. "I mean, I'll walk. I need the exercise."

After we'd both hung up the situation I'd gotten myself into spanned out in front of me like a high walled maze. Navigating social situations was always Rob's forte but now I'd have to deal with it all alone. I was also going to have to have words with him about improper phone usage.

Rob was still missing when I showered and dressed, though.

I began to get nervous when I looked down the hallway and couldn't see him. Now I wished I'd never agreed to switch shifts with Jess. If I was working my usual night shift I would have had the perfect excuse for tonight and would have been able to go looking for Rob.

I waited in my room, perched on the edge of my bed, waiting until the last minute before I had to leave for work. He never appeared. My chest tightened and loosened with each possibility that ran through my mind.

I walked down the stairs to the front door slowly; each step felt like a weight was pulling me but I didn't know if it was up or down. I was going to have to go to work without him. My brain throbbed as I tried not to think about whether he'd actually gone. Forever.

As I left the house my panic had reached a crescendo and so the only thing I could do was scream when Rob appeared at my side, like he'd just been waiting for me on the front step like a stray cat.

I made sure there was no-one around before I addressed his disappearance, feeling relief and guilt in equal measures.

"And where, may I ask, have you been?" I knew my voice gave away my emotions but, as always, Rob smiled through them. He put his arm around my shoulders as we walked down the street.

"Just hanging around the house, spying on your parents and whatnot," He smiled as he spoke but a humourless glint lingered in his eyes. I was starting to notice it more and more now. He made a displeased sound with his mouth that sounded like a hiss hiding a swear word, "Got to say, I never realised they were that vile. How did you turn out so good, kiddo?"

I frowned. I didn't want to defend them but at the same time the way Rob talked about them hit a nerve.

"Sometimes I think they wish I was more like them but I don't think they'd know what hit them if I was..." my voice held only the slightest hint of misery, as I tried to conceal my utter shame of having parents who other people found abysmal. I suppose this is what it must feel like for the parents of criminals and drug dealers, to an extent.

"I wouldn't worry about them right now. Let's just say they're having just desserts for breakfast." Rob's smiled with humorous malice.

I groaned. The image of the TV remote suspiciously moving from one place to the next as Rob swiftly repositioned it around the room filled my head. Their angry voices rang in my imagination, filled with their anger and frustration with not knowing what was going on. In spite of myself I smirked.

"There it is, the famous Amelia McHale smile!" Rob stopped walking and threw his arms around me. He smelt inherently like a living, breathing, teenage boy.

A high-pitched squeal escaped my lips and I looked around the street, worried someone might see us. I could only imagine how strange I must have looked, compressed like one of those poor kittens in a jar you saw on the internet.

Rob's hold ended just as suddenly as it began, his face melted from a broad smile to something more sombre. I shifted my gaze, uncomfortable with the intensity that burned behind his.

His mood swings were often hard to keep up with, as I'm sure mine were these days.

"I forgot to say," I said in an attempt to distract him, "we're going to your house for dinner tonight... so I was thinking... Maybe we can get money to go to at least one of those ghost hunter places on the list."

"So you'll ask Mark for hush money?" Rob's face lit up at the prospect of bribery.

"I might *ask* Mark for some money... if I feel up to it," I lied. "if not you can go and rummage through your room to see if anything is lying around."

Rob rolled his eyes, his shoulders rising and dropping with a sigh.

"So I'm doing all the work?" His voice filled with dramatic misery.

"Well, this was your plan after all, I think it's only fair you make the sacrifice."

I said it before I could hold it back, I didn't know why I had used those words, but we both fell silent as the unspoken conclusion to that sentence.

"Yes, well, I guess I can just this once," Rob kicked at the floor, his unscuffed shoes so unlike his normal shoes which lay in tatters, cold in his room.

"Which one do you want to go with?" He jumped over a puddle, out of habit more than anything.

"Which what?" I didn't jump over the puddle and my canvas shoes soaked up the liquid like a sponge.

"Ghost buster! Are you even listening?" Rob huffed and rolled his eyes at me. The truth was I hadn't been listening very well. The image of his old trainers in his room was stuck in my mind. The barriers I'd made to keep the negative thoughts out had somehow ended up backfiring and the image burned into my mind's eye.

"We'll go with the cheapest," I said after a long pause. "£40 for 30 minutes is probably the best we can do. The very mysterious Claire Voyant better have some answers." I added a spooky mystical voice as I said her name, thankful no one was around to see or hear me.

"Fair do's," He said, as the restaurant came into view. "I hope she's as good as she sounds, for some reason I can only ever imagine psychic women to look and dress exactly like a Romanian gypsy…"

I didn't have the chance to tell him how stereotypical his mind was when Sarah, one of my fellow waitresses, waved to me from the window where she was flipping the sign over to read 'open'.

We'd fallen into a routine whilst I was working. I'd ignore him, he'd try to distract me and cause trouble for a few minutes and then he'd finally get bored when I proved to be better at ignoring him than he was at causing me trouble.

Rob would then either go and sit near the big glass window that was frosted to look like water, which allowed him to people watch to his heart's content, or he'd float from table to table to take part in his most favourite past time of late; listening in on other people's conversations.

I had tried to dissuade him from doing this at first. I gave him the whole lecture about how listening to things out of context and eavesdropping could not only lead to misunderstandings, but also lead to learning things you perhaps didn't want to know.

The biggest case study for my plea was, Jamie, who we went to school with. He'd arrived at Rob's funeral with his parents; we'd know them all our lives, but that didn't stop them from talking about wife swapping with another couple just after the coffin was lowered and people were paying their respects.

Rob felt the need to tell me all the gory details that night, as a fell asleep wondering if I was going crazy. The worst part was that they weren't just discussing the actual act of it, but discussing where they did it, who with, and how much they enjoyed it.

Rob found it hysterical, whereas I found it horrifying. I was the one who had to talk to them and look them in the eye the next time I bumped into them, imagining them throwing car keys in a bowl like some clichéd 70's party, and having sex with other middle aged slightly paunchy parents of kids I went to school with.

Sometimes I hated having an imagination. I shuddered thinking about it now.

Rob refused to stop listening, though. He said he liked knowing what they did and how they lived. I didn't ask whether it was because he couldn't live, himself, even though I was pretty sure that's why he did it. That's why I couldn't deny him that simple pleasure.

Even so, I swore him to the gates of hell and back that he wasn't allowed to tell me about any of it ever again.

The shift came and went and I was still fidgeting with my clothes as I walked up the steps to Rob's house.

I'd already thrown on some jeans and a top when Rob demanded I change into something more formal.

He was smiling at me now as I pulled the hem of my tea dress down, feeling self-conscious. I was relatively tall and didn't think I looked bad in dresses, or anything, but I had always been a tomboy. It was hard not to be when my playmates were Rob and the twins. I still felt a little childish when I worse nice things; as though I were only playing dress up.

I felt that self-conscious shame, like turning up to school in my uniform when everyone else was in casual clothes, which made me hesitate at the door.

Rob rolled his eyes and knocked for me.

There was a time when I used to just walk in, like it was my own home. I guess times had changed.

After a minute of wondering whether to just run away I was left with no choice but to carry on with the charade I knew was coming. Rob's Dad answered the door and pulled me into a tight embrace.

I didn't know who was more shocked at the physical contact. Me, him, or Rob, who stood next to me with his mouth agape.

Mr Wood ushered me into the hallway, which smelled like Christmas.

"I'm glad you're here, come in…" He seemed scatter-brained and distracted, which- just like the hug – was not like Mr Wood at all.

Before I'd even had a chance to react he was on the move again, like a toy you wound up and let run across the floor.

"I've got something for you – let me just go and find it…"

He disappeared up the stairs and I was left standing in the hallway. I looked at Rob to see his face mirrored mine, eyes wide in confusion.

"Poor old man's lost his mind…" Rob said, a soft smile lit up his face for an instance until the darkness of his eyes turned it into something else.

Before he could say anything else I let myself into the living room where Dean and Mark sitting watching TV.

I said hello and was met by a grunt from Mark and a smile from Dean that made me feel exposed in some way, like I'd never worn a dress in front of him.

Rob chuckled behind me and threw himself onto the sofa with not even a hint of cushion indentation. He used to do that when he was still really *here*, causing the whole sofa to groan in despair.

Seeing my escape I left him in the room, closing the door as I went. I could hear Mrs Wood in the kitchen and I followed my nose as I made my way down the hallway and into the large bright room.

My mum always refused to believe that Florence actually cooked meals for her family, saying that she must have a chef who came in to help. She never could admit she was a terrible cook, and her jealousy always reared its ugly head.

Watching Florence, she was every bit the picture of the domestic goddess. Her hair was pinned back with loose tendrils falling into her eyes. She tried to push her hair back but it was no use. Every time she moved it out of her eyes it fell back down with the determination of naturally unruly curls.

I stood in the early evening light of the kitchen for a few moments like I sometimes did when I was waiting for Rob. I used to pretend she was my real mum, in the moments before the illusion was shattered I was content.

"Oh, Amelia, come over here!" She beckoned me into the room breaking the illusion as usual.

I walked over to where she was preparing the food and hopped up onto one of the kitchen stools. She was rolling out pastry, homemade no doubt. Her hands, apron and bits of her face were lightly dusted with flour and she looked homely and inviting. Her eyes crinkled into a smile, like Rob's often did when he was alive, and she motioned to her hands.

"I'd hug you, sweetie, but I don't want to ruin your lovely dress! You look beautiful, such a young woman now..." She also looked at me like her husband had, with a nostalgic expression, as if she was expecting me to leave at any moment. Leave and never return.

"Oh, it's OK, really!" I said, leaning onto the counter and getting discarded flour on my elbows.

I couldn't help but smile as she continued to work on the pastry; rolling it out, spinning it around and rolling it in the opposite direction until it stretched out on the counter like a pale squishy blanket.

The concentration on her face masked the grief that had taken up a permanent residence. It settled on her face like a weight; her eyes dark and her lips pursed with the doom that shadowed her life now.

I kept finding myself mimicking those features, the frown, the distant stare when the room went quiet. I didn't know if I was doing it for real or if I was copying her as a way to blend in. Emotional contagion is what the therapist I'd seen once had called it. I had never gone back after I told him that but still told my parents I was visiting Dr Theobald every week anyway.

I pulled myself back from mental oblivion to see what it was Florence was making, and saw she had a huge pot on the stove which was stewing meat and vegetables and what smelt like coppery, rich and tangy sauce.

There was a large old fashioned looking brown bottle on the counter which was labelled 'Ale', but with a homemade label, not a store kind of label, proving that although Mrs Wood was just like any other housewife, she still had the kind of connections that could get ale made outside of a large factory chain, and most probably the best cut of meat direct from the farmer, rather than having to go to the local supermarket or butchers.

"What are we having for dinner, then?" I said, trying to conjure up a casual tone which left a metallic taste in my mouth.

"Here, do you want to help me?" She said, not answering my question as she pressed the pastry out with her fingers, leaving small indentations around the edge in a pattern not unlike distraction.

I moved around the counter as she opened up the over, which blasted heat on to my unprotected legs. Mrs Wood slotted her hands into oven gloves shaped like manicured hands, and nodded at the pastry on the worktop in front of me.

"Grab that and throw it on top of this, will you?" She said holding her hands up like a surgeon would before going into the operating theatre.

I looked at her in horror.

"What?" I asked, my lip curling in disbelief. "But... I'll wreck it!" I said taking a step back. Mrs Wood smiled and rolled her eyes.

"You're not *that* accident prone. I've seen you - graceful like a ballerina..." She winced as she smiled at me. I laughed at her playfulness, a full laugh and not one I had to force.

"Like a crippled ballerina maybe." I muttered back, but I picked up the pastry as best I could at the edges and lifted. It started to droop in the centre and I knew I only had one shot to get it off the counter and onto the top of the pot.

I moved as fast and fluid as I could, lifting, moving, stepping, placing. It worked out OK and I think we both breathed a sigh of relief.

I then brushed egg on the top which Mrs Wood said would give the crust a nice shine and she slid it into the over with her gloved hands.

"There!" She said, face lit up happily, "It's a steak and ale pie... well, it should be..." She threw the gloves down and pulled her apron off, revealing her white shirt and grey skirt combo, being ever glamorous and understated. She grabbed us a couple of Diet Cokes, the glass bottles frosted with icicles from the over-working fridge and we sipped from them whilst cleaning up the kitchen.

When the kitchen looked spotless again I followed her into the living room. The boys were watching TV and for a moment I almost forgot Rob wasn't really here, well, not to them.

All three boys sat on the huge overstuffed sofas, reclining with their long lean bodies, looking more like brothers than ever.

I had to remember not to join Rob on the sofa, or even speak to him. I smiled at the boys and Mark grunted at me again. All I could do was roll my eyes and avert my gaze. I didn't know why he was back to being cold with me but thankfully I didn't have to worry about it too much because he soon got up and left the room.

Florence followed him out saying something to him under her breath that I couldn't quite catch.

I slumped on the sofa and, kicking off my shoes, tucked my feet underneath me.

"So, how's your week been?" I asked Dean. He turned to look at me, which made me nervous, I couldn't ever recall a moment in the past when he would have turned to me, instead of just talking to me with his eyes still glued to the huge TV in front of them.

"It's been OK, you know?" He ran his hand across his face and I noticed he looked tired. I also noticed him look at my dress again. "You look nice," He added, the corners of his mouth curved up. "What have you been up to?" He swept past his dress comment, leaving me no time to react and he was *still* watching me as he spoke. I felt my cheeks begin to turn pink and my words came out in a hurried tumble of too much information.

"Same as always, working, hiding from my unbearable parents, working some more..." I timidly pulled my skirt down to my knees and grabbed the remote that was in between us, focusing my attention back onto the TV. I mindlessly flicked channels like I was looking for something in particular but in truth I didn't even notice any of the images that flashed up as quickly as I zoomed past them.

Randomly I finally settled on some reality TV show with models. He flicked his gaze to the TV and shook his head with a laugh.

"Ah, I don't think so Melia." He turned his gaze back to me, and held his hand out expectantly, like I was going to give him the remote like some docile child.

Instinctively I pulled it close to me, wrapping my hands around it and cradling it near my chest like a child would their favourite toy.

"NO!" I snapped, and laughed. Me and Rob had always gotten into these kinds of fights but mostly it ended up with one of us hurt or storming out, refusing to watch what the other had put on, but this felt more like teasing and a sly smile crept onto my face. It was a smile that dared him to try to get it back off me.

Dean returned that smile and I knew I was in trouble. He was muscular and tall and could probably pin my arms in a second. I doubted very much I could wrestle him off like I could Rob, who was certainly scrappy, but less muscle mass that his older brother. He first just grabbed at the remote, which I snatched away just as fast. Shaking his head he reached over and tried to grab it again, using slow and controlled movements. He was just playing with me.

"No, Dean, let me watch this," I pleaded with him, putting the device behind my back and out of his reach, "Please?" I tried to smile as sweetly as I could but I could tell it had no effect. I heard Rob choke on his laughter at my playfulness. But I didn't spare him a glance. Dean took that opportunity, when I was trying to bargain, to pounce on me, all of a sudden his hands were all over me, tickling and poking at my ribs. I screeched with laughter as I abandoned my grip on the controller and tried to push him off.

"You've brought this on yourself!" He bellowed, as he continued to mercilessly grapple with my ribs. I squirmed underneath him and finally managed to push myself onto the floor and scramble away, thankful for my dress not ripping or else exposing my underwear. I huddled up on the floor, with my knees to my chest at the armchair in the corner.

"Stay away!" I screamed, as he gracefully pushed himself off the chair and lopped over to where I was, all thoughts of the remote control abandoned in our struggle. He laughed lazily and held his hand out to me.

"Come on," He grabbed my hand and hefted me up, wrapping his arm around me, "squirmy." He threw me back to the sofa letting me watch what I wanted as we chatted about nothing, waiting for dinner. The entire time my heart was hammering, mostly because the wrestling. I pushed away the other reasons.

Rob had been quiet, sitting and watching us and the TV, occasionally joining in with the conversation. He seemed bored of never being able to actually join in the conversation though and mumbled something about going to find Mark, which made my heart beat erratically for a few seconds. It was so easy to forget he was dead, and I think he forgot sometimes too. I was distracted by the TV when I heard Dean say my name. I blinked myself out of my daze and looked at him.

"Huh?" His face was hard to work out, looking confused and slightly embarrassed as well. He wasn't the kind of guy who got embarrassed easily, so I was automatically on edge at what might come out of his mouth, yet I still wasn't prepared for what he said.

"You and Mark... did you guys...?" He left the unspoken question hanging in the air and my brain wouldn't process what those missing words could have been, as the very thought of me and Mark doing anything together was foreign.

"Did we what?" I asked, feeling like I'd missed a huge chunk of the conversation... had I fallen asleep? Was I in the twilight zone? He seemed to notice my stupidity, but instead of laughing at me he looked more serious and frustrated, as though it was my fault he had to ask the question again.

"The other day, when I saw you coming out of his room..." He looked away from me. I could see he was biting the inside of his cheek. Rob did the same thing when he didn't want to say something. "Did anything happen between you two?"

I scrunched my face up in disgust and then laughed.

"Anything happen? Between me and Mark? What are you talking about?" I stopped laughed when I realised he was serious and my stomach did a little backflip, leaving me lightheaded.

"Well, it's just that you came out of his room late, and... you'd been in the garden a while..." I stared at him, speechless. Aghast, actually, if people still felt aghast.

"I was just wondering, that's all." Dean frowned, he seemed intently focused on the pattern of the carpet.

"No, nothing happened, we were just talking," I wish I could have told him everything about that night. I knew if I did we could laugh about it and I wouldn't feel like I was stuck in some awful lie but I couldn't betray Mark. "I swear, nothing would ever happen between us, that's just gross. He's like a brother to me." I shuddered at the thought of Mark kissing me, it just seemed so wrong. Picturing Dean, on the other hand... I turned away to hide the blush spreading on my cheeks.

The tension in the room built up to the point even the TV sounded like it was screaming for it to stop.

"He said that too. Y'know, that you guys just talked...It just seemed like he was keeping something from me." Dean couldn't hide the fact that that might be possible. As twins they shared everything with each other and even though I knew Dean sometimes hated how Mark could overshare, the idea of his brother hiding something was enough to cause that crease between his eyebrows.

I found myself looking at that crease differently, his entire face seemed to change before my eyes. For my whole life I'd seen Dean and Mark as one but now he looked like a different person.

I'd never really noticed how his lips curved into a natural smile, or how his arm muscles flexed under his t-shirt when he was fiddling with the TV controller. I mentally chastised myself, not knowing what was going on with me today.

"He's not really my type, anyway!" I said, jokingly punching him in the arm to try to lighten the mood. That made him smile and he relaxed again. I just needed to get him past this moment, and then we could both move on and forget about the mortification factor.

"What?" he said teasingly, in a very Rob like manner, "You don't think he's good looking?" He asked me, his smile returned sending shivers across my skin.

I met Dean's gaze and sneered at him with indifference.

"I've seen better," I mused. I tried to play it cool but the warmth of my cheeks told me I wasn't that great at bluffing. His smile confirmed it. Damn my fair skin!

He opened his mouth to say something but stopped when Mrs Wood took that moment to come into the living room to call us for dinner.

When we walked into the dining room Mr Wood was already sat and was reading a familiar worn book, with a black leather cover and gold embossed writing on the spine. I couldn't make out the title, but I knew I'd seen it somewhere before.

CHAPTER 8

"Put that away," Mrs Wood tutted, "Honestly!" She rolled her eyes and went back into the kitchen, re-appearing every few seconds with glasses and cutlery.

"Here, let me help!" I said, rising from my seat, but she shooed me away and after a stern look from his father Dean got up to help his mum.

Mark arrived a few seconds later, with his phone in his hand, thumb jumping erratically from one place to the next - probably texting his latest 'girlfriend'.

He went through a lot of girlfriends. It wasn't that he wasn't a nice guy, and he did have a sense of humour, but he wasn't charismatic and I don't think he ever really tried to be.

The girls he tended to meet were interested in his muscles and the label of a sportsman's girlfriend. They all seemed to live by the rule that if he treated you mean, he was keen. Of course, Mark wasn't really keen on them.

He liked what he got and when they wanted too much, he cast them aside. Still, it worked for him and I could tell this latest one was getting awfully close to the cast aside pile, as he shook his head and slammed the phone down. Rob followed him in and raised an eyebrow at me.

I think I was still flushed from earlier and I could tell from his probing gaze he wanted to know what had happened in his absence. I had to sneakily shrug my shoulders but I couldn't hide the grin that was forming on my face. I didn't know why, it was unstoppable and I had to put my hand over my mouth and lean on my elbow to try to look both normal, and hide the fact that I was a grinning mess.

Rob sat down in the empty seat beside me, at the head of the table. Where he used to sit when he was alive. Rob's mum had put a place mat out, but no plate, still, the fact that the mat was there was depressing.

Mark looked up at me then, and his face twisted into one of annoyance. He glared at me. I glared back.

"What?" I mouthed silently.

He shook his head, as though I'd done something to annoy him and I was instantly angry that his bad mood could bring me down too.

Mr Wood hadn't noticed any of this as he'd picked up his book and started reading again when Mrs Wood had left the room. He quickly jumped up though when there was a clatter in the kitchen and Mrs Wood cried out.

"Andrew!"

He strode into the kitchen muttering under his breath, and I took the opportunity to confront Mark on his bitter face, just at the same time he decided to launch his own attack.

"What?" We both said in unison.

"I can't wait to hear this!" Rob said, leaning forward on his elbows with wide, amused, eyes. I shushed him, which he only smiled more at, and Mark seemed to turn an angry shade of red, thinking I'd shushed *him*.

"Not you," I said, but that didn't make things any better, and he launched into his tirade.

"What do you mean? Not me? You better not tell anyone about the other night, Amelia, I mean it..." Before he had a chance to threaten me I cut him off.

"Mark! I'm not going to tell anyone, and I'm surprised you even remember it -" He rolled his eyes at me. "Don't roll your eyes. Your secret's safe with me, don't worry, I won't tell anyone you got smashed on your brother's birthday memorial. Not that anyone would blame you, but heaven forbid we ruin your perfect record of being the only sober asshole at the party," I snapped, "But don't think I'm going to lie for you every time you mess up!"

I pointed my finger at him to emphasise my point, and immediately felt like my parents. Urgh. My hand dropped but I continued to glare at him.

"I don't need you to lie for me!" he mumbled. I shook my head at him but inside I was revelling in the fact that he didn't have a decent comeback. We could hear talking in the kitchen and lowered our voices.

"Look," I continued, "I just wanted to help you out, I wasn't going to tell anyone. You don't have to worry," I tried to make myself sound more sympathetic. I really did understand his situation, but I just didn't like the fact that the only way he thought he could deal with it was by being aggressive.

"Fine. Thanks." He said, but he was still moody and sulking when everyone came back in with the piping hot food.

Mrs Wood sat down on the other side of me, Dean sitting opposite, and she fanned her face with her hand.

"Oh, we almost lost the pie, didn't we Dean?" She laughed, and I could see the pastry top was slightly skewed to one side, but otherwise looked amazing.

No one commented on the tension in the air between me and Mark, but I know they noticed. Dean looked between the two of us for most of the meal, as we all chatted about our week so far. It was like any other day

I'd gone for dinner. Dean's frown grew deeper and deeper and by the end of dinner he seemed dejected and miserable.

Later, as we were cleaning the plates up, I approached him.

"What's up?" I looked around to make sure no-one was listening in. Rob was smelling the leftovers and glanced over his shoulder at me.

"I know what's up with him - but I'm not going to tell you!" He said those last words in a sing song voice and winked, turning back to the food and making himself a nuisance. I ignored him, as usual.

Dean was scrapping left overs into the bin. He placed the plate on the side and I rinsed it and stacked it into the dishwasher, we moved as a team and he regarded me, shrugging.

"Nothing's wrong," He said, but I could hear the lilt in his voice, like when you ask someone if they want something to drink at your house and they say no, like they don't want to burden you. I frowned at him,

"I know something's wrong." I said matter-of-factly, "You can either tell me now, or..." I was going to say I would get Rob to tell me, but managed to bite my tongue.

"Or what?" He said, raising one eyebrow. I shook my head and shrugged, nudging him with my shoulder. Rob muttered behind me and it sounded like he said 'get a room'. He was a dick sometimes.

"Come on, tell me, what is it? Did I do something?" I don't know why I asked, I just had a feeling that something I did might have upset him.

I'd never worried about upsetting him before, but today was different and I was confused. He shook his head at me this time, his dark hair catching the light of the room, making it shift with gold and bronze tones. I'd never noticed how his hair was a multitude of browns before, it was lovely.

"No, it wasn't you, it was just Mark being his usual grumpy self, he just pisses me off - did you two have an argument or something?" He'd finished with the plates by now and moved onto the cutlery, rinsing it and handing it to me - our fingers brushing against each other's every now and then, causing my heart to flutter.

"Me? And Mark? Argue? Now where would you get a silly idea like that from?" I used my very best sarcastic voice, which always came out in a southern belle American accent, he smiled at me and chuckled.

"Cute," he said, causing my face to warm in what I knew would be an unflattering blush, "I just thought maybe something had happened -" Before he could finish I cut him off.

"For the last time, nothing has ever or will ever happen between me and *him*! That I can promise you, you nut case!" I was a little annoyed that he'd thought the tension in the room was any kind of passionate tension, because it had been a very aggravated tension. I didn't want him to think me and Mark had any kind of romantic feelings for each other. Normally I'd probably just laugh something like this off, but I felt a little bit hurt at his accusations and the fact that he hadn't believed me the first time.

"OK!" he said, holding his hands up. My eyes watched as the soap suds slid down his arms, "I was just checking, really. I just... thinking of you two together just made me feel a bit -"

"Wrong? Sick?!" I concluded for him, but he looked hurt.

"I was going to say jealous." He was serious and looking right at me. Not knowing what to do I panicked.

I never pictured this scenario happening, and everything around me blurred into a soundless haze, although I was acutely aware that Rob was now sat on the counter watching and smiling at me, with his know-it-all smile. In a second the past week flew past my eyes, and all of a sudden I saw signs I'd never seen before. The smiling, the touching, the laughing, and the play fighting. I was so stupid.

I was lucky today was the day of great timing, because at that moment Mr Wood came into the kitchen and ushered me out of the room, helping me avoid any kind of awkward moments. I quickly escaped, leaving Dean standing and staring, and Rob followed.

"Jeez, Melia, that was cold. He's probably still stood there, like a statue!" he seemed to be enjoying this very much.

"Can I meet you in the living room?" I asked politely, despite the fact he never asked me to, I always addressed him by Mr Wood and not Andrew. It just felt strange to do so. He looked down at me and smiled kindly,

"Come up to the study," He started humming to himself, "But don't be long, I'm getting old, I need to sleep after I eat."

I couldn't help but laugh. Although he was quite stern at times, it was moments like this I could see little bits of Rob appear. And since Rob's death I think he had changed, not dramatically, but maybe lightened up a bit. I walked to the bathroom at the bottom of the stairs and locked the door. Rob had come in with me, obviously knowing I wasn't really going to the toilet, and sensing the need to talk things out.

"What was that?" I whispered, sitting on the closed toilet seat that was covered with a pink frilly cover. The whole room glowed pink and had frills everywhere. I think this is the only room in the house Mrs Wood was allowed to help decorate, as the rest of the house was cosy and slightly modern. She had more of a cute and frilly theme she wanted to implore, but she'd been assigned this small downstairs bathroom. The pearlescent sink glowed in the soft lighting. Rob stood and leaned against the door.

"That is something that's been brewing for a while, I think," he said, thoughtfully, "Come on, you can't say you didn't notice?" I shrugged meekly and he hit his palm against his head.

"Amelia! Come on, you guys have always had a thing going on, I thought you were doing it on purpose!" I was aghast. Had I? I didn't know. I mean, I liked him, but up until this point I never even thought about him that way... did I? I was confused and I leant forward and covered my face with my hands.

"No! I didn't have any idea!" I mumbled.

"What?" Rob asked, obviously not understanding my girlish talking into hands moment.

"I said," I breathed as I released my face, "That I didn't have any idea! Why didn't you tell?" I wailed at him dramatically. "What the hell am I going to do?" I hid my face again, feeling my cheeks burn.

"You're going to go back out there and kiss him!" He seemed to like this idea and his exuberance over it caused my heart to do a backflip, in anger.

"What? And you'd just be OK with that? You die and then I just hook up with your brother?" He shrugged.

"Better Dean than Mark, I say" He joked.

I frowned and stood up, looking in the mirror. My face was cooling and I took a moment to straighten my dress out and smooth down my hair, and then I stalked out of the bathroom and went upstairs to the study, not talking to Rob.

He followed, though he knew not to press me to talk to him, so he kept his mouth shut as we ascended the oak staircase up to the second floor.

I followed the dark red carpet down the hallway to the end and found the office door ajar but Mr Wood wasn't there. I turned to see Rob's bedroom door was slightly open as well and when I peeked through I could see Mr Wood standing in the middle of the room with his back to me. I hesitated, with my hand hovering just over the door handle. I could push the door farther open and walk right in but there was something stopping me.

I hadn't been in Rob's room since he had died. Every memory from our childhood was locked in there. Pictures on the walls, movies we'd watched, everything that marked our lives was out in the open like pins in a map, marking our history, tracing our steps.

Rob was like a statue behind me. I could feel his gaze over my shoulder, watching his dad in his room. A sight I don't think either of us had ever seen. It wasn't that Mr Wood was a bad father but he hadn't been a part of Rob's interests like he had with the twins. We didn't speak of it often, but I knew Rob ached for his father's approval and seeing him in his room so solemnly could only bring back memories we all could do with forgetting.

Without looking back at my best friend I gently swung the door open and stepped into the room.

Mr Wood turned at my arrival and seemed to come to his senses as though he'd been lost in his own thoughts. He shook his head to clear his thoughts but his eyes gave him away, the slightest hint of tears shimmering in the light.

I didn't comment, merely walked into the room to take it in again, like going back to a house you used to live in when you were younger, everything seemed familiar but not at the same time, it was like I'd forgotten something, like something was missing.

Rob entered the room slowly behind me, I could hear his gentle foot-steps on the floor. They were as tentative and unsure as I felt but at least we were going through this moment together. I twinge of guilt shot though me; for Mr Wood this room would always be empty.

"Sorry Amelia, I just..." He trailed off and gestured to the room, a pained expression aged his face. I nodded, not saying a word. I understood. My eyes traced the room, in inhaled the familiarity. Most of all I tried to avoid look-ing at Mr Wood's broken-hearted face.

"I've been coming in here almost every day you know, reading his books, looking at his photographs..." He was talking to himself mostly and he wan-dered around the room, picking things up and placing them back down like they were made of the most delicate materials.

It was then I noticed all of the books; scattered around the bookshelf, stacked next to his small sofa, piled on his desk in random assortments. Thinking back to dinner everything clicked, the book he'd been reading was from Rob's collection. I knew it was familiar.

"He was good, wasn't he?" I looked over to where Mr Wood stood, about to tell him that *of course* Rob was good, what else would he have been? But then I noticed he'd been looking through Rob's makeshift portfolio, a collection of his favourite shots.

The sight of them filled me with bittersweet memories, like flashbacks, printed in an array of black and white and intense colours, so vivid and full of life.

"Yeah, he really was." I smiled as Rob put his hands on my shoulders and peered over my head. We looked at them together, silently. I picked up some of the most recent ones he'd taken of trails of traffic, like stars, racing down the road. I ran my fingers over the gloss of the photo paper.

"Hey! Fingerprints! Come on..." Rob squeezed my shoulders and I stifled a laugh for fear it would turn into a sob.

For his benefit I placed the photo back into the folder with care next to the box full of cinema tickets.

"I keep reading these books trying to figure him out. I just want to know him... I wish I'd known him better..." Mr Wood perched himself on the arm of the small sofa where me and Rob had watched so many late-night movies together, he seemed like a giant in here, trying not to break anything. "What was he like?"

I wasn't really ready for this conversation but I couldn't see any way out of it now. To be honest, I'd been expecting it for the past week.

Rob moved past me to stand next to his father. He stared down at him with an expression I couldn't read on his face. They had never understood one another but they were both so much more similar than either of them give themselves credit for.

I didn't really know what to say but I the words began to fall from my lips before I could stop them.

"You knew him, I just don't think you saw him the way he wanted, or he wasn't who you wanted him to be." The honesty of it shocked both of us. Silence followed and a moment where I wondered whether it was worth just leaving the room.

I had a mind to back pedal, try to soften the hostility of my words with the niceties you offered people who'd just lost loved ones but he put his hand up in anticipation.

"No, you're right. You're right, I didn't. I wish I had Amelia, I really do," He sighed and his posture crumpled underneath him with the weight of my words. "I suppose it's too clichéd to even think that you don't know what you've got until it's gone. I just wish Rob had known that I loved him. I wish I could have told him how proud I was of him wanting to do his own thing."

I tried to hold back the tears that stung at the back of my eyes, threatening to spill down my cheeks like acid.

"I'm pretty sure he knew." I said, the bold-faced lie everyone tells when confronted by grief.

Mr Wood nodded and got up, standing side by side with his son without even realising it.

Rob's face still held that unreadable expression. The blankness of it stirred up memories of darker times.

"Come on then, there's no point in dwelling in here, Florence does enough of that for the both of us, I'm sure."

The Mr Wood I knew was back, his straight backed, straight faced normality that shielded the man I'd just seen from view like a suit of armour.

✳

"He's gone..." I didn't like the way he kept on repeating my name. The shock was overwhelming and hearing the words out loud made me feel like I was falling even though I was firmly planted on the ground. Heavy as the world. I put my free hand down to steady myself.

"What?" I repeated. He didn't say it again though, he knew I'd understood. I was numb. My face was numb. My hands were numb – I couldn't feel my legs. I couldn't feel Tony who had knelt down and was rubbing my back. I couldn't feel anything but the distant absence of pain in my chest. It was dull and empty and entirely wrong. Mr Wood's voice cracked as he continued. I could hear Mrs Wood sobbing in the background and hushed voices trying to soothe her.

"I'm going to come and pick you up from work, I'll call your parents and let them know what's going on? I'll be there in five minutes..." He trailed off or I dropped the phone. All I know is his voice subsided into a high-pitched ringing in my ears.

Tony put his hand on my elbow and helped me stand, moving me to a chair someone had brought in from the dining room.

I sank into it, not seeing anything properly, the tears in my eyes distorted the room, making it shine and swim like I was underwater. I was drowning.

I took comfort in the fact that no-one around me had faces anymore, they were just ink blots in a sea of colours. Jane, another waitress, came in and put her arm around me.

"I just heard, are you OK?"

I didn't give her an answer, I couldn't speak. I stared straight ahead and she squeezed my shoulders and rubbed my back – I didn't know why people kept rubbing my back. Tony reappeared with my coat and bag and he handed them to me, which I took, but mostly because it seemed like that's what I should do. My brain didn't quite know what it was supposed to do with them so I hugged them to my chest.

For a few seconds I thought it must all be a joke, they were joking; it was Rob's stupid idea – proving that sometimes when he calls it is an emergency. But no, Mr Wood would never play such an awful joke – I remember when Rob had once covered himself in ketchup and lay at the bottom of the stairs to scare his brothers; his dad had found him and gone ballistic. We weren't allowed to play in the kitchen for a long time after that.

Mr Wood pushed the door open, the wood brushed the plush carpet, making a '*throosh*' sound you'd associate with a cosy room. And it was cosy. It was also very dark.

It seemed the curtains had been drawn and a projector, one of those old-fashioned ones you usually saw on TV or in a movie, was set up on the desk.

When Mr Wood built an office, he meant business. Files upon files were stacked on the desk and underneath - the filing system seemed too intricate for me to figure out, and I couldn't even begin to try as I had no clue about the banking world.

Mr Wood sat down on the old black leather desk chair, which was tatty around the edges and fit around him like he was wearing it, rather than sitting in it.

When we were younger me and the three brothers would take it in turns, sitting in the chair and spinning around until we were dizzy, seeing who could walk the farthest before falling down in a fit of giggles.

We had so many memories in this house, opening a new door just unleashed floods of forgotten times. I mentally shook myself to return to the present.

I turned my attention to the projection screen; the projector looked like an old-fashioned piece of equipment but it was just a façade. The images that lit up the screen didn't belong to an old and grainy black and white film but a crystal-clear video from a DVD.

I smiled when I realised the film was from my seventh birthday when we'd all gone to the zoo. My parents were even in the film, laughing with the Wood's and holding balloons that I remember we'd begged for and then not wanted to carry once we had them in our possession because they slowed us down; we'd run, but were tethered to these bobbing tangling weights that caught us in trees and other people's balloons.

Me and Rob were holding our hands out to the person filming, who I recall was Mark. He was reluctant to actually do the job though and his attention and his filming hand kept travelling to other things. As a 12 year old boy, it was the obvious distractions; girls.

We were waving, trying to catch Marks attention and then, to my instant horror, pretending to impersonate the animals and putting on a little skit, acting out how we thought the animals spoke to each other. Cringe-worthy stuff, I groaned audibly.

Mr Wood turned to me and smiled, the encounter in Rob's room apparently buried away.

"Hard to imagine you were that young, isn't it?" He mused, eyes travelling back to the screen, and the image that flickered in my peripheral like unrelenting memories. I perched on the edge of the desk jokingly hiding my face in my hands.

"It's so embarrassing!" I groaned as I watched my younger self feed the animals in the petting zoo area.

"I've been watching these old videos a lot recently..." His eyes flickered as they followed Rob on the screen, so small and young, preserved forever to haunt us.

Whilst he was distracted I glanced around the room to where Rob was stood. He'd not come into the room fully, lingering in the doorway like a shadow. He didn't watch the screen or seem that interested in the video, he watched his dad with his blank faced mask that sent shivers through my body.

"Where did I put it?" Mr Wood said to himself. I turned back to him and saw he was looking for something in a drawer.

I moved closer, curiosity getting the better of me. When he sat back up I noticed Rob had appeared next to me; silent as ever he moved.

"Here we go!" Mr Wood exhaled in one long breath, like he'd been holding it whilst he was searching.

I squinted in the low light and he seemed to read my mind, flicking a switch under the desk which brought the room into a bright glow.

He held a small key up to the light; bronze and kind of dirty looking. No key I would imagine fit any of the locks in this house.

"What does it open?" I asked, though I had a feeling I was going to find out.

Rob was equally as interested as I was, getting as close to the key as he could without touching his father.

"I've never seen that key before, it's not for the house," He whispered, coming to stand by my side. His face had resumed its normal appearance, the blackness of his eyes had gone completely and the bright blue irises shone in the soft light. "Why did he hide it?"

The tone of his voice suggested he wasn't happy there might be secrets in his house. Rob hated not knowing things, it was one of the main causes of our very rare arguments.

"This," Mr Wood said, regarding me calmly with a tone I couldn't quite fathom, "Is a present. For you."

"A present for me? Why?" I reached for the key but he snatched it away and stood up quickly.

"Follow me!" He boomed, his authoritive voice filled the room, making me jump. He turned the projector off with the flick of a switch under the desk and led me out of the dark room, back into the brightly lit hallway.

We passed Mark on the stairs who smiled at his father and scowled at me.

"What was that about?" I whispered to Rob, behind me. He shrugged.

"Dunno, you know him, moody as hell..." He paused and smiled, putting his hands on my shoulders and leading me down the stairs, "You're talking to me again." It was a statement, not a question. I shrugged.

Mr Wood beckoned me to the mud room I'd been in early this week, although the last time had me hefting his heavy middle child on my shoulder and trying to stop him from commando rolling into the hallway.

I followed, unsure of the outcome of our journey, having to jog small steps every now and then to keep up.

Luckily the weather had warmed up, as expected, and though it was now reaching evening time the heat hung in the air like warm sheets drying in the sunshine.

We walked across the stepping stones that marked a path around the house but he didn't lead me towards the garden, he led me around to the side of the house where the three-car garage sat.

It was an impressive building in itself, built in the same style as the house and the size of one, really, but instead it housed the family cars; Mr Wood's 4x4, Mrs Wood's smaller coupe and the sports car Dean and Mark shared.

I assumed that's where we were heading but Mr Wood strode past it.

"Just over here!" He called. His long stride had him several paces in front of me and he kept looking over his shoulder, as though making sure I was still there and I hadn't disappeared.

I smiled encouragingly every time he did it, though I didn't know what I was encouraging him towards.

Rob strode at my side, muttering the whole time about secrets and hidden keys, trying to figure out what his father could have been hiding. I ignored him as best I could.

When Mr Wood finally stopped, I wasn't surprised we hadn't known what the key was for.

We stood at the door to the old wooden shed that had been on the property when they had bought it, the original garage, but unused and fallen into disrepair.

We'd never been allowed to play in this garage and had been convinced, as kids, that it was haunted by the ghost of the previous owners. Even when we'd later learned that the previous owners never died we still carried on the story just out of habit.

Mr Wood stood before the door which was all beaten up planks; weathered and greying in the diminishing sunlight.

I shivered, in spite of myself, as I pictured ghosts swirling in the shadows of the abandoned garage.

The irony wasn't lost on me; being scared of the ghosts I knew weren't there, when the ghost who'd been following me around for the past few weeks didn't stir so much as a peep out of me.

I looked at the old lock on the door; the rusted soul mate to the key.

Rob kicked one of the rotten planks that made up the doors.

"That lock seems a little bit pointless." He said. I looked down and saw his point. The doors looked ready to fall apart at the slightest knock, a lock wouldn't keep someone from getting in.

"This lock must be as old as me." Mr Wood said as he pushed the key into the lock and jiggling it with some intent.

A jolt of unreasonable fear ran through me as I mentally re-watched every horror film Rob had made me sit through.

Rob sensed my tension, as usual and grabbed my wrist.

"Careful! Dad's going to murder you and hide your body in here," He joked, "I always knew he had it in him, but I always assumed it would be Mark who killed you... or Dean... You know, jilted lover and all that."

He laughed at his own joke and I went back to not talking to him.

The lock finally clicked open with the sound of old rusted metal upon metal and Mr Wood pulled the doors open.

The fresh cool air that had been held inside this rundown place burst out, creeping into the warm air and adding an unnatural chill that sent goose bumps up my arms.

"Come on then," Mr Wood beckoned me with a wave of his hand.

He stood at the dark opening like a gatekeeper to another dimension. There was no light from the garage, in fact, light didn't seem to be able to penetrate the room at all.

The age-old foreboding we'd imagined as kids made me hesitant.

"I'm not going in there, something's going to eat me, there might be spiders!" I said.

I squinted to look inside but couldn't see past the dust swirling in the air disturbance like an ancient snow storm

"Nothing's going to eat you!" He said, in good jest, "But yes, there's probably a million spiders in there." He walked past me and disappeared from view, the shape of his bulk was only just visible as the darkness smothered him.

CHAPTER 9

"Well, come on!" Rob said, fading into the darkness after his dad leaving me standing outside as the men walked into the unknown.

Hesitantly I edged towards the doors, shrinking away from the entrance in fear of dropping spiders.

I could hear the sound of movement and a sudden *whoosh* sent a cloud of dust flying towards me. Coughing, I waved my arms in front of my face.

Rob and Mr Wood began to cough, out of sight, the dust seemed to affect the living and the dead alike.

"Sorry!" He called, "Are you coming in?"

Using my hands to cover my head I walked over the threshold, closing my eyes as I went from the lightness outside to the darkness within.

When I opened them, blinking in adjustment to the gloom, I was stood beside Rob.

"Cool." He breathed and I followed his gaze to see what caused the smile to lift his face.

It was black and the glimmer of light that slid through a crack in a wooden roof panel made it look glassy and fluid, like a thick liquid.

Reaching my hand out I ran my fingertips along the front of the black car that was spotlessly clean in an otherwise filthy garage.

The smooth cool metal slid under my hand like ice. My eyes widened as I took in the beauty.

"What is it?" I asked, looking into Mr Woods smiling face, he was rubbing his hands together to beat the chill that seemed to have settled into this place, which didn't make it seem any less spooky.

"It's a car," He said with a wry smile, running his hand over the top of it with a sort of fatherly pride. "And it's yours."

I couldn't help but just stand there, aghast, my brain taking a full minute or two to process the words.

"I can't have a car..." I said, instinct made me reject his generosity. Call it a hereditary trait.

"It's yours," He said, not looking at me. He clicked the door open and bent into the car, searching for something.

When he heaved himself back out of it he was holding a set of car keys. With a swift arm movement he threw them to me. I only just caught them with my fingertips and held them in my hand, looking down at them with trepidation.

"I bought it for Rob... for his birthday," He said, looking down at it and sighing. "But, well, if he's not here to have it I know he'd want you to have it. You two shared everything anyway."

He wasn't looking at me, more looking past me, into the dying day outside.

Rob walked around the car with appreciation, running his hand over its black armour.

"He's right, if I can't drive this beast, you have to have it! Besides, if you get it technically *I* get it!" He was enthralled by the sleekness of it, which seemed more like an animal than a car.

"I suppose." I said to Rob. Mr Wood looked at me, snapping out of his trance.

"Hmmm?" His eyes expressed the sorrow of this moment. Passing on a gift, in general, was too much. I could see what this meant to him so I did what I did in every sad situation I found myself in recently. I smiled through it.

"You're right, Rob probably would have wanted me to have this... but it's too much, can't you just sell it? Or give it to Mark or Dean?" Saying the words I knew I was supposed to say despite the automatic desire to get in the car and drive as far away from here as possible.

Every practical, reliable, bone in my body was suddenly straining at the urge to give in to my inner rebel, but I forced my hand out to give the keys back.

"You're joking, I wouldn't trust either of them with this!" He said, waving my hand away. "No, I want you to have it. It's a shame you passed your test and didn't get to have a car."

My driving test had come and gone months ago, me and Rob had passed together.

I looked at the keys and then at Rob, who was now looking relatively giddy at the thought of getting a car, even though he wasn't really.

"I can't take this home though," I argued despite myself, "My parents would kill me..."

I was torn and my annoyance at my parents burnt in my mind. Mr Wood seemed to agree with this, though I could tell he was trying to be tactful as he chose his words with care.

"Yes, well, you can park it here if you want, it'll give you an excuse to keep coming over at least." His face mottled pink. He wasn't an affectionate man and the gesture wasn't lost on me.

"I don't need an excuse to keep coming over, this place is like my home!" I smiled as I realised the truth of it. This place was more a home to me than my actual house, and Rob's parents had done more work raising me than my own.

"Yes, well, in any case, you can have the car, keep it here and everything will be fine." He seemed to want to move past the emotional scene, so he pried the keys out of my hand and got in the front seat. "Step away and I'll drive it out of here for you."

He clicked on the ignition and the car growled with life, purring like a cat and then leaping forward, excited to be released from this dank prison.

"I can't believe dad got me a car..." Rob mused as we followed it out, "I mean, I honestly thought he didn't even know when my birthday was, but this is -" He was cut off when the car engine stopped and Mr Wood appeared.

Although it was now a dimming light and the stars had started to appear it was still bright outside and the car came into full relief in the glow of the lights from the house windows. It was pure black, curved with chrome accents, in the light I could see the leather interior and that rebellious part of me squealed.

"What kind of car is it?" I asked, sitting in the driver's seat as Mr Wood moved out of the way for me.

"A 1965 Ford Mustang Fastback," he said with some pride, though it meant nothing to me. I was just impressed with how much it seemed to glow.

"It's so pretty." I murmured to myself. My hand slid around the steering wheel and pushed at the gearstick, clicking it into the slots.

"It gets good mileage," He said, though I didn't care at this point, "and don't worry about maintenance, I'll take care of all the costs." I gave him a sharp look.

"No, I'll pay for everything... I've got money saved." Though it hurt me to say, and would hurt me even more to spend. Still, I still had enough time to save more money for my escape, I would probably just have to choose somewhere closer to home that was slightly cheaper.

Mr Wood shook his head but only slightly, and Rob punched my arm through the door.

"He's trying to be nice!" He said with a frown.

"We'll worry about all that later." Mr Wood said, dismissively. I knew I'd have a fight on my hands, "Why don't you take it for a test drive?" He suggested.

Before I could answer he left me and the car alone. I watched as his back retreated towards the house. The slope in his shoulders told me all I needed to know, Rob had the same walk when he was lost in thought.

"Yessss," Rob hissed, breaking the tension only I seemed to feel. He raced around the front of the car and slide into the passenger seat, "Let's hit the road!"

I laughed, letting any residual feeling of depression fade away as I turned the engine on and revved.

The front of the car rose up and we lurched down the dirt track that led to the drive. From there we were away. We drove out onto the tree lined street, cruising at a snail pace, as I got used to all the buttons and levers.

❋

When we eventually rolled back to the house, pulling the car in to the wide driveway, Rob couldn't stop excitedly talking about what having this car would mean to our potential freedom. I was still worrying about the cost of petrol, but I was doing my best to push those kinds of thoughts to the back of my mind for the time being.

I locked the door and slid the key into my pocket as we headed up the front steps. The circumstances for getting the car twitched in the back of my mind like a moth hitting a lightbulb but I pushed it aside.

When we walked through the front door Mrs Wood greeted me, throwing her arms around me and grinning from ear to ear.

"Do you like it?" She beamed, unable to hide her glee, "I knew you'd like it!" She didn't wait for a reply, her arms tightening in a bone crushing hug.

"Yes, thank you, it's too generous, I love it!" I pulled back and smiled at her as she tucked a piece of hair behind my ear.

This is what it felt like, having a loving mother.

I hated myself for even thinking the words, for even being jealous of Rob and taking pleasure in a moment that was brought on in the aftermath of his death.

I sobered up almost immediately and pulled away from Mrs Wood's embrace.

If she sensed my unease she didn't mention it. Instead, she led me into the kitchen for coffee.

"So, what are you going to do with yourself? Your birthday isn't far off, do you have any big plans?" She asked tactfully. I could tell she had been planning on asking it for a while, the question seemed rehearsed.

She hid her face behind her coffee cup as she sipped the hot black liquid. I took a sip of my own coffee to buy some time.

I never intended on lying to her, it's just I never planned on being asked on what I was going to do with my life, even though it's kind of an appropriate question to ask.

"Ummm... I don't know really. I hadn't thought about it. I might go travelling," I tried to sound nonchalant, though I think I came across as skittish and avoid-y, "who knows?"

I needed to get out of this conversation before I dug myself into a hole.

I committed to the story of travelling she would want to help me plan, and I didn't feel good about keeping up a lie and letting her waste time.

As predicted, her eyes lit up at the mention of travel and she stood, too quickly for me to stop her. My worst thoughts seemed to develop before my eyes like the terrible photographs Rob used to develop when he got his first camera.

"Oh, travelling, that's a great idea. You know, I have pictures of when I went travelling in my twenties, have I ever shown them to you?" She walked to the door and lingered, her summer dress swung at her ankles, mirroring her excitement. "I'll go and get the scrapbook!"

She disappearing into the hallway before I could say no.

I let my head sink into my hands with defeat. There was nothing to be done for it now, I'd have to fix the situation later.

I knew she'd be gone for at least ten minutes. I'd seen the photo albums the other day and they weren't as well organised as they usually were; scattered all over the bed and table in the spare room in a bid to find a photo of Rob for the prayer cards; smiling, rather than making stupid faces, as per almost every photo of him.

"What's wrong with you?" I jumped to find Mark had snuck in and was stood with his muscular back to me. He was bent into the fridge, looking for food.

"Nothing." I mumbled, though the shame of the lies I was telling were beginning to weigh heavily on me.

I looked at Rob for help, out of habit, forgetting that he wasn't really *there*.

Mark pulled his hand out of the fridge and set a bowl covered with cling-film on the counter. He grabbed a fork and came to sit next to me at the breakfast table.

"Doesn't seem like nothing."

He peeled away the clear plastic, which was coated in drops of condensation, and threw it to the side with the same lack of interest I felt myself, these days.

I watched him as he ate, unable to understand where this sudden interest had come from.

"Trust me, it's nothing." I said. I snapped with such a bite to my voice that Mark looked up, shocked.

Even in our constant state of bickering I never snapped at him. My temper seemed to float closer to the surface these days.

"Like the car then?" He asked, chewing whilst he spoke. I pulled a face at him to let him know I didn't appreciate the food show he was putting on. Typically he ignored the subtle request to not do it.

"Yes, actually. It's a little too generous though." I admitted and he shrugged without looking at me; his shoulders stayed hunched as he continued to plough through the leftovers.

"Rob would have wanted you to have it, you know. If he couldn't."

Mark was a man of few words normally so the increase in speech, let alone pleasant speech, knocked me back. I forced myself to blink away the tears that suddenly stung my eyes.

"Yeah, that's what your dad said," I left out the part about Rob also agreeing, "but still... it's such a nice car. I'm not sure it's my style."

Mark rolled his eyes and huffed, audibly.

"Whatever," He bristled, holding up his fork at me like it was a tiny trident. "If you don't want it I'll take it. Think how many more girls I'd get with it!"

I arched my eyebrow and we laughed together. This happened sometimes, what Rob liked to call the Eye of the Mark Storm. It was like it you set two metronomes ticking at different times. At some point they'd line up; tick-tocking, if just for a moment, in perfect rhythm.

"What? You're winning smile and warm personality isn't doing the job? You need a sexy black sports car to hook them in?"

He shovelled more food, making a point of chewing with his mouth open.

"Well, those things help, but that car would just push me into another level, that's all."

He took another bite of food and looked at me. It was a different look than I was used to. Not a scowl, but his brow furrowed like he was fighting in internal battle.

"Sorry I was a dick earlier." He met my eyes, the sincerity was unnerving and I looked away, anywhere but at him.

I waited for more, thinking he'd make a point of apologising for how much he tormented me for basically the duration of my life so far but it seemed that was asking too much.

"It's OK," being the forgiving docile girl I was it was all I could say. Years of forgiving Rob for various faults had hammered that response into me like reflex. "Maybe if you keep this up I'll let you borrow the car."

I smiled at him. It was semi-forced for a reason I couldn't pinpoint, like most of my smiles recently.

He didn't seem to notice or if he did he had the decency to not say anything.

He went back to the fridge, his empty bowl left behind, just as Dean appeared at the door.

"There you are. Can we talk?" He stopped in his tracks as Mark popped his head out from behind the fridge door.

"Do you want a Coke?" He held a bottle out to me, only noticing his brother when he closed the fridge again. "Did you ask me something?"

Mark sat next to me, passing the open bottle to me roughly, making the liquid fizz up and drip down the sides of the curved bottle in a sticky mess.

Dean leant in the doorframe, his arms folded across his chest defensively. I saw his eyes drift at the table with the food and coffee sat between me and Mark, his expression was unreadable.

"It's OK Mark, you drink it. I have to go, anyway." I patted him on the shoulder in an awkward farewell and slid past Dean, into the hallway.

As I walked towards the front door the twin's voices followed me, muffled and low. Moments later the kitchen door opened behind me. I didn't have to turn to know who had followed me out.

"Amelia, wait," He took a few long strides and caught my arm easily despite my head start.

"What?" I twisted my arm away from him and fixed him with a glare that should have told him to leave me alone. It would have worked on Mark but Dean was more like Rob than I realised.

"What do you mean, 'what'? Can't we talk?" He shoved his hands into his pockets and stared down at me with an intensity that sent shockwaves through my whole body.

This would have been a perfect moment for Rob to reappear and I mentally screamed his name, hoping to discover an unknown power.

"What do you want to talk about?" I played dumb, waiting for my dormant power to activate. It was either Rob appeared or I became invisible. I was holding out on the latter.

Dean tilted his head to the side and regarded me with a sadness I saw in my reflection more often than not these days.

I didn't want to deal with this but neither power kicked into gear so I put on my brave face, the one I wore when I saw my old friends in the street... He took a step towards me and seemed to think better of it, taking a step back again.

"Why does it seem like every time I turn around you and Mark are having some kind of heart to heart?"

I'd been trying not to look directly at his face but with those words I glared at him.

He starred right back at me, lips pressed together like he was waiting for me to react. The strange flutter I'd started to notice when we were together forced my cheeks to burn. I knew it was irrational but I swore he could hear how my heart picked up speed.

"That's what you want to talk about? Seriously?" I tried to keep my voice quiet, and not let my annoyance increase the volume any more than I could help, "you're unbelievable!"

I turned on my heel and stormed to the front door, desperately hoping Rob would appear at the perfect moment so I could storm off quickly. Otherwise I'd no doubt have to linger outside for him and that would be awkward to say the least.

"Wait, no - that's not what I wanted to talk about, I was joking!" Dean laughed as he strode after me, catching me by the arm again.

We both realised the mistake too late. I had anticipated his grasp and turned towards him just as he went to pull me to a stop.

I turned and he pulled and all of a sudden we were crashing into each other.

My hands went to his chest automatically, and his hands slid to my waist. I didn't know what I noticed first, the fact that his body felt more toned than I remembered, or the realisation that I was wearing a dress and the thin material was all that was between his hands and my bare skin.

Our eyes locked and I felt the blood rush to my head. At the same moment we made contact Mrs Wood appeared in the hallway.

I pushed Dean away or he took a step back, it was hard to tell who moved first.

From the look on Mrs Woods face she knew she'd just interrupted something.

"Oh, Amelia..." She began, I could tell she was trying to act casually but the lilt in her voice betrayed her embarrassment, "I found the pictures of that time I went travelling... I'm sure I could give you recommendations, though they might be outdated!"

She smiled at me, the smile she'd often smiled at Rob, a smile she saved for her family and here she was, offering it to me like a warm bed on a cold night.

My gut tightened as the situation took a turn for the worst. Dean's eyes bore into the side of my head. I refused to look back at him.

The silence hung heavily in the air. I felt like I was trapped in time, everything seemed to stop, even my heart.

"Where are you going?" Dean's voice cut into the moment and time resumed its march into the unknown.

"Is it OK to look at them another time? I have a bit of a headache." I ignored Dean but stole a look at him. His face was unreadable again, blank and void of emotion; the mask was a mirror of Rob's and it cut into my soul.

"Amelia?" Rob appeared at my side, finally. He looked between us all and seemed to sense that he'd missed something. He reached for my hand but I pulled it away, pretending to absentmindedly push my hair behind my ears.

"Of course, how about this weekend?" Mrs Wood was solemn, like she could see Rob with us, or maybe it was because she couldn't.

I nodded and smiled.

"Sure, I'll see you then."

As soon as we were out of the door and walk-running down the driveway Rob bombarded me with questions. I answered each one as we walked back to my house, leaving the car on the driveway, but I gave nothing away.

"For the last time, Rob, nothing happened between us. Are you going to tell me where you were the whole time?"

I knew the only way to deflect attention from myself was to place it on him. It was a technique that usually worked, up until the last year or so, anyway.

Rob skirted the question like a pro.

"If mum is going to help you out with planning our escape this could be a good thing!" He said it with such enthusiasm, the old Rob back, that I didn't tell him why my insides twisted like barbed wire when he said 'our escape'.

I fell asleep to the tornado of regrets in my head, and lived through a million ways I could have dealt with the situation that was my life. The next few days were monotonous as I worked and avoided my parents, and Rob in a way.

He didn't seem to notice how I'd pulled back from him and spent a lot of time researching flights and apartments whilst planning different ways he could haunt my parents.

I didn't hear from or see any of his family until my scheduled Saturday visit.

✤

"Mr Wood's here..." Tony's voice broke through the silence that was deafening; my own thoughts had just become a painful white noise.

I could only nod and he once again grabbed my elbow and helped me up. He mentioned something about not having to worry about work and he'd sort out the rest of the week's shifts and I could let him know when I was ready to come back. None of it registered, I could only focus on Mr Wood standing in the doorway to the restaurant.

The whole room disappeared, the staff melted away, the customer's ear-splitting chatter tuned out.

We looked at each other, silently. His face was red and his eyes bloodshot. He was impeccably dressed as usual, meaning he must have been at the office earlier, must have been given the news over the phone like me.

I saw myself in him and in that moment I could see him look at me in the same light. There was something so broken in his appearance I wondered if that's what I looked like. I knew it was, I felt it.

When I reached him he didn't seem to know what to do, so he took my coat and helped me put it on. The weather was so nice outside it wasn't necessary, but I didn't say anything, just pushed my arms through the sleeves and followed him out of the door.

He was parked right on the curb outside and I climbed into the passenger seat.

"What happened?" I asked, it was barely a whisper and I wasn't sure he'd heard me. I wasn't even sure if I was asking him or some power in the universe.

He put the car into drive, pushing the gearstick harder than necessary, and peeled away from the curb he spoke, not taking his eyes off the road.

I didn't even know how he could operate the car in the state he was in. His hands gripped the steering wheel so hard his knuckled pulsed white and his usual distinguished features was shrouded in a crumpled mask of what seemed like utter loss.

"There was an accident, Amelia. Rob was at home, alone…" His voice was gruff and quiet. It was unnatural. All of this was unnatural.

I stared down at my hands, folded in my lap so uselessly. Alone. Rob had been alone. I swallowed the lump in my throat that threatened to choke me.

"Alone?" I whispered, the word itself sounded like death. "How?"

I wasn't sure if I was asking how it happened, how I'd left him alone, how he could have done something. There were too many of them to specify.

"It's not…" His voice broke but he tried to disguise it with a cough and he continued. "He wasn't… It was self-inflicted."

He finally said it, confirming the fears I'd buried deep down inside for the past few months.

Rob had been changing in front of me. Sad, happy, sad, nothing was stable, he wasn't stable. I should have said something.

Bile rose in my throat but I forced it back down.

Mr Wood sniffed and changed gears. I looked out of the window at the scenery as it rolled past, I had expected us to head for their house but we were heading into the centre of the town.

"Where are we going?" I asked as. Mr Wood indicated at a roundabout. Steadily manoeuvring through the traffic.

"The Hospital. Florence is already there with the twins."

I nodded, feeling stupid asking questions.

My breath caught in my throat, chugging in and out unevenly. I couldn't breathe but I didn't care. I only knew I was crying when the tears landed on my hands. Everything was numb.

I'd always made sure to ask Rob what he was doing when I was at work. He always had answers, replying something like 'oh, this or that', or else just tapped his nose and changed the subject. I never thought to ask properly. Why hadn't I known?

I knew then I was a bad friend, to not know what my best friend had going on in his life. So caught up in my own world, and problems.

I stewed on these thoughts for the remainder of the way, putting up walls between me and life. Mentally pushing the world away.

We pulled into the hospital and found somewhere to park. Mr Wood got out of the car, me following suit.

After stopping in the reception to ask for directions we blindly walked down the halls, not talking, until we found the morgue.

Mrs Wood, Dean and Mark were all sat in a row in a grey walled waiting area. At our arrival Mrs Wood stood up and walking to her husband, collapsing into his arms she cried; something it looked like she had been doing ever since she heard the news.

I didn't know what to do, so I walked to her empty chair and sat down next to Dean. I couldn't look at him or any of them for fear of breaking down, so forced myself to stare straight ahead. Not taking it in, pretending I wasn't there. What was happening? My head spun.

A faceless doctor came out to speak to Mr and Mrs Wood, looking very serious mixed with that almost fake looking sympathy.

I quickly glanced at the twins, afraid too much eye contact would cause me to lose it. They looked terrible. Their usual handsome features were tainted with the horror of the event they were living through. They looked exhausted.

Mrs Wood let out a hysterical sob and Mark buried his face in his hands.

The white noise started again, my ears tuned into a high-pitched ringing that I fell into, letting it wash over me.

The bile rose again and I ran to the bathroom and threw up before crumpling onto the floor and dying of grief, myself. Why, Rob? Why?

My chest caved in on me, breaking me in two.

CHAPTER 10

I'd worked a double shift on Friday and I was paying for it today, I was so tired that when I woke up I felt like I was still in my dream, everything seemed hazy and cast in half light.

It took me a few minutes to realise that it wasn't a dream haze I was stuck in, it was the dullness created by the storm that was raging outside. The clouds had squashed away the great weather we'd been having and was now punishing us for enjoying it so much.

I moaned in misery as I rolled over.

"Morning!" Rob called. He was overly chirpy, suspiciously so.

I squinted up at his smiling face, almost maniacally stretched into a grin like a carved pumpkin.

He was sat on the edge of my bed counting out the money I'd made in tips last night.

I'd made a good amount from the dinner shift; the hot weather really drove people to find shelter in cool places. We always made sure to blast the air-con and it always paid off.

Rolling over to my side I cringed at how much my hair smelled like fish.

"What time is it?" My eyes refused to put anything into real focus and I tried to lull myself back to sleep with thoughts of warm weather and the beach.

"It's like, eleven or something," Rob answered. I peered up at him from my snug cocoon of a bed. His smile remained as he mouthed numbers to himself. "One hundred and forty three pounds! Bam!"

He whooped to himself as he put the neatly stacked money on the desk.

I couldn't muster the strength to cheer with him so I gave him a sleepy smile and pulled the covers over my head, trying to lose myself in the warm flowery washing powder in my sheets rather than the stinky fish smell that clung to my hair.

I felt his hands slide under the covers towards my feet and I jerked them up.

"Hey! What's wrong?" His voice was muffled and I shrugged the covers down a little so my head was unobstructed.

"It's Saturday, I'm going to your house today. Dean might be there... do you think he'll be there?" I prayed silently that he wouldn't be.

Guilt bubbled up for a million little things I didn't want to think about. The top one being Dean with Rob coming in a close second.

He was leaning on me, needing me to get through the death of Rob and all I was doing was pushing him away.

I didn't want to be his crutch and I definitely didn't want to be part of this strange relationship substitute. It had plagued my thoughts during my shift at work and as I fell asleep my brain swirled the situation around and around until I couldn't even remember what the problem was anymore.

"Um, hello? He's almost definitely going to be there!" Rob said, reaching under the covers to grab my feet, finally grasping one and shaking it.

I glared at him. I was worried Dean was using me as a crutch but what if it was the other way around?

"But, I mean, he might *not* be there. I mean, he has a life." Rob back peddled but it didn't work. I knew Dean. He'd be there, waiting.

Like Rob, Dean was a 'live for the moment' kind of person. He didn't hesitate. Unlike Rob, though, Dean didn't live his life in two extremes. Happy and sad. Dean was just happy. I couldn't ruin that by encouraging whatever this was.

"I'll just have to tell him straight then." I said. Determination to finish things was often a good trait to have. It certainly helped me out at school, I just never thought I'd have to use my steely reserve to tell my best friend's brother to leave me alone.

"And what does *that* mean?" Rob asked with a wry look on his eternal boyish face.

I threw a pair of socks at him in protest.

"It means I'll tell him that we can't take these... 'feelings'... seriously," I made the air quotes, hating my own dramatics. "I'll tell him that grief makes people act strangely and it's OK, but we can't make any rash decisions at a time like this."

Rob rolled his eyes at me but when I got out of bed I saw his smile fade and a darkness replace it. He stared out of the window at the dark clouds like he could see something I couldn't.

❋

Possible scenarios for the day ran through my head as I picked out clothes.

After some time thinking too much about what to wear to the house I settled on jeans and a hoodie; clothes I hadn't had to wear due to the recent heat wave, but luckily could cover myself up in now it was raining.

The usual playfulness me and Rob had in life sparked up again as I mooched around my room. I threw socks and other various clothes at him and he dodged them and threw then back but harder and with the kind of competitiveness his dad had wished he'd shown in sports.

It was like the normal Rob was back again.

He hummed to himself as he dodged the flying grenades. He swatted them out of the air in one swift motion, his lithe arms and hands moving with grace like a cat.

He'd decided to play matchmaker, in a way, and had laid out clothes he wanted me to wear to go to his house. I had thrown the black jeans and very fitted black vest top he'd picked in some bid to make me look like a Parisian sex kitten back into the wardrobe with minimal fuss.

Rising to his intentions would only lead to more prodding and teasing than I could put up with.

The idea that Rob was actually on board with this crazy idea troubled me in a way I couldn't explain, but it just niggled at the back of my mind like an itch you just can't find no matter where you scratch.

"Clean this up." I said, pointing to the clothes and soft furnishings that now lay strewn about the room from our childish game.

"Why is it always my job?" Rob said in a well-rehearsed teenage whine.

Ignoring him I went to the bathroom to brush my teeth and apply a little bit of makeup without him noticing.

I passed my mum in the hallway but she brushed passed without a word. That was becoming standard.

Sighing I walked back into my room. Rob was perched on the bed with a handful of my tip cash clutched in his hand.

When he heard me push the door open he looked up quickly, his hands froze gripping the notes to his chest.

"Amelia," He said my name, drawing out the 'me' and the final 'a', singing my name the way a kid asking his mum for more sweets would, "What would you say if I told you I had an idea?"

I gave him a droll stare and walked to my desk to tie my hair back into a ponytail.

Experience told me the best thing to do was stay non-committal. The last time he'd had an idea we'd ended up sneaking out to a late-night party that got us both into a lot of trouble.

"I'd say 'Oh god, no!'" I couldn't help but laugh, "Why? What are you doing with that money?"

"Well, what say we put this extra money to good use?"

I almost told him it wasn't really extra money; the chide rested on the tip of my tongue only halted by the eagerness in his voice.

Instead I gave him my full attention, noticing for the first time in a long time how normal things could be between us if I just ignored the gaping hole that caused every beat of my heart to echo through my bones.

"We can go and see those psychics, try to figure this out. See if any of them are the real deal." He spoke quickly like a kid trying to trick a parent into something by giving up so much information; the more words used the more likely for success.

It didn't escape me how his eyes searched mine for help, whether he knew he was doing it or not.

Suddenly it was like a balloon had popped at a party and my fantasy of normality deflated with it. Guilt scratched at my insides like a caged animal.

"You don't need to ask my permission to search for answers, Rob." I said. It was true, in a way, but these days I wasn't sure who was the one stuck in limbo and his request for possible escape made me feel breathless. "I don't want to spend a load of money on some fake bullshit for no reason, though. We'll research and try to find some testimonials first."

He nodded eagerly and I crumbled a little bit more inside.

Having been so self-involved over the past week, worrying about all sorts of stupid things I'd totally pushed aside the whole idea of trying to find out why Rob was still here.

I watched him as he started my computer up, getting the pad with the list of names on so he could start researching them as soon as he could. He hummed to himself as he typed in an internet search engine; trying to find people who could vouch for the so-called psychics.

The rain hit my window in little drip drops, and outside was sullen and grey, but it suited my mood just fine so I told myself I couldn't be miserable about it.

All I wanted to do today was just curl up in my room with Rob and maybe watch a movie, like we used to. Except we usually did it at his house. I scrunched up my eyes at the thought of his house and Dean.

Dean was good looking, and I did think of him as a brother of sorts, but something had changed between us and I needed to try to put it all back. I was going to have to remind Dean we were like family. We couldn't go breaking that relationship and ruining everything just to suit our current situation.

I glanced over at Rob and found I couldn't look at him. He looked so determined I had to dig my nails into my hand just to stop myself from crying.

An hour or two passed and Rob had scribbled more than fifteen testimonials down, marking them under the names we had as either little ticks or crosses so we knew what we were dealing with.

Unfortunately, they all seemed to be unhelpful. For every person who said they thought the psychic was legitimate there was another who said it was a scam or hoax. In which case I didn't know why they'd bothered going to see the person in the first place if they didn't believe. We looked at each other in despair.

"Well there's only one thing for it," I said, grabbing the pad and closing my eyes.

I wheeled my hand in the air as if I was conducting some sort of invisible orchestra and pointed to the page, pushing my finger onto the paper to make sure I'd done it right.

"There, we're going to see Claire Voyant. Oh! That works out well, it's the closest one to us, and I guess we can drive there in *our* new car." I had to remind myself to smile. At least we were moving forward with our investigation.

"Good, I like the sound of her the most, such a clever play on words, don't you think?" He was teasing and spoke as though he were criticising a good wine, or a book. I rolled my eyes.

"Do you wanna go now?" I asked, looking at the time. We had about 2 hours until I was due to go to the house to see his mum and I needed something to take my mind off things.

"I thought you said you wanted to drive?" he scratched at his face like he had stubble on his chin, but his facial hair hadn't grown since he'd died. In fact, nothing about him seemed to change, except his expression. Even his clothes; the suit he was buried in was un-crumpled and clean despite his lack of care. Something I'm sure we could as Miss Voyant about.

"We could go and sneak the car off the driveway - it'll be fun. In fact, I bet you could just do it if I hid in the bushes down the road..." I stopped talking because he was giving me one of those 'don't be ridiculous' looks that parents gave their kids when they were trying to talk them into getting a puppy. His expression softened after a few seconds and he put his hand on my arm.

"You're going to have to face him later anyway. Besides, I don't know what the big deal is, just confess your love for one another and have at it!"

I huffed and stifled a scream as I walked away from him; plonking myself back into the desk chair.

"You don't understand." I didn't want to say it aloud but it just slipped out. I rested my chin on my hands and leant my elbows on the desk, feeling like a miserable teenager, rather than an almost fully grown woman.

"Of course I don't because you won't explain! Why do you freeze up when it comes to talking about this?"

There was something in the way he looked at me that made my cheeks flush. It was true, as much as we were best friends we'd never really, truthfully, broached the subject of relationships and boys. It was something I purposefully glossed over. Our friendship worked best on blissful ignorance.

I opened my mouth to answer him. I was going to say it was none of his business, but the doorbell rang.

I frowned. We never had people over, and it was too late for a delivery. I leaned over the desk and looked out of the window and there, parked in front of my house was Florence's very parental looking car.

Even though I had no clue what she was doing here I couldn't help but be thankful she hadn't driven Andrews 4x4 here. That would have given my parents ammo for snide comments for at least a month.

"Who is it?" Rob asked. He leant next to me to look out of the window and I inhaled his smell, yet another thing that lingered in this life. It was so real to me and I had to ignore the voice that told me I was going insane.

His face matched mine when he looked down to see his mother's car, and then we both looked at each other in horror as I heard my own mum walking towards the front door.

We tried to keep our parents away from each other as much as possible. It wasn't that they couldn't get on, it's just my parents *wouldn't* despite the fact that his parents were always polite, even when faced with my parent's blatant rudeness.

It was a horrible embarrassment for everyone so we made a rule when we were about fifteen that we'd keep them apart as much as we could to save everyone the bad experience.

I raced to the door with Rob hot on my heels. By the time I'd reached the top of the stairs the front door was already open.

I descended the stairs at a thundering pace, jumping the last one out of habit. Landing with a thump I sprinted down the hall to be faced with the back of my mum, the smiling shining polite face of Florence Wood, and the handsomely dark and brooding face of Dean. Damn him, he'd sprung a surprise attack.

I pulled the front door open wide so I could greet them, yanking the handle out of my mum's hand, as she'd only opened it a crack like they were Jehovah's Witnesses trying to convert her.

"Amelia, don't let all the cold in, we can't afford to heat the street as well as the hallway!" She said, trying to pull it back towards her. I bit back a snappy retort. They carried on their conversation, which I'd missed in the flight down the stairs.

"I'm so sorry we missed the party. Amelia didn't tell us until it was too late, and we didn't have time to find anything decent to wear..."

I looked down so I didn't have to face anyone with the shame of my mother and her terribly hidden dig at me.

"Of course, don't be silly," Mrs Wood said, waving her hand to imply it wasn't anything to worry about, "It was only a few people anyway, nothing fancy. But you did miss Amelia's speech and she looked beautiful. Did you see the dress I bought her?" Even though Mrs Wood was trying to be nice, light and breezy, I knew the mention of the dress would irritate my mum.

I cringed.

"Oh yes, it was beautiful!" I didn't want this exchange to go on any longer, but I feared I couldn't stop it, "It's still strange to see Melia in pretty dresses though, she's always been such a tomboy!"

My mum laughed and Florence laughed out of politeness, but I caught sight of Dean's face and went cold inside. He wasn't smiling. He was looking at my mum like she had just said she wanted to kill all the puppies in the world. Rob was shaking his head but kept quiet, he was good at letting things ride out, but I wasn't.

"Yes, thanks mum!" I said, trying to usher her away. She took the hint and moved back, waving at Mrs Wood and Dean, but she didn't leave the hallway, she started tidying, as though she did it all the time.

"Hi," I smiled at them both, but didn't meet Dean's eye. I focused on Mrs Wood who was holding a big book with stickers all over it. "What's this?" I asked, as she handed it over to me.

It was heavy and on further study I could see it was a photo album. My brain told me to run, but I didn't know why until it was too late.

"Well, I have to cancel today I'm afraid. I forgot I had a dinner date with some friends of mine from the charity drive. Dean's just driving me over there because I'm going to have a few cheeky glasses of wine," She winked at me as though I was in on a secret with her, "but I didn't want you to be left 'hanging' as Mark would say. So I thought I'd drop these photos off of some of the places I went travelling to." I inwardly breathed a sigh of relief, but it was premature. "Hopefully it might help you decide where you want to go when you go…"

I smiled but I knew what was to come. Simultaneously me, Rob and my mum spoke.

"Thanks!"

"Oh no!"

"What?"

I pivoted on my heel and turned to face my mum, who'd been lingering just behind me. I shrugged but Mrs Wood answered for me.

"Hasn't she told you?" She smiled, as though she didn't notice how mortified I was, "She was thinking of going travelling."

Mrs Wood spoke as though it was nothing to even think about, travelling was something that was just done, it wasn't a big deal. But to my mum, who'd never left the country and always complained about students spending their parent's money on getting drunk and spreading diseases, it was like a punch in the gut.

I could also see the hurt in her eyes. Florence had known, I'd talked to her, but my mum was left in the dark.

This photo album was getting heavier by the second.

"Travelling? Where are you going to get the money for that?" She demanded, her face a mottled red colour. The colour of rage I was sadly used to.

"Oh, you know I'd always be happy to -" Mrs Wood began before my mum cut her off with a glare.

"If you think you're going travelling, think again. We don't have money for that, and you can't leave me with your dad. You know he can't work. We need to keep food on the table, or maybe you'd forgotten that because you're never here, you're either at that mansion letting people pity you, or you're god knows where with god knows who!"

Dean exhaled through his nose, sounding like a snorting horse, but I quietened him with a quick glance and shake of my head, pleading with him with my eyes to keep quiet.

"It's called work, mum. I go to work."

"Don't you dare take that tone with me," She bore down on me like an eagle going in for the kill, her finger pointed in my face like a razor sharp talon. "You think it's OK to run off playing games, trying to make the rich family love you so they might make your life better, might take you in to replace the son they lost, well grow up Amelia. This is your life and it's time you took some responsibility!" She stormed off and I heard her find my dad and start retelling the story. Her voice carried at an embarrassing volume. I looked up and saw Rob going after my mum, and I saw Dean silently fuming and Mrs Wood looked at a loss for words.

"Well..." I could feel the colour rising in my cheeks, my heart hammered with the humiliation my mother always seemed to cause. I bit my lip and looked away, refusing to cry in front of them.

"Oh Amelia, I'm so sorry!" Florence said breathlessly, putting a hand to her face.

I shook my head and smiled. It was a defeated smile, but a smile nonetheless.

"It's fine, don't worry. I suppose she was going to find out anyway."

I just had to count my blessings she didn't know when I did go travelling I wasn't coming back.

Realising that was how the Wood's would find out the same way filled me with guilt. Mrs Wood hugged me and I could tell she didn't know what to say by the silence that was almost as bone crushing as the grip of her arms around me.

"I really have to go, unless you want me to cancel?" She pulled away and looked at me like a mother might look at a daughter. At least that's what I imagined it to look like.

How she managed to keep in such high spirits when my monster of a mother had pretty much insulted her was beyond me.

"Don't be silly, I know what she's like, I'm used to it. I'm sorry you had to hear that..." I sighed and shrugged, at a loss for anything else to say.

"Well, don't get into any fights with them. Stay out of their way and come over tomorrow instead."

She waved and walked back to the car using her handbag as a make shift umbrella and still managing to look glamorous as she side stepped a puddle.

Dean lingered on the front step. I was too dejected to care about what had happened between us so when he went to move towards me I didn't step away. It was him who hesitated.

"Don't go anywhere." He said taking a step back. My face must have echoed how pathetic I felt because he reached for my hand and gave it a squeeze before walking back to the car.

I don't know where he thought I was going to go. I didn't have any plans on going out in the cold weather now anyway, so I closed the door with a light click and took the photo album up to my room. Rob appeared a few minutes later and he immediately pulled me into his arms.

"What. A. Bitch!" His voice was muffled, lost in my hair and sounding a million miles away. Or maybe it was me who was miles away this time.

I sank into his embrace. I could hear my mum and dad arguing now and knew it was going to be a bad night of raised voices and slamming doors. I just hoped they'd steer clear of my room.

"I just want it to be March. I need it to be March, Rob. Let's just go away now!" I pulled away from him. He looked like a half-remembered dream through my tears. I'd never felt so humiliated in my life.

"No, Amelia, we stick to the plan and when March comes around we'll have so much money we'll never have to come back."

It was unspoken but I knew what he meant. *I* might never have to come back.

His fate was still hovering over us like the dark clouds outside. We still didn't know what would happen to him if and when I left. Could he come with me? Would he still be here?

The whole world seemed to weigh on my shoulders and I crumpled onto the bed hoping everything would fade away and leave us alone together.

We lay in silence, all thoughts of our escape banished from our lips but it didn't stop my mind from clinging onto every moment that had just passed.

I heard another car pull up. This time I heard an engine growl; deep and bone rattling. Rob got up and looked out the window again.

"Huh... it's our car..." He said. I'd fallen into a black hole, or at least that's what it felt like. His words didn't make much sense at first and I had to drag myself to the window.

Wiping away the condensation from one of the panes I looked down into the miserable evening and saw it too. My new black car, all shiny with rain drops and street lamp reflections that were glistening in the dying sunlight like fallen stars.

I opened my bedroom door a crack and could still hear my parent's voices raised, but not shouting. They were still discussing me.

"I hope they don't come out!" I said, as I tiptoed out of the door and down the stairs. Rob laughed behind me.

"They aren't getting out just yet!" He said and I shot him a look of horror.

"What did you do?" I whispered, sternly. No doubt whatever it was would be blamed on me later. He winked at me and drew his eyebrows up innocently.

"I didn't want them to start battering you with their negative energy so... I kind of locked them in the living room!" He said with a laugh. He sobered up when he saw the look on my face.

"What did you do?" I let him push me down the hallway towards the front door.

"Don't worry," He whispered as we passed the living room door. My parent's voices drifted out in snide tones. "I followed your mum into the living room and locked it from the inside, then I climbed back out through the window. When they finally figure it out they won't be able to blame you, my sweet!"

He seemed very pleased with himself. It was a good trick, but just because I hadn't done it didn't mean I wasn't going to get in trouble for it somehow.

Passed the potential parent hazard I unlatched the front to find a dark figure standing on the front step.

Dean was wearing a hoodie with a black leather jacket over the top. With his hood pulled up he looked like a shadow in the gloom. A soaking wet shadow. Rain clung to him, drenching his skin and hair; large drops slid down his face and I couldn't stop my eyes from lingering on his mouth.

"What are you doing?" I tried to add some attitude to my voice to compensate for the fluttering feeling that was settling in my stomach. I don't think it worked though because before I knew it his hand was clasping mine. It was warm and wet, vivid with life.

With a yank I was suddenly half running down the path behind him.

Luckily Rob followed quickly. When I looked over my shoulder he'd closed the front door and was close on my heels.

I turned back to Dean and we stopped at the car.

When he opened the passenger door I managed to yank my hand out of his. Although his grip had hurt with its intensity I also felt numb to the pain, or perhaps I just didn't care enough to feel it anymore.

"Wait!"

He glared at me, his hands clasping into fists.

I'd never seen him like this. He seemed more like Mark who was prone to bouts of anger.

Rob surveyed his brother with curiosity. He was wide eyed and still. Just looking at him made the cold weather seem even more chilled.

"You aren't going back there Amelia, your parents - " He finally found his voice only to lose the ability to form words. He slammed his hand onto the roof of the car and breathed heavily. "Just come out with me, let's go somewhere, anywhere. I can't stand the thought of you staying in there with them."

He'd only left my house twenty minutes ago so he must have raced home after taking his mum into town and raced back in my car as quickly as he could.

His face was so sincere and caring I could barely look at him, even Rob had backed away and was staring away into nothing.

When Dean opened the car door I climbed in without a word. Dean walked around the car, my eyes followed him in the rear-view mirror but stopped half way when I saw Rob had appeared in the cramped back seat. There was no time for questions.

Dean slid into the driver's seat, revved the engine and drove us away and into the rain. I didn't look back at my house.

CHAPTER 11

Dean drove the car like he was a part of it, he switched gears and seemed to know where all the buttons were making me wonder if he had already taken it for a joy ride.

We drove in silence. Normally I would have found it unbearable with that quiet mass between us throbbing like a stab wound. Luckily for me Rob decided it was the perfect opportunity to nag me seeing how I couldn't talk back.

"Just tell him you like him already." He whispered into my ear so close I could feel his breath on my skin.

I gave myself a headache trying to block him out but it was like his voice buzzed inside my skull.

I felt bad for Dean as I stole a quick glance at him, even in my own misery his feelings shone through.

He looked calm but his knuckles were white they were gripping the steering wheel so tightly.

We drove for what felt like hours, but I knew that was just my mind being stupid. When we drove by the big clock on the bank in the town centre it told me we'd only actually been driving for a few minutes.

The street lights breached the car's small windows and lit up the interior as we passed under them, casting an orange glow on Dean's face and making his chiselled features even more annoyingly handsome.

I hunched into my seat and I wrapped my arms around myself, suddenly aware of the cold in the air.

Rob finally shut up, losing interest in the fact that I couldn't talk back.

He sat in the back humming to himself and commenting under his breath about how he hoped he didn't have to sit through something embarrassing. I was silently wishing the same thing.

"Are you cold?" Dean asked with a gruff voice. He coughed and tried to fiddle with the heaters but he couldn't get them to work.

"I'm fine, it's OK." I lied.

I wasn't fine, I was a nervous wreck.

My parents were back at home, arguing because they thought I was going travelling. Luckily they didn't know I wasn't coming back. Mrs Wood thought she'd gotten me into trouble, Dean thought my mum was out of line and so he'd taken me away. All of these people I'd affected with my lies, and all of these people I didn't want to be around right now, despite how they felt about me. I just wanted to be alone. Well, not totally alone, with Rob.

Rob understood me, he was a huge part of me, but I got the feeling he didn't want to be around me all the time.

I hadn't missed the way he starred into space, the way the darkness seeped out of him.

In life he'd hidden those parts of himself. He'd make excuses and go home or go walking without me. That's how I'd missed it, he was so good at hiding.

145

In death, though, he didn't have the luxury to leave me. I could feel it, he wanted space but was afraid to take it. I felt sick at the thought of him finding answers through this psychic woman but how could I stand in his way?

A horrible black hole expanded in my chest as I felt the weight of that thought seep into my being.

As much as I loved Rob did I even want to be with him forever? Tied to a girl too selfish to let him go, did *he?*

I felt that blacking-out feeling speckle my vision and I struggled to breathe.

"Can you pull over?" I tried not to sound panicked, to keep my voice calm and normal, but I don't think it worked.

Both Dean and Rob looked at me, their green eyes peering at me, putting me under their family microscope.

 I never used to be this fragile but this was the second time I'd broken down in 24 hours and I hated myself for it.

Dean found a place to stop and I fumbled with the door before I managed to swing it open and stumble out into the night air.

Gasping for air I jerkily walked to a bench that was on the side of the road. The wooden planks were slick with rain but I didn't care. With the shortness of breath came the shakes. I was a wreck.

I heard Dean get out of the car but at this point my head was in my hands so I didn't see where he'd gone. A moment later his warm arm wrapped around my shoulders and without even thinking I sank into him with my eyes closed and I tried to imagine Rob's arm around me instead.

Guilt once again cut into my heart, and I wondered if maybe I *was* using Dean as a replacement for his brother.

Instinct kicked in and my eyes searched for Rob. He was trapped in the car because getting out would attract attention and it hit me that maybe I was the car, in some stupid over the top symbolic way. I was holding him hostage, even in death.

I shot him a look that I knew he'd understand, it was my 'I'll be OK' face and he nodded at me. I was struck with a clarity I didn't realise I needed.

"Dean..." My eyes watered and my throat seemed to close as I fought back the tears I never wanted to shed.

I was going to tell him what I should have said earlier. That this wasn't what he wanted. This wasn't what I wanted.

It was all a lie.

His face came down and his lips brushed mine. It wasn't a real kiss. Not like the ones I'd experienced when drunk on a night out with friends. Not like the kisses I'd shared with Matt, whom I'd briefly dated from the restaurant. This was something more. It was tender and soft and didn't go further than a brush of the lips but felt more intimate than anything I'd ever experience.

I recoiled like I'd been stung by a wasp and I couldn't stop the heat spreading across my face. I shook my head and groaned.

"Dean!" It was a sigh, but not one of pleasure. I faced him and shrugged his arm of my shoulder. "I can't do this with you."

His face was unreadable as he pulled his arm back. I felt my skin freeze where his warmth had been moments before.

He avoided my eyes as he pulled away and that moment of intimacy seemed to shatter between us like glass turned to sand, blowing away in the wind.

"Why not?" He asked quietly.

He was staring at the car, directly at Rob like he could see his younger brother looking out at him. I wish he could see him, maybe then this would be different.

I'd never seen Dean display any kind of misery. Even after everything that had happened he'd been like a shining beacon of hope for all of us but somehow I was the one who broke him.

"I don't know how to explain," I wanted to be honest but trying to speak my feelings out loud seemed impossible, "It's just too soon..."

He looked at me; confusion clouded his features.

"But you and Rob never... I mean you guys weren't..?" He couldn't finish his sentence and I was glad of it. I blushed again, uncontrollably.

"No, no, no! That's not it," I felt I was lying somehow despite the fact that it was true, "We were never *together* but... I don't know. I can't just use you to replace him. And you can't use me either. Can't we just be friends?"

I tried to make it sound final but it sounded meek and unbelievable when I said the words. Dean took a moment to process my statement and when he answered me I could hear the bruised feelings.

"I wasn't using you. I'm sorry if it felt like that."

The bluntness of his answer hurt me more than I'd thought it would. In spite of the internal war my brain was waging with my heart I knew it was for the best that I nipped this thing in the bud before it got out of hand.

"I know you weren't but, well, I think grief makes you do things and say things you wouldn't normally do or say. We shouldn't -" It hurt to say the next words, "do anything stupid, just because we miss Rob, y'know?"

This time *I* looked away, to hide the fake-ness of it all. Because I *did* want to be stupid, I just couldn't let myself. I couldn't ruin this family, and I couldn't face my feelings for Rob *or* Dean. I had to do what I do best, which I squash the feelings I don't want and wash over them with something else. A distraction.

"I swear that's not what I was doing, Amelia. I've felt like this for a while. Ask Mark, ask..." The unspoken name hung in the air and I glanced at the car.

Rob...

Had he'd known this was going to happen all along? He'd been pushing me into Dean's arms and I hadn't caught on. The betrayal I felt was crushing and my head swam.

What else had Rob been privy to that I wasn't?

What was it Rob did when he wasn't with me?

My mood plummeted even further and I stood to leave.

"I have to get out of here. I'm going to walk for a bit, I'll make my own way home." I got up but Dean grabbed my hand which I jerked away like the contact would cause him to suddenly know my true feelings.

"You can't walk around at night on your own and you can't go home." I couldn't tell him I wouldn't be on my own.

I felt like coming out with the truth and just exposing myself to everyone. Letting them think I was insane was better than pretending I'm not. Perhaps I am, I considered it when Rob had first appeared.

"I'll be fine. You don't have to worry about me."

He didn't seem to buy it and he stood; towering above me.

Even though he and Mark were twins I'd never really thought they were alike. Mark was hot headed and sometimes scary; Dean was channelling him tonight.

"I do have to worry about you, after everything that's happened I worry about you more than I thought I ever could." The honesty of this statement filled me with anxiety.

He meant it, I could see it in his eyes, but even though I wanted to hear it from him I knew Rob was watching us from the car and that was enough to make my feelings waiver. I could never have anything with Dean if Rob was around. It was unimaginable.

"Fine. Walk with me, do whatever you want..." I knew that wasn't the best idea as soon as I suggested it. I couldn't leave the car and I couldn't leave Rob locked up like an animal. "Actually, I'm hungry." I said, quickly.

As if on cue my stomach growled even though the thought of eating made me feel queasy.

Dean nodded and took my hand again, careful not to hold too tight as though that might make me snatch it away again.

"Come on, I'll take you to get something to eat." He walked me to the car and opened the door. I looked over and caught him smiling to himself as he got into the driver's seat.

"What?" I buckled up, trying to hide how my hands shook.

He looked at me and tucked some hair that had come loose behind my ear.

"I don't know who's losing their mind more. You or me" He smiled, but it was kind of sad.

"I guarantee it's me." I sighed, leaning my head against the cold damp window and watched my breath fog up the glass.

"What happened?" Rob asked from the back seat. I couldn't answer but I looked at him through the side mirror and shook my head at him. To make matters worse Rob leaned back in his chair, smiling from ear to ear.

I frowned as I remembered Rob's part in all of this. He had some explaining to do.

We drove further down the road and parked. The rain had stopped and the orange glow of the street lights echoed in every puddle and drop of water on the ground. All the cars shimmered in the sunset warmth that was being cast down upon them and the world seemed to be smouldering.

We walked in silence again and I was amazed at how comfortable I was with it even with the tension that hung between us.

"So what do you feel like?" Dean was the first to break the silence and his deep voice sent a crack in the atmosphere, making this dream landscape seem far more real than I would have liked. I eyed the street and realised we were right near my place of work. I didn't want to go there.

"Pizza... let's go to Alfredo's." I pointed at the small restaurant, with its steamy windows and glowing sign. It was a small place and I assumed no one we knew would be there on a Saturday night, as it was a little too far from the local bars to be threatened with the hungry drunk crowd.

When we got to the door Dean reached forwards and held it open for me. I lingered just long enough for Rob to sneak through.

I didn't know how this was going to work. Rob might have to stand the entire night or something.

Luckily the place was quiet with only a family of four sitting at one of the tables near the window, which was so full with condensation it obscured the view of the street. It made it seem like we could be underwater.

A tall and skinny waiter showed us to a table but I didn't pay attention and when a menu was handed to me and I was asked what I wanted to drink I looked up at his face blankly.

"Diet Coke, thanks." Dean ordered for me.

"And how do you know I don't want wine or even just a water?" I asked. I was annoyed at his presumption but I couldn't put my finger on why it irked me so much.

"I dunno," He shrugged, looking at his menu as though it held all of life's answers on it, "I guess I just know what you like..."

His smile made all of the annoyed parts of me melt and when he looked over his menu at me I felt the flutter of butterflies in my stomach.

It was like an out of body experience; I saw us sat together from outside and realised what this was.

Somehow we'd ended up on a date.

This whole thing had turned on its head. I'd tried so hard to push him away and convince him we shouldn't do anything stupid and yet here we were.

The look on his face told me he'd just come to the same realisation. He looked like he'd just disproven Einstein's theory of relativity. Damn it.

The restaurant's smooth Italian music was like alarm bells in my ears and the slow flickering candle between us like a warning beacon. I found Rob and with a subtle nod I directed him towards the bathroom.

"I'm just gonna clean up." I gestured to my appearance and pushed the chair out from the table just in time to knock the waiter who'd arrived with our drinks. He managed not to spill anything but his face spoke a thousand words. I knew what it was like to serve idiots who didn't look where they were going, and now I was one.

I slipped past the waiter as quickly as I could and walked quickly across the room to the bathroom.

The light was dim and the mirror murky with age so I couldn't really assess the damage of the rain. I wiped at my face and stared at my reflection. Rob had squeezed into the room after me and shuffled around me to sit on the lidded toilet.

"Well, this has turned into an interesting evening." His slender finger poked at me and I batted his hand away without looking at him. If I looked at him I might explode with rage.

"Stop it!" I snapped. "And don't think I don't know about your part in all of this. How many times have I told you to stay out of my love life? And now this? And he's out there and now it's like it's a date or something!"

I knew I wasn't making total sense but I couldn't help it. I glared at my face in the mirror and crinkled my nose.

My face wasn't the one I was used to looking at every day. My eyes showed the desperation I was trying to push down. I hated how they gave me away.

I also looked more pale and tired than ever; it was hard to believe this was the same day I'd woken up to. I felt like I'd lived a lifetime in the space of a few hours.

I pinched the bridge of my nose and took several deep breathes. Time to face the music.

The notion was literal. When I re-entered the restaurant the romantic music that was playing swelled as though someone had planned it.

It was like plunged into a warm bath. The air was warm and the smell of garlic bread and red wine hit me hard.

When I sat back down Dean shifted in his seat, his fingers tapped on the table erratically.

"I didn't plan this... just so y'know. You look like you think I did but swear I didn't." He picked his glass up and took a sip, mirroring my uncertainty of the situation.

"I know." I felt like I was being too blunt but I thought that was my best bet of getting through the evening unharmed. He nodded at me, seeming to understand my mood and we both seemed grateful when the waiter arrived to take our order. I didn't even have to look at the menu to know what I wanted. I always had the same thing, more or less.

"Margarita pizza, please!" I smiled up at the Italian looking man, who was rather large around the middle and ridiculously stereotypical of an Italian waiter. I handed the menu back and sat on my hands, absentmindedly chewing my bottom lip.

"Please can I have the ham and pineapple pizza?" Dean ordered in his usual polite manner, smiling at the waiter like he was an old friend. He had that ability to make everyone around him comfortable.

I looked at Rob without even thinking and smiled. I mentally started. Thankfully when I looked to see if Dean had noticed me smiling at nothing he, himself, was smiling at nothing.

Just a pair of grinning idiots awkwardly sitting in a romantic restaurant.

"What?" I tried to pull the edges of my mouth down but found I couldn't. Rob snorted and hid his face in his hands, shaking his head. I ignored him.

"I couldn't help it, sometimes it's nice to remember the little things about Rob. It makes it easier to deal with."

And there it was. The bitter truth to the whole situation. I was instantly brought back to the matter at hand. Not the stupid love life dilemmas that seemed to have occurred, but the reason we were here in the first place.

My eyes once again wandered to Rob and he looked back up at me, he dropped his hands from his face which was no longer open and happy but dark and stormy with the thoughts he kept trapped in his own brain.

It was like I could hear Rob's thoughts, or maybe it was a projection of my own thinking, but I could have sworn right then that I hear Rob think he wished he hadn't died. It was a revelation I hadn't been prepared for because ever since it happened he'd never once mourned his own passing.

I felt the familiar burning of tears behind my eyes but for once I couldn't stop the flow. The warm drops slid down my cheeks before I could wipe them away.

"Oh, God, I'm sorry, I shouldn't have brought him up, I mean, it's not the best time or place." Dean stumbled over his word awkwardly, which was so unlike him.

He grabbed his napkin and handed it to me. I took it but didn't do anything with it as his hand had captured mine and he squeezed it. It was warm and comforting and it made my head spin.

"*I'm* sorry!" I sniffed and looked at him, smiling as though to prove it but I didn't feel the smile reach anywhere past my lips. If I was honest with myself I wasn't sure if any smile recently had been real. I pushed the thoughts away.

Dean leant back in his chair and ran his hand through his dark hair, in a very Rob-like way. I tilted my head to watch him, lost in the memory of the many times I'd seen Rob do that when he was alive.

Since he'd died, I realised, I'd not seen him do it once and that thought hung in my mind like a dagger over my heart. There was something in that, but I didn't know what it was.

"What else do you think about?" I asked, trying to lighten the mood.

It only just occurred to me that I'd been avoiding talking about Rob since the funeral. People usually remembered the dead, talked about them and shared memories to help them get over the pain, but I'd never had to do that.

I still had him and I'd never sought anyone out for the ritual.

From the look on Dean's face I realised he hadn't either. Whether by choice or not, he'd not actually talked about Rob since the party.

I saw a light in his eyes at the mention of his brother and that's how the next three hours passed.

Reminiscing about Rob in the dimly lit restaurant was like medicine for a pain I didn't know I had and yet I felt it ease away at every laugh and anecdote.

Rob helped us along, filling in the gaps I would forget so I could recount stories flawlessly, even helping me help Dean along with his memories.

If Dean found it strange I'd be able to recount stories I wasn't there to experience he never let on and we were laughing and joking long after the family that had dined at the table near the window left.

Dean settled the bill for us. He didn't mention the fact mine hadn't been touched save for the few nibbles I'd taken before I felt queasy. Even the chocolate cake he'd ordered didn't appeal to me. The only think I'd managed was my Coke and a few cups of coffee.

"You know, it felt as though Rob was here tonight," Dean drawled as he rounded the car to let me into the passenger side door. By habit I hung back just long enough to let Rob sneak into the back seat.

"Yeah, me too." I hated the fact that I couldn't tell him Rob *had* been there, was still there, and wasn't in the foreseeable future, going anywhere. But I kept quiet.

The streets were deserted as we drove back from town. We sat in silence again but this time it was far more comfortable; thoughts of impossible romances pushed aside to no doubt worry over later.

The car purred the way a sleeping cat might purr if it was large, black and made of metal. The sound of it was soothing and I felt my eyes give into the heaviness I'd been carrying around. Dean had put the radio on and both he and Rob sang along to the song. Though all I could make out was unintelligible droning, the music jarring me awake ever now and then when the bass thumped.

"...Amelia?" Rob's voice called at me and his hand touched my face. Without thinking I batted it away.

"Stop it, Rob!" I slurred, repositioning myself in the car seat so I could lean my head on the window.

The car.

I snapped my eyes open. We'd come to a stop at a crossroads and the streetlight overhead shone into the car, making the world outside its beam diminish into greying nothingness. Dean shook my shoulder slightly.

"Melia, wake up..." He gently coaxed me. My hand flew to my mouth to make sure I hadn't drooled or anything and I sat up groggily. I'd only been asleep a few minutes but it had felt like hours, like I'd been pulled under a heavy ocean.

"Did I just call you Rob?" I glanced in the side mirror to spy on the backseat where the aforementioned boy sat. Dean smiled at me and turned the radio down so the smooth sounds of the instruments only just made it to our ears. With the quietness of the music and the paleness of the world outside the car it really was like we were in our own world.

"Yeah, were you dreaming?" His hand absentmindedly moved to tuck a piece of hair behind my ear, out of my face. Though it seemed casual I couldn't help but notice the heat that emanated from his palm and the precision of his fingers. They lingered at my ear and just when I thought he might move to touch me again he pulled back and rested it on the steering wheel.

I shook my head, undoing his attempts to reveal my face.

"I don't remember," I answered honestly, "You just reminded me of Rob, poking me awake." I smiled into the mirror to tease Rob for his tactless ways. Dean nodded and frowned in thought.

"What's wrong?" I slid around in my chair and unbuckled my seat belt so I could actually face him without the constricting material pulling at my chest.

He turned to looked at me dead on and his frown increased, his tanned skin looked sallow in the orange glow of the lights.

"Do I remind you of Rob a lot?" He asked, though it seemed like he didn't really want to know the answer.

"I guess... sometimes," I answered, puzzlement creeping into my voice, making my words rise in question, "But you all do..." I trailed off because Dean had turned his focus on the radio now, tuning in and out of stations but not really listening to them. Like he was searching for something in particular to say and he hoped the radio might give him the answers he needed.

"Maybe you're right, then." His eyes were firmly fixed on the radio dial. There was a lull in the background music and my brain snapped everything into place like a jigsaw puzzle finally revealing it's masterpiece. "People always say grief makes you do crazy things."

He was saying it to himself, I could hear the conviction in his voice. Though it was exactly what I'd been telling him all along hearing *him* say it was different.

"You can just drop me off at home." It took me all my strength to keep my voice calm and kind because I wanted to scream and pull my hair. I wanted to yell at Rob for causing so much trouble and making this situation into something that caused me physical pain.

Instead I buckled myself back in and turned the music up on the station we'd finally landed on. It was a pop channel and a corny love song rang out.

Dean flicked the station off and revved up the engine again.

"You seriously want to go back there to that house?" His brow crinkled with concern. I shrugged and sighed, squeezing my eyes closed for a few moments as I tried to compose myself, "Come back to our house tonight, we can sort it out. Mum and Dad-"

"No. Dean, no. I appreciate the thought, really, but I can't get your parents involved in this. Really, it's fine." I smiled one of those fake smiles again. If it saw through it he didn't say but I felt Rob's cold touch on my shoulder as he squeezed it. Solidarity. Me and him against the world. At least it used to be.

Dean nodded and re-started the engine, driving us home in silence that pressed a tangible weight onto every inch of my skin.

I would have given anything for one of us to break the tension, instead we both sat with all the unsaid words flying past like the dimly lit houses outside.

I was expecting a stand-off with my parents when I creaked the front door open but they'd reverted to the old tactics of ignoring me and I went along with it, closing myself off in my room for the night. Thankfully Rob decided not to rehash the night's events, leaving me to fall asleep with thoughts of escape and Dean.

�֍

The events after this moment were all a blur, I couldn't quite place what had happened in any kind of chronological order. I knew I had been taken home, though by whom and when was impossible to tell. I remember crying myself to sleep, or what I assumed was sleep but felt more like drowning.

Seeing Rob swimming and being dragged under waves; being pulled away from me by the rip tide and me getting dragged further away.

Rob waving at me from a bridge and then jumping off. Him falling. Me trying to catch him but he was always too far away.

I woke in a sweat and Rob was stood over my bed looking sad; disappearing as I blinked him away.

The remainder of the week was equally disorientating and jumbled. Rob's family were around, or more accurately, I was around them. I went to their house every day, sat with them to help them plan the funeral - none of it felt real. Mrs Wood was with me a lot, and we comforted each other and she hugged me often, saying she hoped I'd still spend as much time at their house as I used to. I would nod and say of course and we'd hug and drink tea and plan an event neither of us were really prepared for.

The only time my memories and actions snapped back into place was at the funeral. It was relatively small despite the family money - nothing over the top. The attendees included his closest family, a few friends from school and some friends from the random art groups he was a part of. It was a week before Rob's birthday so Mrs Wood had decided that they would honour his birthday more than his 'death day'. Her words, not mine.

We'd gathered at the local church and had a very short ceremony; His brothers, dad and uncle carried the coffin in. This was the first moment I kind of realised this was all real. I hadn't seen his body before at the hospital - I was advised against it.

Now, as the coffin was carried past me and Mrs Wood started up her daily sobbing routine, everything suddenly had colour again. It was like the sepia tone my life had sunken into was permeated with technicolour.

This moment. The coffin, the funeral. It was real, and I was OK.

I hugged Florence as the ceremony played out before me with prayers and anecdotes. We moved onto the graveyard and gathered around where he was to be buried; next to his grandparents.

This part I remember well because this is when he appeared to me as a newly formed ghost; or figment of my imagination as I interpreted it.

He stood across the grass from me, an apparition like from the movies, and smiled his annoyingly familiar 'I know something you don't know' smile. I tried to ignore him. I just had this horrible premonition of my future. Me being the crazy girl who saw the ghost of her best friend for the rest of her life. So I ignored him. He continued to smile at me as the people gathered around me mourned.

The burial was quick, considering I was stood there for most of the time wishing for it to end. We all hugged, and people went back to the Wood's house for a few drinks and to comfort each other. I rode back in a car with Dean and Mark. They were both in the front, me in the back with my new delusion sitting next to me.

CHAPTER 12

My parent's frosty attitude hadn't melted by the morning so I was able to wander around the house in the glow of victory. I'd finally found a topic that had shut them up enough to grant me peace and quiet.

The downside was that whenever I wasn't in their direct eye line I could hear them muttering to each other and I knew that sooner or later their icy exteriors would drip away and I'd be left with their raging inferno of an argument which they were no doubt planning this very instance.

"Rob?" I whisper-shouted his name when I came back to my room after doing a load of washing and I couldn't see him in his usual lounging place in front of my computer.

When he didn't appear I called him again, quietly, in the hallway.

He appeared moments later; heaving himself up the stairs two at a time with that kind of boyish exuberance I could never muster.

"You rang?" He smiled, his hands thrust into his pockets as he walked around the room. He was looking around at things as though he'd never seen them before. I narrowed my eyes.

"Where have you been?" I asked. I feared the answer.

"Nowhere... just wandering!" He sat at my desk and started clicking the mouse. A game of solitaire opened up and lit his face up in a devilishly green glow.

He didn't appear to be in a sharing mood and I decided not to ask for more information. From past experiences I knew better than to ask why he looked like he'd just done something devious.

"Right... well, I was thinking, if you're done doing whatever the hell it is I don't want to know about, we could head into town and visit that Claire Voyant character?" I wiggled my fingers at him and instantly felt bad at being so sceptical when his face lit up.

"Really?" He jumped up and grabbed my shoulders. I braced to be shook but he just planted a huge wet kiss on my unsuspecting lips. I reeled back from him and wiped my mouth.

"Rob!" I squealed. Rob's lips on mine were *not* what I wanted, despite everyone we'd ever met thinking otherwise.

"Two kisses from two brothers in the space of 24 hours. You floosy!" He laughed at me and I flushed a deep shade of red, my stomach did a flip at the memory of Dean.

Grabbing my bag I stormed out of the room in mock disgust. I didn't bother to turn to see if Rob was following me because a few seconds later I heard my bedroom door close and quick steps hurry down the carpeted stairs after me.

"I'm going out!" I yelled into the whispering house. No reply came, which didn't surprise me and I launched myself out of the door and into the fresh air. It wasn't quite as cold and miserable as the day before but the sun was still hiding behind some ominous looking clouds. The air nipped at my un-coated arms but I wasn't going back into the house for the sake of warmth.

I started to stride down the road at a brisk pace to get warm.

"Hey! Wait!" Rob jogged up behind me and pulled at the hem of my t-shirt, "Meliaaa!" He whined, drawing out the last syllable like a child. I slowed a little, but not because he couldn't keep up; as a ghost he seemed to have no problem performing strenuous activities.

"Stop pulling!" I swiped at his hand but missed. The street was empty and peaceful as we walked, which I was thankful for as it meant we could talk without being stared at. Not that we wouldn't be stared at if someone saw me walking into a psychic's shop? Office? I didn't know what they were called.

"I was only teasing," He smiled as he threw his arm over my shoulder, "I know you're no floosy, quite the opposite."

I didn't laugh but I wasn't really that mad at him. I suppose I just liked to carry on with our bickering ways. Better Rob like this than a stormy looking cloud of doom like the ones that floated overhead.

"I know, doofus!" I bumped him with my hip and ducked under a branch that was hanging over a fence, "I'm not really mad. But stop pointing out my... innocence!" I wasn't ashamed of my inexperience but I didn't like to talk about it with anyone, not even Rob. Some things were just private. I remember when Rob had told me about his own 'experiences' and I'd had to drink a lot of tequila that night just to make the embarrassment go away.

"Sorry, Mary." I let the joke slide and he didn't push it any further so we walked along the road and into the middle of town where only a handful of people were out and about.

Most people were probably staying in for Sunday dinner or in the pub watching some kind of sporting event. I saw it before Rob did, the purple front of the shop in between a chemist and a 24 hour mini supermarket.

I don't know what I expected but it wasn't this.

"It doesn't look particularly magical, does it?" Rob took the words out of my mouth like he always did.

Upon closer inspection there was a slight glow emanating from the window which did add to the mystery a little but when I saw it was only due to the cheap fairy lights hanging on the wall the hopes that I had hanging by a thread smashed to the ground.

"I guess it's now or never!" Rob was practically running when we reached the door.

I hadn't known whether it would be open on a Sunday but there was a woman sat behind a little counter just inside the door and a little sign in the window with curly handwriting told me they were, in fact, open.

"It's open!" I said, surprised. If there was a hint of scepticism in my voice Rob didn't notice. He was practically glowing and I wondered whether he'd always looked like that as a ghost or whether this was something new.

Rob looked inside, his cupped hands against the glass like a kid. Without warning he knocked on the window. I instantly ducked away from view to stand in the doorway of the chemist, which was closed.

"Stop!" I tried to yank him away from the window but he batted my hand away.

He pressed his face further into the glass, looking around as if he might be able to ascertain if this was a good place or not, like he had any kind of authoritative knowledge on psychic shops.

"We're going in anyway and I wanted to see if she could see me. She doesn't look psychic..."

I ignored him and tried to straighten myself out; wishing I had chosen something smarter to wear. Maybe that would make it seem like I wasn't crazy which is probably what she was going to think I was.

My thoughts were cut off mid wardrobe-worry because Rob was trying to pull me back towards the glowing lights.

"Come on, towards the light, Amelia, everything is better in the light..."
He was trying to sound mystical but it sparked a question in me I'd never
thought to ask before. I yanked my arm out of his grip.

"Did you ever see 'the light'?" As soon as the question left my lips I
wished I hadn't asked.

If Rob had been glowing earlier it wasn't evident now. He looked dark,
his expression was sceptical and he folded his arms across himself, creating a
barrier between us.

He took a step towards me and then stopped, held back by an invisible wall.

"I don't know if that's how it works. Maybe we should save those kinds of
questions for the professionals..." His voice was void of his usual playfulness,
back to the Rob I found myself scared of. His eyes were black portals to a
place I didn't want to go.

He turned on his heel and walked to the door, leaving me biting my lip
and fearing whatever answers may come.

A little bell jingled upon entry and I immediately thought of that quote
from *It's a Wonderful Life.*

I rushed in behind Rob just in case the woman, who I could now see was
younger than she appeared, had seen the door open by itself.

When she looked up I saw her face; makeup so thick she had added ten
years to her age with the cosmetics.

She stared at me as I approached and I felt my cheeks redden. What
was I going to say to this woman who was now looking expectantly at me
as though I should be saying something to her rather than just standing in
the doorway?

I was still caught up on what Rob had just said. His words buzzed around
me like flies lingering in the shade of a tree on a hot day.

"Can I help you?" She asked with the attitude only a young teenager
could muster, she even curled her top lip up a little like Elvis when she spoke.

I couldn't help but smile at her forced bravado which seemed to annoy her even more than my presence.

"Hi, I'm looking to speak with Ms. Voyant... if that's possible? Are you her?" I silently prayed we hadn't walked down here just to talk to a kohl obsessed tween.

I started to feel the dizzying effects of the candles that lined the room in the few short seconds I'd been standing there. It would have been generous to call it 'cozy', it was just the door, the candles and the desk, not even a seating area which made me wonder if that was due to the lack of space or the unwillingness to be seen there by passers-by. I didn't have time to think about spatial issues as the girl looked at the book on her lap, closed it and then consulted an appointment book which, from my viewpoint, looked empty.

"Do you have an appointment?" She didn't look at me, but instead looked out of the window at the passing cars. It was like a fish tank in this room, and my palms started to sweat.

Rob had been hovering at my side, silently, but at the mention of an appointment he took it upon himself to test the waters.

He disappeared through a retro beaded curtain before I could think of a way around this roadblock. The clichés just kept on coming.

The girl looked at the beads as they parted and frowned before turning back to me.

"Erm, no...?" I looked at the appointment book again annoyed at the girl's attitude. Surely she wasn't going to make me book an appointment when the calendar looked as clear as her face might have been if she hadn't covered every pore with makeup.

"Right, well, you have to have an appointment to see Claire." She lifted her heavily groomed eyebrow at me.

A small laugh escaped my lips which brought a sneer to her face but I couldn't help it. I was just so glad to find out that this girl wasn't the acclaimed psychic.

She began to say something which was no doubt going to be snide but before she could utter a syllable a woman dressed in a floaty dress with a ridiculous amount of red curls cascading down her shoulders and back appeared from the beaded curtain like a performer might appear on stage; game face on.

"Is my 3 o'clock here yet?" She called in a musical voice, her dark round glasses sitting on her pixie nose, making her seem more librarian than omniscient.

She didn't wait for the answer from her nameless secretary. When she saw me she reached her hands towards me, beckoning me into her embrace.

"Oh yes, here you are!" She sang, closing the distance between us and taking my clammy hands into her own smooth palms. I looked back at the receptionist, who at this point had gone back to her book and was rolling her eyes.

"Oh, no, I don't have an appointment!" I confessed, though it didn't seem to matter to this woman, who I took to be Ms Voyant herself.

I was pulled thought the beads and into a back room which was more like what I expected from a fortune telling point of view.

There were of course fairy lights all around and more candles than a church altar.

She led me to a very low table with cushions on the floor instead of chairs.

I wasn't shocked to see stacks of colourfully illustrated tarot cards and a crystal ball on the table, nor was I taken aback by the fabrics that lay strewn around, making it seem like we were inside a genie's lamp.

"Here we go, take a seat!" She dropped my hand and swept around the table to plonk herself on the floor. I took my cues from Rob, who had already made himself at home; sitting cross legged on a cushion and I tried to confess again.

"I think there's been a mistake. I don't have an appoint-"

She didn't let me finish; instead she just waved her hands at me and shushed. Closing her eyes she took a deep breath in, inhaling the warm spicy-scented air, and then smiled wryly before opening her eyes. She produced a tea pot and three cups from beside her and placed them on the table in front of us.

She began to pour the tea but stopped at the third cup, leaving it empty. She looked at it and at the seat where Rob sat and frowned. Maybe she was worth the trip, after all.

"You don't need an appointment," She stage whispered to me like she was scared the young girl outside might hear. She passed me the cup of tea and picked up her own, blowing on it to cool it down. I followed suit and hoped my awkwardness wasn't too apparent.

"It's just something I like to do to make the punters think I'm all mystical and to annoy my step daughter. She hates it!" She laughed and it was the kind of laugh that put you at ease.

"So, back to business. What can I do for you? No appointment? No flair for the procedures - something tells me this isn't the usual visit, yes. Even I can tell that much!" She laughed again and I smiled. Rob laughed too.

"I like her!" He smiled, his face lit up with hope.

"Um…" I stalled. I hadn't really thought this far ahead.

A million explanations and questions ran through my mind but I couldn't decide which was the right one to start with. Rob nudged me and I automatically shot him a warning look. Claire, and her cool hazel eyes, observed me as though I was the most interesting thing in the world. My face turned red under her scrutiny.

"Don't be embarrassed!" She gushed, waving her hands as if to dismiss anything that could be considered a 'bad aura', hanging around in the air like a smoky cloud.

"I can assure you I've heard the worst, seen the worst. No one here will think you're crazy. Well, no one in this room. I'm afraid Imogen thinks everyone who walks through that door is crazy. Most of all me..."

"I'm not embarrassed, I just don't know where to start..." I placed the cup down and shrugged my shoulders.

"The best place to start is to tell me what you're looking for today. A tarot reading? Aura cleanse?" Claire spoke so calmly, like this was the most natural thing in the world.

"I'm not after my fortune being told, I never liked the idea of knowing what was or wasn't going to happen. No offense!" I added in a rush, although Claire didn't strike me as the kind of woman who took offense that often. Again, she waved her hands at me. It seemed this was a habit of hers.

"Not to sound too obvious, but they *do* say the beginning is the best place." She spoke in quite a regal fashion which clashed with her spiritual, hippy-ish demeanour. Clearly she was someone from quite a good background who dabbled with this hocus pocus as a hobby. I didn't know whether that made me more comfortable to talk to her or less.

"*They?*" I asked, sceptically which made her snort with laughter. She managed to compose herself as I turned a dark shade of red.

"Not 'the spirits' if that's what you mean," She sipped her tea with a smile. I felt stupid for even questioning who she meant but the situation was making me feel awkward. I didn't want to waste my time, but Rob seemed to like her and so I decided I might as well go all out, even if this didn't pan out, at least it would be good practise for the next person we went to. I cleared my throat and sipped my tea and tried to organise my thoughts.

"A few weeks ago my best friend died," I'd decided not to tell her any names or exact dates. I didn't want her to know who I was or who I might be talking about in case it got back to the family. All of a sudden the decision to come to this place, so close to home, seemed like the worst one I'd ever made. Claire didn't do the usual 'I'm sorry' routine, so I ploughed on with my story.

"It was...traumatic... for everyone," I struggled to find the right words but she encouraged me to continue with a nod; like a doctor listening to a patient describe ailments.

"When the funeral came and went...well, he came back." I stopped and looked into her eyes to see what her reaction would be. Rob also had stopped his constant fidgeting and was looking at this 'Claire Voyant' with longing in his eyes. I felt a pang of nausea and my stomach muscles contracted. I didn't know when I'd last eaten and a distant voice in my head told me that was bad.

"And by came back you mean..." She trailed off, waiting for me to fill in the blanks. Her face was unreadable yet I did my best to figure it out, I didn't take my eyes of her.

"Reappeared. Not back alive, just... not gone... A ghost?" I said the G word like it was a curse. Hesitant to say it out loud. I didn't realise until then that I needed her approval. I needed her to tell me I wasn't crazy, that this was all real. She bit her lip and looked at the beaded curtain that separated us from the world outside.

"Are you done? Is that it?" She asked snippishly. The silence hung in the air, Rob looked between the two of us.

"What just happened?" He murmured to me, but I obviously couldn't answer him.

Claire got to her feet, sweeping her dress up so as not to catch it on the flames, her face was now readable and she was very pissed off. She stormed around the room, blowing out the candles and flicking a switch so that the overhead light came on, drowning out the fairy lights with the superior glow.

"I'm sorry, what did I do?" I asked, following her and standing up, I looked around the room but I couldn't see any hidden cameras, then again I wouldn't.

"Is this supposed to be funny?" Her eyes glistened in the brightness of the room and her cheeks were flushed with her sudden anger.

"I'm sorry if I've done something wrong... I've never been to a psychic before, I don't know what the rules are. Shall I go?" I motioned to the beaded curtains which swayed in the slight breeze created by her sweeping movements. Claire held her hand out at me and closed her eyes for a moment. When she looked back at me there was something else there. I think it was the same look I saw on my own face in the mirror sometimes; distant recognition of someone you used to be.

"Wait! Imogen didn't put you up to this?" She stared me down, imploring me to tell her the truth, which I did easily.

"What? No! Of course not, to be honest I've probably walked past this place a million times and never even knew it was here. I promise!" Rob and I shared a look of confusion and he frowned at me. I knew what he was thinking. Why would anyone play that kind of joke? Claire sighed and lowered herself back to the floor, waving me down with her. She started to light the candles again and it wasn't long before the hot and warm smells of cinnamon and vanilla were wafting their way up my nose again.

"I'm so sorry!" She waved her hands in front of her face the way emotional women did on TV when they were either going to cry or laugh.

"It's just, sometimes Imogen thinks... well, I think she just likes to wind me up sometimes, bless her." She picked up her tea and downed the lot, pouring herself another one. She shook herself out and her hair shimmered with the movement.

"When I was younger I used to see ghosts. Imogen likes to tease me. In fact the other day she prank called me and played static down the phone whilst she rambled on like a crazy person!" She laughed and picked up the tarot deck and started to shuffle. I looked at Rob and he smiled at the woman's unknown help.

"I knew I liked her!" He laughed and leaned forward, captured by this woman's presence.

"But that's beside the point. You say your friend reappeared, what exactly do you mean? You can sense his spirit still around? Hear his voice?" She stopped shuffling and looked directly at me, her eyebrows raised high and the clarity in her eyes was unnerving, "see him?" She tilted her head and placed the cards in front of her.

"Yes... to all of those, really. I can see him." I felt as though I'd finally been freed of a burden. Not that Rob was a burden, but being the only one holding onto his form was taxing, I hadn't realised it until now.

I'd never said it out loud to anyone else.

Oh god, I hope I'm not crazy!

Claire smiled at me, that kind of smile you only saw parents give their new born children. It was unadulterated, joy. Pure and shining like the little candles that dotted the room.

"I'm not crazy, am I?" I had to ask because that was something else I had never mused out loud to anyone other than Rob. This sudden release of secret words had a cathartic effect on me and what I imagined to be my soul.

"Oh heavens, no! Well, I hope not anyway. Although sometimes I do meet crazy people, but it's not polite to say so - I'm sorry, listen to me, getting carried away. So where did you see him?"

Taking a deep breath I prepared myself to upload the biggest secret I'd ever carried around.

"Come on Amelia, use your words!" Rob was getting impatient. His eyes were wide and urgent; pleading with me to help. I batted him away with a dismissive hand.

"Everywhere. I see him all the time."

Claire reached across from me and took the teacup from the table. It was half empty and she discarded the remains into the teapot quickly and observed the inside of the china.

I leant forward and was taken aback when her head snapped back up and her eyes drove deep into mine.

"Not just his familiar places, somewhere his spirit might linger, like his home?" Claire twisted the cup in her hands to look at the leaves from another angle.

"No, everywhere. His house, my house, my work, the street, the coffee shop. Everywhere."

I didn't realise I'd been gripping my hands together until I stopped talking and I felt the little marks of my nails that had been left in my palms.

Claire frowned at me and looked around the room, dramatically casting a glance over her shoulder. If it had been anyone else I would have thought they were making fun of me, but I knew she believed me. I could feel her belief rolling off her like a heat wave.

"Well, that's strange. It's mostly unheard of to see them all the time..." She trailed off and looked back at the tea cup as though it held all the answers.

"What do the tea leaves say?" The question came out more sarcastically than intended but I didn't like the way she reacted to my answer.

If other people didn't see ghosts all the time and not just in their 'familiar' places it could mean that I was actually crazy.

My brain started to throb, maybe I could have a tumour. Rob could just be a tumour that's pressing on my brain right now. Irritating and formidable just like he had been in life.

It would make sense but it also wouldn't because Claire said it herself; she had received a prank phone call and it could have only been Rob calling unless it was a coincidence, but then, what about all the other little bits of proof I had? Rob could touch things, push things even lock people in rooms. Was this real or had I done it all myself in some sort of craze induced trance like in the movie Fight Club?

The lights started to dim as my internal debates melted my brain.

"Oh, my - here, have some water!" Claire handed me a water bottle from under the table and I took it and gulped it down without hesitation. "I'm sorry, sometimes I get caught up. I was trying to trance, to see what I could make of this all. It's not often a person will see a ghost all the time... wait a second..."

She fixed me with her hazel stare and I felt like someone being hypnotized by a snake charmer. Rob was right next to me, though I didn't remember him moving from his seat, and he was rubbing my back.

"He's here now, isn't he?" She asked, looking over her shoulder again. I didn't ask why she though he would be standing behind her, it seemed rude.

"...Yes" I admitted, hoping it really wasn't a tumour that was driving me insane.

Reflex kicked in and I turned and looked right at Rob. His eyes shined in the candle lit room; he looked happy. Hopeful.

Claire sat back and blinked, her face full of concern and what I thought could have been sympathy.

"I don't even know your name." She said quietly, like as afterthought. She buried her hands into her hair making it even wilder. She used her hands a lot, but it was an endearing quality.

"Doesn't the teacup tell you?" Rob said, leaning forwards so his elbows rested on the table.

I hid a laugh as I repeated his question, hoping she wouldn't take offence.

"The teacup? No, it can't spell. I could ask the crystal ball but it's quite temperamental..." she took the joke in her stride.

I could tell Rob liked her by the way his face lit up at her joke. His eyes followed her movements with the curiosity of a young boy watching a magician.

It was easy to feel at ease in Claire's presence. I hadn't felt it immediately, having been caught up in all the glitz and glam of the room and the trinkets that were dotted around. Rob had seemingly spotted her matching kindred spirit straight away.

He was good at reading people, I should have known to trust his judgement.

"It's Amelia," I didn't give her my last name and hoped she wasn't one to read the local paper in too much detail.

"Well, Amelia, this is quite a case you have. I was going to read your cards but I don't think I need to, especially since you don't want to know your future. But... well, I don't know what I can help you with."

She looked sad again and swirled the tea leaves around in the cup, as though washing away bad thoughts.

I was dumbstruck. A moment passed where I didn't even know what to say. This wasn't going in any way I'd expected.

"I don't know really what I need help with, I-" I tried and failed to give an explanation. Before I could finish speaking Rob cut me off, slamming his hand on the table and making the cups rattle. The tarot deck slid apart, several cards fell from the table altogether.

"You need to ask her the rules, what I can and can't do, where I can go, what's going to happen to me...why am I here?"

His words came out in a rush like he'd been preparing for this for a while, maybe since he first arrived back here to haunt me. Guilt burned in my heart.

"I'm sorry," I said to Claire, "He was just reminding me why we came." I smiled at him, silently telling him to calm down with my eyes. Claire looked from me to Rob's empty space in silent awe as she slid the cards back into a neat pile.

"So you just... converse with him. Whenever you want?" She was clearly trying to keep up and was, so far, taking it quite well.

"Pretty much. He's there when I wake up, there when I go to sleep. Always with me. Solid as a solid thing and he can touch stuff..." I gestured to the recently trembling table, "but he definitely can't walk through walls. Mark that under 'tried and tested'." As soon as I started to tell her about it all the stress of keeping the secret faded away.

"Can't taste food, though... that sucks." Rob frowned, like that was the worst part of this whole thing.

Claire's eyes were wide like I'd just told her I could talk to God.

"Amazing!" She chimed, "Just... amazing!" She reached out and then pulled her hand back quickly.

"Can I... I mean, can we try something? An experiment?" She laughed nervously and placed a tea cup in the centre of the table.

I looked at Rob who smiled. With a shrug he reached out and pushed the teacup.

Claire jolted in excited shock and laughed again. She shook her head, sending her red curls spiralling around her.

"You've not told anyone about this? You've kept it a secret - which I understand. I mean, who'd believe you but a loon like me? Why hasn't anyone else seen things move?"

She raised a good question but there was no real answer to it. All I knew was what I could assume.

"We've been careful, mostly. And I think if people see things move they just assume they imagined it. I read about it on the internet, well, Rob did - it said something like 'people only see what they want to see, but if they opened their eyes to all the possibilities they would see everything and it could drive them crazy'... something like that anyway!"

"Yes, well, people *will* only see what they want to see," she mused and smiled at me and the empty space beside me, "God, what a trip today's turned out to be. I know what we need!"

She put her hand under the table and pulled out a bottle of tequila.

"For the nerves." She filled a glass, her hands shaking whilst she did it.

It was almost like Rob was alive and we were just three people talking, except I was intensely aware Claire couldn't see him, though she tried.

I could see it in her face; her brow furrowed like she was trying to reach out with all her senses but I didn't think it was working.f

"Why do you think I can see him all the time?" I asked in a small voice. Rob shifted uncomfortably beside me but I couldn't bring myself to look at him.

Claire frowned. I could tell it wasn't something she was accustomed to, her face crinkled in a way that made her seem younger than she probably was.

"Well, ghosts usually haunt," She turned her nose up at the word like it was a curse, "their homes, or graves, somewhere they are particularly connected to. I suppose, although I'm just guessing, that Rob could be with you because you two were extremely close in life?" I nodded, though I didn't need to. It was the only explanation.

"Perhaps he's with you because even in death you are his home; soul mates... I don't mean to intrude," She quickly back peddled when my eyes bulged at the word, "Not that you are really soul mates in the general consensus. Not lovers like people would have you believe soul mates are, but an actual pairing of the soul in its purest form. It's very rare!"

Everything about this seemed to be rare. How did we get so lucky?

I looked at Rob who was equally as consumed with thought as I was. Were we soul mates? What happened when one of the souls died?

"So what does that mean?" I asked aloud, needing to clarify the situation, though I felt like I knew where we were heading with this conversation, but having someone else say it, out loud, might bring me a little bit of peace of mind.

"It's hard to know, I mean, like I say we're wading through unchartered waters here, as far as I know, certainly not in my lifetime... but it has been said that some ghosts stay to tend to unfinished business." I rolled my eyes, and gestured to Rob, forgetting the fact that she couldn't see him.

"Unfinished? His life is unfinished, he died before he even got to 18. That's as unfinished as unfinished gets!"

I had lost all concept of the meaning of unfinished in that one sentence but it felt good to rant. The cruel fate that had delivered this circumstance was awakening feelings I'd suppressed.

"Yes, that may be true, but when we come to unfinished business it hardly ever relates to the deceased my love -" She stopped talking and looked at the vacuum of space beside me.

"It's you Melia, you're my unfinished business..." I turned to face him and met his gaze, I had only seen such sureness and seriousness in him at his darkest points, it wasn't a look I liked to see blazing behind his green and hazel eyes.

I shook my head and bit the inside of my lip to stop from saying something I'd regret.

"Well, what if I don't particularly want to be your unfinished business? What does it even mean? You have to save me from my dreary life and then you move on to the 'other side'?" My voice was thick with emotion and my chest felt tight, "then you're done and I'm left here alone..." I let my words trail off and I looked away from Rob.

I turned my attention back to Claire, who was trying to keep up with the one-sided conversation,

"And if he were to leave me; would he disappear? Do you think he could he go somewhere without me?" It wasn't that I wanted him to leave, there was definitely the part of me that wanted him here forever, but the thought of potential freedom to be able to do things without his judgement was appealing.

I cringed, hating the way my brain worked.

Claire's shoulders rose as she inhaled deeply. She massaged her temples like she was channelling in on the headache that was forming in my own head.

"I can't see why not, he's here from what I can tell, I don't know why he wouldn't be able to leave you and then return." She hesitated, biting her bottom lip. "This happened to me, once. I was younger than you but I could see my grandmother after she passed."

My mouth hung open, so that was her truth; the reason why she was caught up being Claire Voyant. This admittance shattered the aloof illusion that enveloped her and I saw through to what she was and what I could become if I wasn't careful.

"The rules are never clear so I assume, and that's the key word… I assume he'd still be here, but, well, would you want to try it? He came to you for a reason, perhaps you should try to figure out what that reason is."

"What was the reason for her grandmother?" Rob asked. The gravity of what she had said felt tangible, like a lead weight that was tying her to this world she'd created for herself.

"And your grandmother?" I prompted both for my sake and for Rob's. He sat forward, his eyes like saucers. It was possible he wasn't alone in the ghostly world, that was huge.

"That's a story best left untold. She was here, she left…" Claire's eyes misted and she ran her hands through her hair again, pulling the ends over her shoulder.

Her experience had marked her and left her like this. Would it do the same to me? I bit down on my lip and clasped my hands together, staying silent whilst I let my doubts run through my mind.

We couldn't risk Rob leaving my general vicinity, I knew we couldn't yet I could tell, with Rob squirming beside me, he wanted to. He wanted to test his unearthly leash, pull at it as hard as he could, and consequences be damned.

It was how he was in life, too.

"And I imagine the longer he's here the more he'll learn to control whatever his abilities are. He can affect objects without struggle. Perhaps, unlike films, he will have to learn to *not* touch things. Learn to pass through objects?"

She was trying to help but my mind was adrift now with Claire's own untold experiences and the weight of being Rob's possible 'unfinished business'.

The walls were a lot closer than I remembered them being. I feigned a look at the clock on the wall but I didn't see the time.

"I think you've left us with more than enough to think about, we'd better leave if that's OK?" I aimed the question to Rob, hoping he would sense my discomfort. "How much do I owe you?"

Grabbing my purse I rooting around for the money I had stashed. I had about £50 in notes and I unfurled them and put them on the table.

Claire seemed in two minds, hesitating, her hands curled around a tea cup.

"No, I don't need you to pay me, I haven't helped you." She looked at her hands before her gaze fell onto Rob's empty space. My stomach contracted and I pretended not to notice her teary eyes.

"Seriously, take it, I'd feel bad otherwise." I got up and Rob followed, but not happily.

"Come on Melia, I'm sure she can help with my other questions!" He tugged at my arm and I snapped at him.

"No, she can't help us," I turned to face him, his eyes were dark and broody again, "It's great she believes us and everything, but what use is that? We need to know the rules of this, I really don't think you're here to somehow fix my life!"

I stalked back through the beaded curtain, whipping it out of my way with the back of my hand. The wooden chains crashing back together with a clatter.

In my head I chastised myself for my loss of temper, but I couldn't stop the words from tumbling from my mouth.

Rob and Claire follow me through the curtain; its lengthy arms clacked together twice.

If Imogen noticed the extra exit she didn't react to it, she just looked up at me with the perfect teenage scowl on her face and went back to texting on her mobile phone, thumbs moving faster than I thought possible.

The sky outside looked like it was going to break into joyous sunshine again and I thanked God for it, but swiftly tried to un-think the thought, as I remembered I was mad at anyone who might be responsible for this crashing chain of events.

CHAPTER 13

Claire held the front door open for us, the bangles on her arms and rings on her fingers glinted in the sunshine. I found the light distracting and shrank from it, looking anywhere else.

"Well, Amelia, if you or Rob need my help in any way, just call me, OK?" She handed me a business card which had the store number and her own personal number on it next to a crystal ball logo which had a black crow perched atop it, ominously.

Imogen didn't seem to notice the mention of anyone else and I burned inside at how ignorant some people could be.

I tried to be friendly but I could tell my smile seemed more of a grimace as I took the card and slid it into my pocket.

When we stepped into the street I felt relieved; totally the opposite of how I think I should have felt.

We'd gotten answers, to an extent, but I was more stressed than before. If that was even possible.

"Why the hell were you such a bitch in there?" Rob rounded on me, his voice louder than it should have been. It was like he was shouting inside my head. I inwardly shrank back at the intrusion.

I had no answer and I fumbled for an explanation in my head, the words caught in my mouth and felt sticky and thick like cotton wool.

Before I could concoct an explanation two figures appeared before me, blocking out the sunlight.

My heart dropped to my feet and I felt the blistering sting of nausea.

"Hi!" I heard my voice out loud and cringed at the awkwardness of it, I tried to laugh it off and only managed another strange grimaced smile. I just couldn't seem to get a hold of my stupid emotions today.

Dean and Mark stood before me, each holding a shopping bag.

They'd been chatting and laughing but at the sight of me and a glance at the door I had emerged from, not to mention the person who was gazing out of the window at me, their faces changed into identical confusion.

I tried to shuffle out of sight of the big glass window and managed to sandwich myself between Mark and the wall between the shops.

"What are you doing?" Mark's eyebrows knitted together and his eyes shifting to Dean, as though he could provide an explanation.

Casual, I thought to myself. Look casual. I felt like a criminal caught at the scene of the crime.

"Nothing, just came out for a walk..." My arms folded across my chest, and Rob seethed at me silently, cursing his brothers for the untimely interruption.

He walked away, kicking at the stones on the pavement with frustration, not even looking back at his brothers.

When he had first re-appeared he'd taken joy in talking to them, loving the fact he could say whatever he wanted without repercussion. The novelty faded pretty quickly.

Neither believed my reason for being there. For once their twin-ness was evident, they'd mastered this expression well, which was basically the 'We don't believe you' face.

"What were you doing in there?" Mark asked, smugly, as though he'd just found my diary and couldn't wait to read the contents to the world.

Dean, on the other hand, looked at me with his Oh-So-Worried eyes, eyes I recently realised could cause butterflies to explode like fireworks in my stomach.

"What? Oh, in there? Nothing, just went in to say hello to a friend..." Being casual wasn't one of my natural abilities, apparently.

They pretty much knew everyone I knew, but they didn't call me on my lie. Rob snorted in my peripheral, and shook his head.

I didn't give him any indication that I'd noticed but my mood plummeted. Not wanting to give the boys a chance to ask more questions I started to inched away from them.

"I'm actually just on my way home. I'm not feeling very well, I think I might be coming down with something."

With all my might I tried to muster up a 'sickly' face, but I had I feeling it looked more like painful stomach cramps. Still, I could work with that, so I put my hand on my stomach absentmindedly and inhaled through my nose, as though it might be 'woman problems'.

If there was one thing I'd learnt from hanging out with Rob for so long it was that guys didn't like to know about women's periods.

The sheer mention of them used to drive Rob into a fumbling frenzy and usually he'd leave the room in a haze of stammering words and flailing arm movements. It worked every time.

Mark actually took a step back. It didn't matter what you said was wrong, as long as you were displaying signs of sickness Mark treated you the same way. Sickness was a weakness he said he didn't have time for. If he caught any illness off me I had no doubt he'd hold it over me for a very long time.

Dean responded in the exact opposite way to Mark; he took a step towards me.

His sudden need to look after me sparked conflicting feelings that could do with staying un-sparked.

The world felt like it was tipping and I was the only one who couldn't find my footing.

"Are you OK?" Dean shifted his weight to one side and partially blocked Mark from sight. Whether he'd done it by mistake or on purpose I wasn't sure but the look he gave me was for me alone. That much I knew.

Mark didn't appear to have heard Dean's concern. He was busy looking at his watch and not so tactfully looking at some girls in pretty dresses walk past on the other side of the road.

Dean's hand came up to meet my shoulder, but I shrugged him off before Mark could see. That last thing we needed was Mark getting involved in this whole situation.

I felt like the world's worst juggler.

"Yeah, I just need to get some sleep or something, I'll see you soon..."

I stood there for a moment just starring at Dean before I realised I should leave.

With Rob no longer a solid form of contact my connection to their family had been severed. As I walked away I felt like it was a physical thing; a tie that had been cut.

Rob trailed after me, only speaking to me once we'd rounded a corner and were safely out of the way of any pedestrians.

"What is *wrong* with you Amelia? Are you losing the plot?" His face was wrinkled with worry but also impatience. I took a deep breath and tried to still the churning emotions, the start of tears stung my eyes, threatening to embarrass me further.

"Yeah, actually, I think I am. I thought I could handle this Rob but I just don't think I can. I can handle you. I can handle your family and the grieving, I might even be able to handle your brother and his constant misplaced affection, but..." I cut myself off, as I realised what I was going to say.

He was staring at me with his cheeks a furious red and his mouth set into a firm line. He knew what I was going to say but he needed me to say it out loud.

"But what?" His voice wasn't raised, he didn't shout, it was more of the dejected voice of someone who has tried so hard, only to fail.

My eyes stung but the tears didn't come.

"But...maybe, but... maybe I can't handle it all together."

My voice was hoarse, my throat trying to strangle the words, trying not to say them despite the fact that they were true.

"Can't handle me being here, you mean?" He didn't need an answer, his voice said it all. He understood.

He knew that him and me together alone was fine, but when I had to see his family I had to pretend, it was unfair to them, and to me. I had to lie to everyone I knew and I was drowning in the fabricated world I'd created.

I thought it would be OK, that we could make it like it had been before but I knew now that was stupid. Rob knew it too.

He nodded, not saying anything. The moment seemed suspended in time.

We looked at each other and without another word he turned on his heel and walked away from me. My gut instinct was to run to him, grab him and tell him that I didn't mean it, but I couldn't lie anymore.

Suddenly the tears I'd held onto for so long spilled down my cheeks, the world had gotten darker and everything blurred in my vision, my surroundings sparkled and shimmered like a reflection.

Throwing everything to the wind I ran. I ran in the opposite direction to him. I ran all the way back to my house and after throwing myself through the front door and launching myself on to my bed I realised what I'd done.

Rob had walked away, though. He'd done it first; pushed against the barriers of our situation. It didn't change the fact that I was the one who ripped away from him without looking back.

Grief overwhelmed me, crashed over me in waves that drowned me in my own tears.

We didn't know if he could exist without me. I didn't feel any different and I tried to reach my mind out, trying to concentrate on finding his presence, as though that was something I knew how to do but I didn't. I'd never know if he was still out there.

For all I knew he'd really gone this time.

I turned my lights off and closed the curtains, crawling under my covers awash with my shame, guilt and grief.

Was this it? Was I finally alone?

My broken heart crippled me and all I could think was that he'd hated me and I realised I hated me too.

I was jolted awake by the vibrations of my phone against my desk. At this point any noise was too much for my senses so I rolled over to stop the pneumonic drill from splitting the world in half.

When I emerged from under the covers of my bed my face was warm with recirculated air and slightly damp from my tears. A flash of what I'd dreamt about lingered in my mind's eye and I tried to push it away to no avail. The depressing thoughts ate away at me, encouraging me to dwell on them.

"Hello?" I answered on auto-pilot, not really caring who it was on the other end. It wasn't who I needed.

There was a crackle and other noises coming from the other side, fuzzy like my head. I pressed the phone to my ear and sank back under the covers where it was dark and safe.

"No... Stop, get out. You're a dick." Dean's muffled voice split through the darkness.

The sounds were so familiar to me I had to swallow a cry.

"Dean?" I waiting for him to stop fighting with Mark. I heard more shuffling and then a door slamming.

"Sorry, are you still there?" His voice was quite upbeat and relaxed, and I closed my eyes and pretended that nothing out of the ordinary had happened in the last few hours.

Lie.

The word sounded in my soul like a familiar chant. Lie. Lie. Lie. A heartbeat thudding.

"I'm here," I snuggled deeper under the covers and pulled my legs up to my chest, making myself as small as I could. As small as I felt.

Even though it was becoming difficult to breathe I couldn't surface. To look out into my empty room.

"You sound awful, are you OK?"

Lie.

I cleared my throat as quietly as I could and smiled, stupid really considering he couldn't see me.

I'd learnt a while ago that if you smiled on the phone the person you were talking to could tell, I didn't know if it was true and I tried to imagine Dean smiling.

Rob's face flashed in my mind.

Lie.

"Yeah, I'm fine, I must have fallen asleep, how're you?" The question shouldn't have needed to be asked, but I had to. I couldn't be selfish anymore.

"Yeah, I'm OK. Just trying to deal with Mark, he's being... well, like Mark. Better than him not being Mark though, y'know?" He was talking fast, babbling really.

"What's he done now?" Keeping the conversation as light as possible even though every word felt heavy. It seemed to work, though, because Dean sighed down the phone.

"Oh just this and that, nothing too bad...I just wanted to check you were OK."

I didn't answer him for a few seconds. I wasn't OK but I couldn't tell him that.

I quickly sifted through all my recent memories. Now that Rob was gone a small part of me wondered if I could confide in him but I couldn't. I knew I couldn't.

He waited for my reply, the dead air hummed in my ear. All I had to do was leaf through carefully and pick out the feelings that were relatively normal.

Lie. Tell the truth. Ignore the empty feeling of the room. Ignore how my chest hurt like my heart had stopped beating properly.

"I'm fine, I promise, like I said I think I'm just coming down with something," I lied. "I just... I don't know. I miss Rob," That was true, "and sometimes I feel like I'm going crazy because it's like I can still feel him here and everything's OK," Again, true, kind of, "but today it was like he's gone again. Like I've lost him all over and I don't know what to do. I feel like I can't breathe."

And that was the whole truth, as much as I could muster without direct details.

I choked on my own tears and felt the warmth of them slide down my face; fast and unstoppable like my words.

I felt obliterated, like I was totally lost and I couldn't even see the path I'd taken to get to this point. I was stuck in a maze of riddles and dead ends.

"I know what you mean," He answered immediately.

I closed my eyes. I heard him sit down and imagined him leaning back onto his bed.

"I have days like that. I'm working, or I'm just watching TV and I can kind of pretend Rob is just sat at home playing music, or he's with you. You know, I think of him and you just hanging out in that coffee shop you go to, and I can just pretend everything is fine and you're going to look after him. But... then I remember he's not there. Not at home, not watching TV, not drinking coffee, not with you."

He did the only thing that could break me even more and cried. A sob that escaped his lips and travelled all the way over here to hit me right in the face.

"And then I think of you all alone, sitting in your house with your parents... What the hell happened to life?"

It was rare that Dean got so existential. That was usually Rob's job.

"I don't know."

We sat in silence, the air passing between us and the phones.

Something about it was calming. This was the way we were supposed to get through this. Grief and sharing the pain and helping each other through. My throat closed up again.

"He's not coming back." I was saying this for my own benefit, and I thought Dean would think I was stupid for saying it out loud but he just sighed.

"No. I'm pretty sure that's not going to happen."

The wind ripped through the trees outside and even though my window was closed it felt like it was tearing through my room, destroying everything, the rain followed and lashed against the glass.

Pulling the covers back I forced myself to sit up and gulped in the cool air.

The emptiness of the room weighed on me but I didn't hide from it.

A tear slip to the crease of my lips and the salt hit my tongue. I sniffed and my free hand buffed my cheeks.

"I don't know what to do, I don't know what I'm doing anymore." I let my internal thoughts loose, feeling less crazy as I spoke feelings I'd kept locked up.

Dean sigh again and my heart clenched. I took in ragged and uneven lungful of air as I tried to keep from falling apart again.

"Do you want me to come over?" Dean asked like he was scared to know the answer. He paused. "I mean, well, if you want me to keep you company I will, but if you want to me alone that's OK too."

I bit my lower lip and scrunched up my face. My heart thumped in my ears. Rob. Rob. Rob.

The wind hit the window again and the rain lashed down and I kept my eyes closed as I imagined I was out at sea, the house my ship and the storm outside was casting me further and further off course.

"No, it's OK..." I answered when I felt like I could speak in a normal voice. "I think I need to ride this storm out, pun intended." I forced out a little laugh to try to prove to both of us that I was OK, smashing my head into my hand repeatedly. "Unless *you* want company?"

"Nah, Mark keeps asking me to watch a movie with him so I should probably do that..."

The conversation dropped, the comfortable silence of before was nowhere to be found. It was lingering and sharp and I was acutely aware of the tension that fizzled through the handset.

"OK, well... have fun. I'll talk to you later?" I sounded like an idiot.

"Yeah, I'll talk to you later Amelia."

He hung up before we could converse anymore and my mind went into overdrive over the stupidest things.

Why had he offered to come over if he had plans? Was he mad I said no? Was he upset I didn't want him here or relieved to be off the hook?

The hurricane that seemed to be blowing outside didn't do me any favours and never answered even when I asked my questions out loud. No voice came from the darkness. A huge part of me had hoped they would.

I didn't speak to anyone except the people I worked with for the rest of the week, no parent interaction, no late-night calls from the Wood's house. Nothing. I fell asleep to the sound of the storm and the feeling that the house was rocking in the imaginary waves, I was being pushed out to sea on my little boat with no way back. Where was Rob? What had I done?

CHAPTER 14

I woke up to my parents arguing downstairs.

From the crashing of pans I could tell they were in the kitchen, though what they were doing in there was a mystery, it was only 8am, a couple of hours shy of their normal waking time.

I decided to forgo my toast and have a quick shower before getting out of the house and began the usual routine of gathering up my clothes to change in the bathroom. It was only when I was laden with my outfit choice for the day that I remembered I didn't need to do that anymore.

It was strange how something so small could splinter the ground beneath your feet.

My breathing ceased and I sat down, staring at the chair at my desk.

How I could still be hit with these realisations was beyond me, it had been a week and I was still floored by the smallest things.

I would not cry here. I couldn't sit and cry. I'd never get up, probably never stop, so I did what I always did when the need arose. I jumped into the shower and turned the water up to the hottest setting I could handle.

The warm water hit my face and melt the tears away, I even only let out one audible sob which was a new record.

I was on a new track this week. With Rob gone I was having to act like I wasn't still in the first stages of mourning but it was hard.

I still looked for him everywhere.

I went into my room in my towel, changed, taking my time to appreciate being able to walk around in my underwear, picking out clothes.

I pretended this was a good thing.

Lie.

Not bothering to talk to my parents, who were still shouting on about something in the kitchen, I left the house.

I hadn't spoken to them at all since Dean had dragged me out of there.

My stomach rumbled but I ignored it.

One step out of the house I felt something under my foot.

A white envelope stuck out from under my tennis shoe. It was stark and bright against the grey concrete and it shone under the sun, which was thankfully now out in place of the recent rain.

I scooped the envelope up and noticed it didn't have our address on it so the postman hadn't dropped it. It just had my name on it, in writing I didn't recognise.

The way it was written made it look like it was the start of a sentence. My name, Amelia, was placed in the top left corner and the full stop next to it seemed to have been edited from a comma. Strange.

I opened the seal and found a set of car keys.

Scrunching my eyes against the unfamiliar sunlight I looked up, the car Mr Wood gave me wasn't outside the house. Then again, whoever had left the keys would know better than to leave the car outside my house.

Sure enough, as I scanned the street, I saw it parked on the corner down the road.

When I approached it I saw it was freshly washed. My warped reflection stood before me in different variations. Close in the black paint but skewed and distant in the chrome.

My guess was it was Mark who has begrudgingly delivered it at his father's instruction.

He wanted it, I could tell. Well, if he wanted it, I'd have to make sure to use it to my advantage. Blackmail and Mark were my two favourite things, and had been since we were kids.

Mark was so jealous of anyone else's things that it was a common pasttime to make him work for things, like playing with computer games, or riding new bikes.

He always got his own, of course, but he really suffered from the 'grass is always greener' syndrome. Which is why he went through girlfriends so often. Or other people's girlfriends. I don't think he'd had a girlfriend he hadn't stolen from someone else since he was about sixteen.

I unlocked the car door and started the engine to see the petrol tank was full. I bet that just killed him.

I chuckled to myself as I fiddled with the radio button, I was about to try to change stations, not wanting to sit through even a second of that horrible in between station static, when the car was filled with music.

David Bowie's 'Space Oddity' began playing.

On instinct I switched it off. It was one of Rob's favourites. That's when I realised it wasn't the radio but a cassette tape that had started up.

I hit the eject button and was transported back to the summer me and Rob had spent hours and hours making mixed tapes for no reason other than to have our favourite songs in one place.

My stomach twisted as I realised it must have been Dean who had brought the car, thinking he was being thoughtful by putting this tape in the player.

Reaching over to the passenger side I opened the glove box and threw the tape in, clicking it closed and locking the memories away.

The last thing I needed was Rob's songs right now.

Taking pleasure in the sound I revved the engine.

I drove to the coffee shop down the road and parked right outside, lucky to get the only parking space they had. I walked in and the waitress smiled at me.

"Usual?" She asked, already getting the cup down from the shelf. I smiled back, basking in the warmth of familiarity.

"Please, and can I get some toast as well?" I asked, glancing at the glass fronted cake shelf.

The lights above made the pastry and icing glisten like diamonds. I swallowed back the sick feeling I got when I looked at them.

"No cake today?" She asked, a frown creasing between her eyebrows.

It took me a few seconds to realise she was referring to my recent cake orders; the ones I'd been buying so Rob could smell them, even if he couldn't eat them.

"Nope, trying to cut back!" I said, laughing one of those fake laughs that everyone knows is fake.

As I took my coffee and toast to my usual table I almost tripped over my feet. I stopped in my tracks and mentally pinched myself. Instead of the table I would normally sit at I picked one on the other side of the room.

It took all my might to stop myself from looking over and replay memories of countless conversations, both in life and death, me and Rob had had over there.

Instead I sat staring out of the window, watching people and watching my car as it gleamed in the brightening day.

Despite all efforts my thoughts wandered to the last conversation I'd had with Rob.

These past few days had been hard without him and I'd tried to feel how I *thought* I should have been feeling.

Grief was complicated and layered so intricately like a Rubix cube I didn't really know if I was forcing myself to feel it or if it was real.

Whatever this unfinished business meant, that old cliché, I was sure it wasn't about me.

If he hadn't returned I would have been fine. I would have been part way through grieving for my best friend, perhaps even wondering what could have been if he was still here and we'd grown old together. Wondered if he could have been my future husband; that happened, right? You could go years without realising your perfect match was right there the whole time.

It was stupid to think like that but it was harder not to.

His return, if anything, was what had ruined me. Now I had all the furious memories of us spending secret time together; living in our own world but never being able to really live in the real world.

I wasn't broken before he came back. I wasn't that girl. He was what was killing me slowly on the inside. He was the reason I'd exploded.

All of my emotions swirled in me, and I felt like one of those static balls, the ones where you touched them and the electricity sparked at your fingertips. You could see the reactions but you didn't really know where they came from. Well, not unless you were a science nerd. Which I wasn't.

Rob could probably tell me all about how they worked.

At the end of the day I had to face the facts. I'd been the one to kill him this time.

Not in real life, but in my life, in *our* life and if felt just as bad as if I had actually done the deed.

My chest tightened and my throat seemed to narrow, I gulped my coffee in a bid to eradicate my thoughts but it didn't work. Everything that I needed was absent now.

It was my own fault, and it was Rob's fault. I'd become so dependent on someone I knew couldn't stay.

Yet I missed him. I tried not to miss the crazy situation we'd been in but I did.

I pushed all other thoughts away, especially when Dean's face floated into my vision, with his understanding eyes and his soft words.

Anger bubbled inside me at the thought of not being able to talk to anyone about this until I remembered Claire.

The last time I'd seen her I'd been less than polite. All I could hope was that she was the forgiving type.

My phone buzzed in my pocket, when I looked at the screen I felt a shiver run down my spine.

"Hello?" My stomach churned with anxiety.

"Amelia? It's Claire... Voyant?" She said her last name like I wouldn't know who it was.

"That's really spooky, I was just about to call you, seriously!" Anxieties increased when I realised this was stranger than I first thought. "How did you get this number?"

"It was written on a scrap of paper, wait, didn't you leave that for me?"

She sounded distracted and I could hear chiming in the background. I could pretty much smell the incense through the phone.

"That wasn't me..." Must have been Rob, but when he had time to do it I didn't know, "Since you've called I was wondering if you were free to talk?"

"Of course, you know, I had a feeling you might need a chat. There are some things I need to talk to you about as well..."

She trailed off which had the dramatic effect of making my heart pound a little faster.

"Not ominous at all, I'll come over now if that's OK?"

"Consider my schedule cleared, see you soon!"

Claire hung up and like all good dramatic moments in the movies she didn't even say goodbye.

I drained the last bit of coffee from my cup and got up to leave, thanking the waitress for it.

Worries swirled around my already swirling mind; why in the world did Claire want to speak to *me*?

I really hoped it wasn't more of this unfinished business nonsense.

I decided to move the car before heading over to Claire's, seeing as I was taking up a pivotal emergency coffee parking space.

Once parked further down the road I jogged to the window front where I'd bumped into Dean and Mark.

I walked inside to the jingle of the door-bell and without her even looking up from her magazine Imogen waved me through.

"Hi, I'm here to see Claire." I greeted her in my most cheerful, well-mannered voice that I normally reserved for really annoying customers at the restaurant.

She looked up from her magazine as though I'd slapped her in the face. I could see teenage rage bubbling under the surface and I revelled in it just a little bit.

"You can go right through." She pronounced every word as though they had daggers attached to them.

Amped up on caffeine and anxiety I felt something wash over me. Imogen clearly needed to be slapped with reality and I was more than willing to write 'reality' on my hand in permanent marker.

"But I don't have an appointment, don't you need to check to see if she's free?" I smiled as sweetly as possible, ignoring her flared nostrils and wide eyes.

She was only a few years younger than me but she regarded me with the kind of contempt usually reserved for adults.

"I know you don't have an appointment, I remember you from last time. Like I said, you can go through, she said you were coming in today. She must have seen it in her fucking crystal ball."

I laughed at that. I actually laughed. I couldn't help it, it was so comical that this little girl, with her straightened hair and overly used eyeliner would have such a bad attitude and use such bad language in front of a practical stranger.

Still laughing I pushed through the beaded curtain into the back room, leaving behind the surly teenager with the rage-red cheeks.

The fragrant incense and candles drew me in like I was getting into a warm bath, it smelt like summer and warmth and sweet honeysuckle flowers that grew in Mrs Wood's flower bed.

All of a sudden I was back in the grass, rolling around as Rob held a frog above my head that he'd found in the pond. He'd been laughing until Mark dumped a whole bucket of pond water over his head and run off, which had started a week-long war of pranks and punches under the dining room table.

"Amelia, you're here, that was fast!" Claire appeared from a small doorway I hadn't seen before at the back of the room, a gust of fresh air billowed into the room.

"Hi," I snapped back to reality, "How are you?"

She floated towards me, her feet hidden under her long skirt, and she wrapped her arms around me as though we were long lost sisters.

"Oh, I'm fine, I'm fine. More importantly, how are you?" Her eyes narrowed. She gave me a once over and frowned. "Hmmm. I think we need to sit down, your aura is all over the place..."

Without another word she went to the side of the room and produced a little pot of tea which was still steaming and some small cups.

We both sat cross legged on cushions, me where I'd sat the last time and she resuming her position behind her low table, tarot cards and candles littered the surface.

"Why are you looking at me like that?" I pushed my hair behind my ears and crossed my arms, readying myself for the barrage of supernatural brain-teasers.

"Oh, I'm sorry, sometimes I do that, I was just thinking is all. You seem off balance, here, drink some tea, it's Valerian... it will help loosen you up!" She explained when I didn't react.

She poured me a little cup and I took it, lifting it to my nose. I instantly returned the cup to the table as the smell of stinking feet invaded my nose.

"Oh my god, that's disgusting!" I couldn't stop myself from heaving a little bit, the memory of the smell was almost as bad as the real thing. Claire laughed.

"Sorry, I should have warned you. Never smell the tea! It's gross, but it *is* effective, it really does help you relax."

"What's the point of tea if you don't enjoy the taste?" I pushed the cup further away but kept my fingers on the china. She chuckled again as she shivered visibly.

"Not everything that's good for you is going to taste good, sometimes the best things in life happen after the bad taste..."

She was watching me closely. In order to distract myself from the scrutiny I closed my hand around the cup. Pretending the tea was tequila I downed it in one.

"I'd offer you a drink to wash it down with but I haven't been to the shop today. All I have in is vodka, but you do NOT want to follow that with alcohol, it will hit you harder than a deck of tarot cards." She reached out to put one of her long slender hands on top of mine.

"So, Amelia, why were you about to call me?" She was suddenly all business. Looking at the crystal ball I was hit with the desire to know my future after all.

She followed my gaze.

"You were right the first time. Don't wish your life away, knowing what will happen won't change the fact that you have to live in the here and now to get to the there... oh listen to me, the tea has already set in!" She fanned herself with her hand and sat back to rest on the cushions behind her.

I felt it too; the strange sudden dizziness but not drowsiness, more like the calm you got after a few drinks. It was like being half asleep and the most awake you could be all at once.

"I needed to talk to you about Rob... He's..." I couldn't finish the sentence and my stomach did a backflip.

I closed my eyes for a second and when I opened them her face was filled with sympathy.

"Gone. He's gone hasn't he." She tilted her head to the side and pursed her lips in thought.

I nodded, my eyes thickening with tears that I wouldn't let fall.

"Yes." My voice came out small and whispered. A faint smile played on her lips.

"I had a feeling it had happened." Her hand rested on the deck of tarot cards. They were face down but four were laying to one side.

"Do you think he's gone forever?" I asked, looking away from the cards. Her strange soul piercing eyes narrowed. "I killed him, I killed him again. I... it was my fault, he left because of me and now..."

The guilt poured out of me, threatened to drown me.

"Shhh, don't speak like that, you didn't kill him. He was already gone. If he has moved on you can at least be assured he's gone somewhere better."

I frowned as her words made it to my ears.

"What do you mean, *if?* I thought... didn't we talk about this? I was his unfinished business and all that crap, I sent him away, he walked away and he... I don't know, he disappeared... do you mean he might not really be gone?"

I didn't mean to raise my voice but I realised I'd almost been shouting. We both heard the radio in the front of the shop get turned up a few notches.

"Well, no one really knows what happens but, look, I don't want to be out of line here so let me know if I'm being a B-I-T-C-H," she spelt it out like saying it would make it true, "You have to get on with your life, you can't go searching just in case he might still be out there. If he is, he'll find you. He did before, but... well... you're alive, he isn't, at some point you have to get on with things."

She said it so bluntly I laughed, lost for words.

It was different hearing that said out loud by someone else, different from saying those things to myself in my head. I felt bad when I thought them, my heart panged, my hands curled into fists.

When she said it I had the same reaction but there was also that voice in my head that told me to listen.

"I know." I let out an exasperated sigh, "I know, it's just. I don't know, we were wound up in each other, we were like the same person. I know it's not healthy but we were, and now, what if I'm not enough to be a whole person without him? I don't know if I can give up on him yet, I don't know if I'm ready. I need him -" I wrapped my arms around myself, holding myself together as best I could.

"No!" She snapped, eyes sharp she sat up. "No, you don't need him Amelia, you don't need him to live, you want him to justify yourself but you can't do that, believe me, I have spent so long clinging to the one life I thought I needed to keep me going that I almost missed out on my own."

As she'd brought up her own experience in a round-about way I didn't feel so bad about prying.

"Tell me what happened to you, I need to know."

Claire's eyes shone with tears.

"It was a long time ago," She took a deep breath. After a moment's pause she looked me dead in the eye, determined. "I wasn't much younger than you are and not as strong."

"Who was it?" I dared to ask.

"My mother. She was a wonderful woman. My best friend. The only person I could turn to when the bullying got really bad; red heads were bullied even when I was a kid." She pulled at a curl, making it straight, before letting go for it to ping back into its original coil.

"When she died it was weeks before I'd even leave my room. The turmoil of it all was far too much for me, I was left with only my grandparents to look after me, you see, but they were old and, well, they weren't her. I'm sure I put them through hell..."

When she paused, eyes misted over, I reached forward and put my hand on hers. She looked at me and smiled through her tears.

"When I finally felt able to leave my room and face the world again the first person I saw was her. She was waiting for me in the kitchen like always and for a moment I really thought it had all been a dream, except I couldn't hear her talking. It was like she was behind a wall, so you see how it's strange you could hear Rob so clearly."

"You're right, I know you are. But I can't. Not yet, I can't give up."

She shook her head at me, her red curls shifting in the candlelight, looking aflame.

"I know you can't, I can sense that about you, but it's something you should keep in mind. Why did you push him away in the first place?"

She poured herself another cup of tea, offering me one in a nonverbal manner of inclining the pot in my direction. I shook my head as I stumbled over all the thoughts that tangled up my brain.

"I don't know. No, that's not true, I do know," I pushed down the instinct to bury my feelings. "It was too much. I couldn't be *that* girl, you know, the one who can't let go of her dead friend, the one who loses their friends because no one knows what to say to a person who acts like a crazy person, I mean, my other friends have already stopped talking to me, I can't even remember the last time..."

I stopped rambling when I noticed Claire's wide eyes.

"And I couldn't be his unfinished business. What does that even mean? That I'm something that needs fixing? I don't need him to pity me that much, I thought I meant more..."

My head felt heavy as my emotions swirled like clouds. Every time I thought I managed to suss out what the heartache meant I lost my grip and it blew away, leaving me with fragmented ideas about who I was and what I felt.

"Listen to me Amelia, your feelings are always going to confuse you, but every day I guarantee you'll discover another little piece of the puzzle and you'll start to feel more like yourself. Don't go looking for him, just keep living."

She reached to place a hand on top of mine, her warmth was soothing but it couldn't melt the chill of loneliness I felt now.

"And if he's actually gone now?" I didn't dare to pinpoint how I felt about that.

"I don't know if I believe in 'heaven' per say, but I do believe in an afterlife."

She didn't need to say any more to comfort me, I knew I'd gotten all I needed from her, and all that I needed to say right now had been said. I stood up and my head spun.

Claire was by my side before I could refocus my eyes. She was obviously less susceptible to the herbal tea than I was.

"Before you go I need to tell you something," She wrapped her arm around my shoulders and we walked towards the light from the front door.

"About what happened to you?" I pressed. She'd told me part of her story but not all of it. I knew she was holding back. Part of me was scared to ask why.

"No, there's no need to go over ancient history. What happened to me was different, my life and yours are not mirrored so don't give me a second thought."

It was like she read my mind, which I was sure she couldn't do. I *was* worried I might end up like her. Not that she was crazy but she *was* broken in some way. She had something missing that other people might not have noticed. Perhaps after all of this a mark would be left on me as well; maybe all of the people this had happened to could sense one another in some way.

"There was a message in the tarot cards that I couldn't ignore," she pushed the beaded curtains aside and the bright sunlight blinded me for a few seconds. "I know you don't want to know but I would feel terrible if I didn't at least warn you."

"I'm not going to be visited by three ghosts when the clock strikes twelve am I?" I heard Imogen snicker behind the vampire book she was reading.

"No," She squeezed my shoulder which I took to mean she wasn't insulted by my casual resistance to the occult, "But your ordeal is far from over."

I waited a moment and let the words sink in, trying to grasp what she was saying but my head was too fuzzy to work out cryptic clues.

"What does that even mean?" I pulled out of her hold and turned to face her. With the sun shining behind her she appeared ethereal in a way that sent shivers down my spine.

"Three cards fell when you last left. The first was your past; the three of cups. Friendship," She ticked it off, counting on her index finger, "the second was the eight of cups; change," She counted on her second finger, "and the third was a reversed six of cups."

She paused as though I should know what that meant.

"Which means I'm going to get drunk?" I guessed with a laugh that didn't connect.

"Which means that your past is still a part of your present, whatever is happening isn't over." She looked pale, like recounting the reading was a physical challenge.

"So Rob *is* still out there?" My heart skipped several beats.

"No, that's not what I'm saying but... whatever you started is still in motion, I don't know what that means for you Amelia but you are strong and smart and you will be OK."

Her words of encouragement didn't actually encourage. It was the sort of thing a general might say to the troops before they went into battle and got killed. But at least they went in with bravery and honour.

"That's all you're going to give me, isn't it?" I assumed her mystical warning was what it was; mystically vague. It was what I'd always expected when we first decided to go to see her but this was the first time she'd really pulled the stunt.

"I'm afraid the cards only indicate direction, they don't tell you where you're going to stop." She spoke in well-practiced verse and raised her eyebrows. She was enjoying giving me a reading even though she knew I didn't want one.

I liked her, despite the irritation.

"Right, so I'm just on the train; destination unknown." I tried to act nonchalant but the world shifted under my feet so I don't think I pulled it off.

"Oh the tea is kicking in..." Claire reached out a hand and took my elbow, "let's get you outside. The fresh air might do you some good."

She opened the door for me and the freshness of the day was like a cool glass of water. It didn't clear my head though. If anything the tea was reacting with the oxygen outside. My eyes felt heavy enough to slam shut. Gravity was not their friend.

"What's in that stuff?" I held onto the door frame whilst the world pulled me towards it.

"It's all natural, don't worry. I guarantee you'll sleep well tonight." She laughed, pulling me into a hug.

The surly teen at the front desk scowled as she looked at me, and then went back to furiously thumbing her phone as though she were sending out an indecipherable message in Morse code.

"Go and live your life, Rob wouldn't want you to waste time dwelling on the past, and he certainly wouldn't want you to worry about the future." She whispered through my hair.

I squeezed her back, feeling awkwardly natural in her embrace.

Either the tea or the verbal relief had made me feel better. She was right. If Rob was still here I'd find him like when we were kids and playing hide and seek; he'd show up eventually, even after I'd stop looking.

"Live a little but probably don't drive... that tea hit you harder than most people." She put her hand to her head at this afterthought, but I smiled at her. I wasn't in the mood to be angry about something as trivial as having to leave my car.

"It's OK, I don't live to far from here, I can walk."

Waving goodbye I turned out of the shop and began slowly walking down the street.

She'd given me a lot to think about but the tea made it seem trivial.

It was only when I passed the post office that I realised I was walking away from my house and not towards.

The idea of going home wasn't appealing now, anyway, so I headed towards the town centre, and then I hit a black wall. No, a black t-shirt. Hands were gripping my arms. I felt like I was walking on soft ground, like pillows, and I turned my head up to the human blocking instrument and broke into a wide grin, throwing my arms around the solid body.

"Mark!" An unstoppable grin stretched across my face as I wrapped my arms around him.

"Woah, Melia, are you high?!"

He forced my arms back to my own body and tilted my chin up so he could look into my eyes. He was squinting as he reviewed my face, and I pushed his hand away sheepishly.

"Just had some herbal tea... I think it might have been in the LSD family though, I feel a little... " I drew circles in the air next to my ear and laughed, stretching my arms out.

I felt like I'd been cramped in a box for so long my joints had forgotten they could straighten out.

"What's up?" I heard a voice from behind where Mark's head was. It was deep and echoed in my ears.

Mark turned, blocking my view with his big blocking body.

"Not much, but I think Amelia might be wasted!" He said it with a little concern in his voice, which wasn't expected. Then he ruined it and laughed.

Then Dean appeared.

He was wearing a t-shirt and jeans and he looked, well, the only way to describe it would be hot as hell. His white t-shirt enhanced his naturally tanned skin.

I blushed at the thoughts that ran through my mind. What if he could hear them?

"Are you OK?" He asked, going for my chin with his hand, much like Mark had done, but I was onto their twin trickery and I batted his hand away before he could reach me, pins and needles shooting through my skin where we made contact.

"I'm fine, I'm fine, stop exaggerating, I just had some tea." I waved my hand at them, my hand moving in slow motion.

I looked up at them both to see if they noticed but they obviously didn't. They looked at each other, doing their twin thing again, and frowned. No doubt passing unheard thoughts back and forth.

Almost in sync they looked towards the window to Claire's shop. It felt like I'd walked a lot farther than I had.

Dean put the pieces together before Mark had the chance.

"You're seeing a... psychic?" He asked, running his hand through his unkempt hair.

"No, just visiting, Claire is a very dear friend of mine." I said this with the most sincere voice I could muster, but I felt like it came out like it would when I would tell the customers at the restaurant that no, there wasn't coriander in the carrot soup.

Telling them about my visit to Claire might help in the long run but right now it felt important to keep that information to myself.

The way they were looking at me, like I was already crazy, told me I'd made the right decision.

"Riiiiight..." Mark whistled and wheeling his finger in the air around his ear much like I had earlier.

I slapped my hand on his chest to quieten him, but he only feigned injury. Sometimes I wish he was a weedy as Rob, it was easier to punish Rob.

"Stop that!" I swiped at his hand as he tried to push me back.

Dean was staring at me with a kind of bemused expression on his face, but there was something else, too. His eyebrows knitted together the way they did when he was trying to think of a way to say something without offending.

I frowned back at him and poked my finger into his chest.

"What's up, grumpy pants?" Instead of swatting me away he grabbed my finger and held it tight.

"Meh! Let go!" I struggled to wiggle my hand away from his, happy that he at least feigned a playful attitude.

My head started to swim as I wretched my body away from them both, taking my arms and wrapping them around myself for protection against the twin bullies before me.

"What exactly did you and your 'dear friend' do in there, Amelia?" Dean asked, looking towards the shop like he might be able to see the past if he squinted hard enough.

"Oh, this and that, this and that..." I trailed off as I noticed some of my work friends walking down the street towards us.

Dean and Mark both frowned again and then looked at each other... again. I ignored them, waving at my friends who were fast approaching.

I fished my car keys from my pocket. They seemed to be weighing a ton and making me feel heavier than necessary. Before I could ascertain why they seemed to feel like an anchor Dean quickly snatched them out of my fingers.

"You aren't driving, you're wasted." The humour had gone from his voice. He stowed the keys away in his pocket.

"If you wanted the car why did you even drop it off outside my house, and without a note?"

For some reason, in that moment, the memory of the car being left without so much as a post it note attached to it grated my nerves.

Dean stared at me, mouth gaping like a fish out of water, he didn't get a chance to answer as Hannah and Martin waved and jogged over leaving several others from the restaurant to walk past with polite 'hello's' before going into a bar a few doors down.

When I looked back at the twins Mark was patting Dean's back, he must have been choking on something.

"Hi!" I said, far too enthusiastically.

I normally would have cringed at my own girly-ness but right now I didn't care.

"Hey there girly!" it was Hannah who spoke, Martin hung back away from Mark and Dean.

They'd been in the same class at school but, like most people, Martin was intimidated by them. Not many people took a shining to the Wood family, with the exception of Rob, who most people seemed to love.

My eyes flitted to the shop behind the boys. A familiar shape reflected in the glass but when I turned to look out into the real world there was no one where a body should have been.

The tea must have been causing me to see things.

"What're you guys doing?" Hannah indicated to me and the twins.

I tore my eyes away from the shop window and shrugged, probably a little too enthusiastically, as Mark shuddered with a suppressed laugh.

"Not much, I was just out seeing a friend and I bumped into these guys, where are you headed?"

When she hesitated I realised what situation I'd stumbled into. The awkwardness was enough to make me sober up slightly.

I kept smiling as best I could but it was clear they were out on a work social event and I had somehow missed the invite.

I tried to keep it light, biting the inside of my cheeks just in case the tea had some kind of truth telling effects.

"Oh," She smoothly navigated the embarrassment that coloured her cheeks, maintaining a casual attitude. I followed her lead.

"Not much... it's kind of an impromptu celebration... I'm engaged!" She suddenly beamed, her smile was automatic and un-relentless as it stretched, unrestrained, across her face causing her freckled nose to crinkle.

She held her freshly ringed hand up to my face and I was drawn into a hug I couldn't remember initiating, but I must have done as she hadn't moved and I was suddenly thrusting myself into her arms.

"Congratulations!" I managed, the boys murmured their congrats as well, though it was slightly lesser in volume than my own. Mark, in particular, seemed put out by this announcement, but I couldn't fathom why.

Hannah started to tell me about the engagement but I tuned out. A ringing in my ears distracted me from her story, the words melted into white noise.

I looked over at Dean, smiling at him as I nodded automatically to Hannah's story, but he only half smiled before looking across the street. The way his eyes moved it was like he'd seen a ghost.

Mark was jabbering on about how it was customary for a newly engaged woman to fully hear out other suitors before accepting a proposal of marriage. His previously disgruntled attitude was finally brought to light; he'd taken a shining to her. Probably the minute she said she was engaged.

"Look, I was going to call you but I didn't want to force you into coming out after... everything," She side stepped the taboo subject gracefully. "Do you want to come for a drink? All of you, of course, the more the merrier!"

She truly meant it as well, that was the great thing about Hannah, she was a people person through and through and loved to talk to anyone and everyone; I used to be better at it but now it seemed I was like the black plague of parties.

Martin looked at me, I think for the first time since he'd walked over or possibly even the first time in a long time.

"I'm sorry, I was the one who said you might not want to come, you seemed so sad the other day, I figured you might want to lay low." He shrugged and offered me a supportive arm rub, which I outdid by throwing my arm around him.

"You're always looking out for me Martian!" I said, squeezing his shoulders and pinning his arms to his sides.

When I released him he laughed but he looked towards Dean like he expected him to say something. Dean, however, was looking anywhere but at me. It seemed that after everything maybe our friendship wasn't going to last. I forced the thought out of my head; I could mourn the loss of one brother but thinking about losing another filled my stomach with acid.

"It's been so long since I've just chilled out..." I looked at the brothers, stood like guardians besides me. "You guys in? Let's get some cocktails, come on, we could all use a break."

I reached out to lightly grab Dean's sleeve but he pulled away before my hand reached him. I don't think anyone but me noticed the way he avoided my touch; the rejection stung. Luckily the tea was working as an antidote to the poison of my emotions.

In contrast to Dean's disinterest Mark was practically jumping for joy at the idea of drinking. If Rob had been here he'd have given me *that* look that told me he thought his brother was losing it. The look he given me when I'd attempt to force science fiction movies into his play list on Netflix.

"Yes, hell yes, let's go," Mark bounced on the balls of his feet with pre-game energy. "Dean, come on, let's do shots, Melia, you'll do shots, won't you?"

I couldn't hold back a laugh. His energy was instantly infectious; I refused to comment on his usual tee-total, health conscious lifestyle. It was clear, like me, he needed to forget everything. I heard Rob's voice in my ear, the quiet sting of sibling put downs, the way he'd casually try to make Mark feel guilty about it.

"I'm going to drink you under the table, Mark." I poked him in the chest and he wrapped a giant arm around my shoulder. The polar shift in Dean was casting a black cloud over us, I saw the familiar look of grief on his face. It was Mark's face, or at least the face he'd been wearing for the past few weeks. Selfishly I kept my eyes away from him, not letting myself remember how my own reflection looked every morning.

Mark threw his arm around Hannah as well, turning us into a mismatched version of Dorothy and her friends.

Martin stood aside from us, visibly squirming at Mark's imposing character. It was obvious Martin still felt the typecast from school. He was the quite one, Mark was the popular bullying kind of guy who scared the lunch money out of him.

"Come on Dean, don't leave me with this lot. I'll buy the first round?" Martin was basically begging for a buffer between him and Mark the Meat Head, a nick name from school that I had completely forgotten until now. Mark never knew it was Rob who had given him the title.

Dean looked at me, finally, reading me like he apparently seems to be able to do.

His lips turned up in a tiny smile making his skin crinkle at his eyes. His face was so warm and inviting it made me feel weak at the knees; something I had assumed was a myth until this moment.

"It's OK, I think I'm gonna go home, I don't really feel like a party tonight." He exhaled like it was a casual blow off but inside I knew it was more than that.

Martin sighed as well, and patted Dean on the back as he broke away from our group and headed towards the bar. A wave of new sadness rolled over as my eyes lingered over where Martin had touched Dean, the sympathy was minimal but as loud as an air raid siren to me.

"Come on then." Mark started to follow Martin, his big arms around mine and Hannah's shoulders, pushing and dragging us with him. I slipped out from underneath with the practise of someone who'd avoided being put in a headlock for years.

"Will you look after Mark?" Dean asked. He had already begun to move in the wrong direction; away. I grabbed his sleeve before he could make his escape. Mark and Hannah continued towards the bar, leaving us alone.

"It's only a drink. Please come... I want you to come." I mentally begged him to pretend, just for once, that we could be normal people and not two people with one half of their hearts torn out.

He shook his head and pried my hand away with a little more force than I liked.

"It's OK, you go and have fun. I have things to do anyway. Do you want me to drop your car off at your house tomorrow?" He was acting weird. I was supposed to be the one who was a wreck; Dean was supposed to be the rock but somehow he'd eroded.

His detachment concerned me; his shoulders were hunched and his hands were thrust deeply into his jean pockets. His face and Rob's seemed so similar at times I could scream. My heart did it's usual heavy thump as I tried to suppress the pain. I pushed it back and imagined building a brick wall around it. Each brick reinforced to stop the emotions before they could manifest.

"No, it's OK..." I said, but before I could even finish the thought he walked away. I was standing alone.

If I hadn't been feeling like I was half asleep I might have stood there and watched as he faded into the distance, or just turned the corner, but I couldn't do that.

The ground felt spongy beneath my feet as I ran to catch up with the others. It could have been the tea making me feel unsteady, like the world was turning in the wrong direction, or the feeling that Dean had taken one step away from me and one step closer to some darkness.

Martin waited for me at the entrance to the bar. He held the door and I dived right into the dark room, forgetting the outside troubles for a little while, pretending they didn't exist.

�֍

"I know you can see me." He said. Over and over, creating his own little repetitive song as though he was purposefully trying to drive me insane. I ignored him. Pretended he didn't exist.

As we pulled into the house Mark stormed off, not talking to either me or Dean.

I heard Dean ask if I was OK but words failed to form properly so I nodded and stayed stood at the car, needing the time to breathe. Dean understood without the need for words, as always. He rubbed my arm and left me alone.

I was stood out on the driveway when a poke in the ribs finally made me snap.

"Ow! Rob, stop it." It was instinct, a knee jerk reaction, which made me forget my insanity and actually address him out loud.

His eyes lit up at my acknowledgment.

"Yessss. I knew it." He danced around me in a gleeful gig, waving his arms and kicking his legs. "I'm a ghost and you can see me!" He laughed with exuberance. I could only roll my eyes.

"You're not real Rob, you're a figment of my imagination caused by grief and potentially a family history of mental illness." I leaned against the car and rubbed my head, sure I must have some sort of stress induced tumour growing. He stopped dancing and faced me full on, putting his hand on my forehead like I was sick.

"I must be real Amelia. You don't have this kind of imagination!" He smiled at me and my heart fluttered, threatening to make me faint. I was having a nervous breakdown.

"I'm having a nervous breakdown," I voiced aloud, massaging my temples as though that would help ease the madness within. "Trust you to be the cause of it... dammit. I'll have to go to a therapist, won't I? Why am I asking you?" I sighed in frustration. "You're not really here. You're dead." I whispered.

I closed my eyes and dropped my head, so I didn't have to see him. I couldn't look at him. What if my heart exploded?

CHAPTER 1

The act of ignoring problems was actually a lot easier than I'd imagined. To say me and Mark drank each other under the table is an understatement. In fact, at one point we had both actually been under the table; his idea of a drinking game that made sense at the time.

Mark had decided I would make the best drinking buddy and we'd matched each other drink for drink, despite the fact that he weighed a hell of a lot more than me, and the fact that he didn't drink often we still managed to drink just that little bit too much.

After a few hours we had to call it quits. We said goodbye to the others who I fear had regretted inviting us out, and we left to walk home.

We made it as far as my road when Mark decided he couldn't walk any further.

"Let's just wait here for a while." He lowered himself, ungracefully, to the curb. I plonked down next to him, palming the warm gravel, pressing my hands into the ground so little stony indentations remains even when I brushed the dirt away.

The street was quiet, the only movement caused by the light wind that played with the leaves; rustling and whispering to each other. I leant on his shoulder, and closed my eyes, hearing Rob's voice in every breath of the breeze.

"I think you need a taxi, you'll never make it home like this." My voice slurred against my will, sounding muffled in my ears. The bar had been too loud to communicate with anyone unless you shouted in their ears, which would explain why my throat felt like I'd swallowed broken glass.

I attempted to use my phone, squinting at the numbers, but my eyes wouldn't focus. Mark grasped at it like trying to catch a fly, a moving target. I laughed and pushed it into his big clammy palm to help.

"You're a lightweight Melia! I'll call them myself." He feigned sobriety but I saw through his façade. His eyes were squinting just as hard as mine had been as he attempted to hit the right part of the screen.

It took him more than five attempts to get the number we actually needed, but I didn't say anything. Pissing Mark off now wouldn't help the situation; I was enjoying him being nice to me, it didn't happen enough and I didn't want to wreck it all now.

He called the taxi and managed to explain where he was using very loose descriptions despite the fact I kept repeating the road name. Eventually the taxi company must have just used a location system because they confirmed our exact location and told Mark they'd be here in ten minutes.

We sat on the curb until the car came and I managed to heave him into it.

The driver didn't need to be told where to go; Mark was an almost ce-lebrity in our town, mostly for his athletic achievements, but also for his 'extra-curricular activities'. He was often calling for a taxi very late at night.

I waved him off and started for my house, which at first seemed close enough, but as I walked it got further and further away.

I sat down outside one of my neighbour's houses, my feet not wanting to take my any further. My phone told me it was already two in the morning.

The curb kept me company for another half an hour, helping me try to sober up. Stumbling into the house drunk wasn't a good plan unless I wanted another argument, which I didn't.

My phone vibrated in my hand. A missed call and a voice mail blinked up at me like a beacon. I knew I was sober enough when I could actually read the number on the screen; Rob's home number.

Listening to anyone from the Wood household right now was less than appealing so I ignored it, taking it as a sign I should just go to bed.

Annoyingly I knew something was wrong the moment I approached the house.

The lights were on in the living room, the orange glow spilling out into the street like a warning sign. The curtain twitched as I weaved up the path to the front door so I knew to expect the next moment, I just really hoped it wouldn't happen.

"It's almost three in the morning!" My mum practically screamed as she tore the front door open like The Hulk might tear the door off a car. Her tired eyes bulged out at me, wild.

"I was out with some people from work-" I said, feeling the need to apologise. She looked worried, for the first time in a long time she looked concerned.

"Do you think I'm an idiot? You were out with people from *work?*" She ushered me into the house and slammed the door behind me. The need to apologise quickly melted away.

"Mark was there, too…" It felt like a trap but I walked into it anyway.

"*That* I can believe." She herded me into the living room where my dad sat, equally tired looking. His cheeks were red, a bottle of wine sat empty on the table beside him.

"I just want to go to bed, can we talk about this in the morning?" I waited, wondering if they could even notice that they had already won this one.

"No, not this time, Amelia, this is too much. It's too much." My mum began to cry. For the first time in my life I looked at my mum and didn't see the mask she wore but the broken woman she really was. It was sad but it also made me angry. *She* was the parent, she was supposed to be the strong one, this was just another moment where I felt like I was the only one who was sane.

"Your mother's right. It's time we talked about this. We've arranged for you to go away-" My dad started up, an obviously rehearsed speech. He didn't look at me as he spoke.

"What?!" Now it was my turn to cry. Tears dropped down my face, if it were possible they would have been filled with acid and would have burned me down to nothing.

"You need *help* Amelia!" My mum sniffed, sitting on the sofa next to my dad. He rubbed her back like this was *so* hard for her. I stood, slightly swaying, trying not to throw up.

"I need help?" I was sure she was right but I had a feeling it wasn't the kind of help she was thinking.

"You have a place in Saint Regina's Wellness centre, we're going to take you tomorrow morning-" My dad handed me a leaflet like I didn't know the place. Saint Regina was the rehab centre a few miles away where people went after they'd had a mental breakdown. The last person I knew who'd gone was the old lunch lady who had snapped when her husband had left her.

"I don't need to go to rehab for Christ's sake!" I held back the urge to scream but couldn't hold back a laugh. It seemed it wasn't the correct response because my parents did that look parents do.

"You're drunk, Amelia." My dad shook his head.

"Takes one to know one, though, doesn't it?" I felt bad but at the same time it was a relief to be able to be honest with them, even if the honesty was alcohol fuelled.

Before I knew what was happening my mum was on her feet, she slapped me hard enough to make my teeth hurt. A second later she burst into even more tears; my sympathy for her dissipated.

"I'm not going to rehab, I'm fine. My best friend died, don't you think I deserve to grieve?"

"There's grief and there's you. You are losing your mind, you need help-" My dad, usually the one to take a back seat, was heading the charge on this so I directed my anger at him.

"How am I losing my mind?" I didn't let them see how his words shook me. I flashed back to the car after the funeral and then pushed it out of my head. No.

"You've become a hermit. You don't talk to anyone. You go to work, you come home, you talk to yourself in your room. Don't you think we hear you? Don't you think people notice how you talk to yourself in public? Walking down the street? You spend too much time at Florence's house, it's not healthy. You need to see yourself from the outside. You're aggressive, avoiding any kind of interaction-" My dad was reeling off a list like he'd spent a lot of time thinking about it, gathering his thoughts. My mum, who sat back down, nodded along with him.

The world was, once again, turning in the wrong direction. My body felt the jerk of the universe winding the wrong way.

"Are you done?" I cut him off, holding down the feeling of disgust and fear.

Before they could say anymore I left the room, running upstairs to the bathroom where my body tried to disperse all the betrayal and the last few shots that still lingered in my system.

My parents were still talking about me downstairs, I could hear the murmurs from through the floorboards and words like 'force' and 'crazy'.

Without having to stop and think my body rolled into action. In my room I grabbed two bags from underneath my bed and began shoving clothes in. After a mad dash around the room I picked up five more important things. My laptop, my passport, the money and travel plans Rob had drawn up and finally a picture of me and Rob from his birthday party.

Looking around the room I pictured him sat at the desk, looking through social media for mentions of himself and trying to make phone calls to see who could hear him. I never did figure out what he did when I fell asleep.

Looking again the room was empty, another round of sickness threatened to spill out at the thought that it could have always been this empty but I forced it down.

My escape plan seemed a thousand years in the past and the thought of going through with it now seemed foolish, but at the same time more real than ever. Rob wouldn't have been able to come with me, we'd have had to say goodbye, it just happened earlier than intended.

It also happened to be from the other side of the story; my parents telling me to go, saying goodbye to me, rather than the other way around. It didn't matter; the freedom was the same.

I didn't know what to expect when I reached the bottom of the stairs but it wasn't my mother stood with tears staining her face.

"Amelia, please, where are you going?" She held her arms out like I'd run into them. She must not have remembered that I hadn't done that since I was five years old, that was when I realised she had no comfort to offer me.

Side stepping her I opened the front door. Again, that guilt towards her and the need to say sorry surfaced.

"Anywhere but here." I gave her a chance to take everything back, lingered on the doorstep for the briefest of moments, waiting.

"Once they stop mourning that family will drop you like a stone, Amelia." She always had to have the last word, always had to dig the knife in a little deeper.

The door clicked shut behind me. I didn't even feel the need to slam it, there was no point now. I wasn't going back.

The clarity of the confrontation was euphoric, then my stomach churned and I threw up again on the front step. It was almost poetic.

With my bags on my shoulder I started walking, trying not to care about the way the straps dug into my skin, my aching limbs or my empty stomach.

Despite my mum's words I hadn't planned on going to Rob's house but I didn't have anywhere else to go either and my feet traced the path from memory.

The house was dark as I approached from the back entrance to the garden. There was a shed I could sleep in or the tree house, which was semi-sheltered from the elements.

The treehouse seemed like a better bet. It was a nice night and I was less likely to be caught in the morning by a gardener.

As soon as I was inside the professionally built platform perfectly slotted into the thick tree branches the rain upset my plan.

It started as a light shower which didn't worry me until a loud thunder-clap exploded above announcing a summer rainstorm of biblical proportions.

Huddled inside with my bags was fine until the rain found the gaps age had created in the structure. Part of the flooring started to gather water leaving no space to lie down to sleep. The air cooled to an uncomfortable level and it didn't take me long to realise I wasn't drunk enough to sleep outside.

Leaving my bags in the only dry area of the tree house I climbed back down and crept up towards the house, feeling like a convict on the run.

The previously dark house was now winking at me from afar, like a light-house calling the ships in safely. Mark's bedroom light.

Thanking whichever deity had granted me shelter I slipped through the shadows with as much grace as I could manage with the alcohol still clouding my brain.

Mark would have to help me. He could keep my secret, like I could keep his.

By the time I reached the house and taken shelter under the window my hair was plastered to my head. From a brief glance at my reflection in the glass my face hadn't fared any better; my makeup was almost non-existent.

I took a handful of stones, just small ones, and prayed I could manage to hit his window at least once. After a few tries and a lot of off balanced throws I lucked out.

The soft click of the stone against the pane was another blessing from God. I waited; hoping he wasn't too drunk and that he could still operate the latch.

The lighthouse, the glimmer of light on a stormy night, blinked at me again. Bright and then dark as his face appeared at the window, distorted in the glass so it looked like two people, disappearing just as suddenly as he appeared.

The light in the kitchen blinked on quicker than I would have thought possible unless Mark had fallen down the stairs to save time.

"Finally, I thought I was going to have to break your window," I slipped past as he held the door open, grabbing a towel off the radiator and ringing my hair out. "Can I sleep here tonight?"

I unburdened myself from the backpack I still had on my back and almost walked/ fell into his t-shirted chest.

My hand went out to push him aside but he didn't budge, which worried me. Mark was heavy, but a literal pushover. I was witness to how much he couldn't even stand.

The penny dropped in almost comedic slow motion. I raised my eyes so slowly, praying I was wrong but my luck had apparently run out.

"Oh damn it, no!" I covered my tear stained, rain covered, face behind my hands aware I was standing before Dean like a child caught out after curfew.

He didn't speak to me for a moment, taking in my sodden appearance, my drunken state and the bag of clothes that I hung off one shoulder. Finally he sighed and took the bag off me, pulling my hands from my face gently and taking one of them into his own.

"Come on, just be quiet." He said, leading me through the house. I followed him, trailing him in silence as we walked through the kitchen and upstairs into his room.

When he closed the door behind us I threw myself into his arms and sobbed. The kind of crying where your shoulders shuddered up and down uncontrollably.

The smell of his skin mixed with damp hair told me he'd just showered, I breathed him in, forgetting what we'd said about our feelings not being real.

He was only in boxers and a t-shirt, similar to whenever I'd stayed over in the past. Nothing new, yet this was the first time I'd seen him like this without Rob being my main concern. I stepped away from him, embarrassed at the closeness. I had to tell myself that drunken kisses were out of the question, I wasn't going to ruin it all no matter how tempting it was.

"Come on." Dean pulled me towards the bed and we sat on the edge, careful not to touch.

The fact that he hadn't asked me what was going on was comforting but it put me on edge knowing I was going to have to explain at some point.

I saw myself in the mirror in his room and groaned quietly, rubbing my hands over my face and collapsing sideways into the pillow. It smelt of him and I closed my eyes.

"I look awful!" I mumbled. The call of sleep so strong it was as if I was a weighted anchor thrown into the sea, the only thing to do was sink deeper and deeper into the quiet darkness.

A light poke in the ribs jerked me back to life. Rolling over I watched Dean place my bag of clothes at the foot of the bed. I made no movement to search it for nightwear, exhaustion made me body stone. I kicked my shoes off and curled up on top of the covers.

"I want to sleep..." I closed my eyes again, praying to wake up and find it was a year ago but Dean sat down, making the bed dip towards him, breaking my hold of the fantasy.

"Amelia, don't go to sleep, you have to tell me what happened." He rolled me towards him by my shoulder and pushed the hair off my face.

"I really don't want to talk about it..." I tried to roll over again but he gripped my shoulders and held me face up. The words my parents had said rang in my already ringing ears like a mockery. Every interaction I'd had with Rob, every conversation with his family, they were all tainted by the idea that I was insane.

"Come on, tell me what happened, do you want some water?" The awkward silences that had fallen between us earlier were gone, he was looking at me now with as much compassion as he did that night in the restaurant.

"No, I don't need water, I am water. I'm soaking." It was too late to worry about ruining the sheets now.

"Have you been crying?" He ignored my drunken ramblings, cutting out the niceties.

"Why were you in Mark's room? I came here for Mark, where is he?" I tried to keep the thickness of tears from my voice but I welled up. I had wanted nothing, just to sleep and not explain, for once I hadn't wanted Dean.

He turned his face away from me towards the lamp on the desk. I don't know what look passed over his face but it made me feel like I was being pulled inside out. I thought I might be sick again but I held it in.

"I went in to check on him but he's passed out in his bed. How much did you two drink?"

I groaned, and covered my face with my hands again, not wanting to think back to how much we'd drank.

"Oh God, too much, way too much. I blame him entirely!" I laughed, the humour of the night bubbling up inside.

Dean was quiet but eventually he laughed at my dramatics. It was nice to see his smile. Suddenly things seemed to be getting clearer, even the throbbing in my chest that I'd come to accept as a part of missing Rob seemed to lessen.

"He's going to feel the same in the morning. If I knew you threw stones at his window maybe I would have switched rooms with him..." He said, trying to lighten the mood. I shoved him away playfully.

"I don't do it *that* often, so it would be a waste. I should have known it was you up there, usually he just throws down a rope ladder so I don't have to come through the house." I wiped at my eyes and lay back, looking up at him.

There was a moment, it wasn't a huge one but it stopped time for a split second.

A soft noise outside the bedroom door shattered it. I sat up quickly scared his parents might come in.

"What was that? Do you think it was Mark?" I tried to sit up but my head swam and I fell back down, groaning and pushing the heel of my hands against my throbbing eyes.

"There's no one there, you're drunk!" Dean said, his voice was back to being concerned again, no longer playful.

"Yeah, but I'm not insane, there was someone outside the door!" I said, except maybe I was insane and I had been this whole time. I let out a shuddered breath.

"Why do you have a bag? What are you doing here at three in the morning?" Dean picked up the trail I'd hoped he'd given up on.

"I was running away with Mark, but he's fallen asleep." I whispered, thinking about the fact that at one point Dean might have actually believed such a ridiculous story.

"Amelia, what the hell's going on?" His kind features were shrouded in worry, looking a lot like his dad; family worry lines across his head.

I shrugged, lost for words. His green eyes bore into mine. I had the sudden urge to touch him, to kiss him, to distract him but I didn't. Instead I reached up and buried my hand into his dark hair, so unlike Rob's sandy blonde. He closed his eyes and leaned into my hand for a second before taking my hand and placing it back by my side.

"No, tell me what's going on." He tucked a stray piece of hair behind my ear. His thumb lingered on my cheek, fingers curling under my jaw gently.

The moment had arrived so I took a deep breath and held onto it. When I let it out I let my fear go away too.

"My parents think I'm insane, they were going to send me away." I whispered. I wasn't sure whether saying it out loud made me feel better or worse.

"They think I'm not dealing with... everything, said I had to go to Saint Regina's in the morning. I left... maybe I won't ever go back." I said it more to myself than him.

Dean's breathing was all I could think about in the silence that followed; in and out, deep breathing of someone trying to keep their cool.

"I know it's not nice to say but your parents are assholes. Seriously." He thumped his fist into the bed.

My shoulders hunched into a shrug, it was easier to follow the patterns on the curtains than look at his face right now. My eyes started to well up again, big fat tears sliding down the sides of my face.

"No, Amelia, you aren't crazy, you're fine..." He wiped my face but the tears kept coming. I shook my head, denying his words because I wasn't fine at all.

"I think they're right. I think I might be crazy." I rolled away from him, facing the other side of the room.

"No, they're just not good parents. They aren't good people, you're so much better than them." He was only trying to be nice but his words grated against the words my mum said as I left the house.

"Why? Maybe I'm just like them. Just because me and Rob were friends doesn't mean I'm like you. Once this is all over none of you will care about me." I hated that her words had come out of my mouth but it was the truth. If I went away our connection would be severed. Without Rob I had no one.

"What if we hadn't met until now, would you think I was like them because I grew up over there? Because I work as a waitress?" I sat up, words falling out uninhibited.

He looked at me like I'd slapped him.

"You're getting off topic and you know that's not what I meant, I just meant... you belong here. With us. We're your family, and we always have been." He was so calm there was no point saying any more about it. My vision swam and I felt the nausea from earlier return. "And they're wrong about you being crazy because if you are then I am, OK?"

I nodded. There was no point telling him about Rob, it was over.

"I'm leaving, Dean. I can't go back home and I can't stay here. I'll go somewhere else, I just need somewhere to stay for the night."

He pulled me into his arms, wrapping them around me.

"You can't go somewhere else. Stay here, it will be fine." He pulled back and smiled, warm and reassuring as always.

"Can I sleep in here?" Sleeping was the only thing left to do now. Sleep and forget. This wasn't the time to talk about *things*, I just hoped he'd understand.

"Yeah, I'll sleep on the floor. We'll talk about all of this in the morning." He took a pillow off the bed and found a blanket in a drawer.

Silently I rustled through the random bunch of clothes in my bag, pushing the wad of cash and travel information aside and picked out a large t-shirt.

Looking back at the cash my mind was made up.

"Do you have anything I can wear in bed? I only have this t-shirt..." I held it up and smiled, hoping to dispel the negative atmosphere.

With a smile he threw some PJ bottoms at me. They were massive but at least it would mean I wasn't half naked in his bed. The whole situation now seemed to be a bad idea, and I cursed Mark for not waking up. If only I'd managed to get through this night without having to deal with any more stress.

Whilst Dean got comfortable I snuck to the bathroom that he and Mark shared.

I brushed my teeth and managed to clean my face so I didn't look like such a mess. When I went back into the room Dean had found a sleeping bag on had rolled it out on the floor.

I slid into bed as Dean switched the lamp off. It was so soft and warm that I was almost instantaneously asleep. The last thing I heard was Dean rolling over towards me and whispering.

"Please stay here."

CHAPTER 16

When I opened my eyes it was only four thirty but I was so dehydrated I had to get up.

I used my hands to scoop water straight from the tap. On my way back to bed I thought I heard the scuffling at the door again; I froze.

With as much care as possible I inched to the door to open it a crack. The hallway was empty but I went out there anyway, drawn out like a thread being pulled, following my nose towards a room I knew well.

The door opened with a creek, like it hadn't been opened in a while. I was overcome by the smell of him; stale air freshener and chemicals from when he used to develop photographs in a makeshift darkroom. He'd spilt the stuff on the floor and was banned from doing it in his room ever again. The smell had never really gone away.

I moved through the darkness without needing a light, knowing where everything was, seeing it in my mind's eye, brushing my fingers over the desk and the small sofa that was in front of the TV, trailing my hands along every surface I passed like they were totems, set out to guide the way.

His bed was cold next to the window, the curtains still open to show the dawn coming in. It was just between the dark and the light when everything was slightly rosy and fresh looking. I sat down and pulled the covers towards me.

It was like a tomb in here, nothing moved just in case he was going to come back. I didn't realise I was holding my breath until I felt my lungs burn.

Closing my eyes I lay down, wrapping my arms around myself for warmth in the cold dark room and I let the memories flood into my mind. I couldn't hold back the tears that first welled in my throat like I was being strangled by my own memories, and the hot tears rolled down my cheeks, over my nose and down to the pillow. I sobbed softly, trying not to make any noise, but soon I was gasping for air.

Weeks worth of anger, sadness, happiness. Too much to take all at once, too much confusion and hatred. I didn't know why I felt the hate, whether it was all for my family or whether some of it was for myself. I felt a hand on my shoulder and I woke up, gasping.

Green eyes peered down at me and my heart hammered in my chest. The green eyes melted into Dean's face even though I was sure I'd seen dark blonde hair. I wiped my face and looked up at him with a pathetic blank expression, having nothing to say.

Without a word he scooped me up like I was nothing. Normally I would have screamed and batted him away but I was so exhausted and emotionally depleted I just curled up in his arms as he carried me back to his room and lay me down in the bed.

I kept my eyes closed and tried to imagine I was still sleeping. Pretending until Dean had crawled back into his sleeping bag. It had only taken a second. The moment I walked into Rob's room I knew what I was going to do.

❀

When I woke up the morning was trying to break into the room. The blinds were now being attacked by the morning sunlight. The white streams of light squeezed through the cracks like splinters in my eyes.

I squeezed them tightly, wondering why the sun always shone on me when I didn't want it to, and why the rain seemed to like adding its dramatic emphasis to my worst days.

Dean was still asleep on the floor, breathing in and out with so much intent I wondered if he was pretending to sleep, but after minutes of watching I realised he wasn't. He was on his back, on arm thrown up over his eyes, his toned bicep on display.

His head jerked slightly and I saw his lips curve into a smile. A huge part of me wanted to know what he was dreaming but there was a niggle in the back of my mind which told me it was the last thing I needed to think about. For once it was my own voice in my head and it was the one I listened to.

I sat up slowly, disturbing the small specks of dust illuminated in the dawn. The motes swirled in my wake like a small universe, spinning and expanding. My mind conjured up the thought that I could be a tiny particle on a tiny mote of dust, swirling in the universe that had been disturbed by some other being.

The clock told me it was almost seven in the morning and, though my head was pounding, I didn't feel too hung over. The room didn't spin so much as sway so I managed to time my steps to benefit from the motion. I reached for my bag when the swaying went backwards, and I straightened up on the forward movement, taking myself towards the bathroom door, dancing with the momentum I gained.

I twisted the door handle and slipped through the gap, closing it with the softest of clicks. I waiting for any kind of stirring on either side of the double doored bathroom and jumped when the door behind me was almost ripped from its hinges only just managing to suppress a scream.

When I turned around I was faced with a semi-naked Mark. He was soaked with sweat and only wore a towel around his waist. He had earphones in and was looking down at his iPod.

My hands went to my eyes and I spun around so I didn't see anything I shouldn't be seeing.

"Jesus Christ!" He breathed. "What the crap are you doing in here?" He whispered, thankfully keeping his voice low.

With his hands gripping his towel I turned around praying he didn't feel like exposing himself to me. I kept my hands partially covering my eyes just in case. Vomiting in front of him was probably the last straw in our new friendship.

His eyes went from me to the door and then back again, a smile spreading over his face. I groaned into my sweaty palms, praying I was still asleep, but the vile taste in my mouth was too real to be part of a dream and if this *was* a dream I didn't think it would be Mark stood before me half naked.

"Oh, relax, you can uncover your eyes, it's not like you haven't seen this before... or at least a less impressive version of it." Mark flexed an arm muscle.

I dropped my hands to prove I really didn't care but from the look on his face I knew he took the action as an admission.

"That's not what this is, now move!" I pushed past him, hand slipping in the slickness of his chest. I wiped my hand on my leg only to realise I was still wearing my mishmash of pyjamas. Great. Mark followed me into his room, closing the bathroom door behind him.

"Why are you all sweaty?" The tried and tested method of getting past Mark was to distract him by talking *about* him.

"I went for a run, not all of us are utterly incapable of normal routine after one night of drinking." He pointed at me and the closed door, pursing his lips questioningly. "And what is all this about?"

He gave me a once over that made me feel guilty for no reason.

"It's none of your business." I dropped to his bed and leant forward with my head in my hands. It felt like it was growing and shrinking at a rapid rate. I groaned at the obvious sign of imminent death. Mark let out a sigh and handed me a glass of fizzing orange liquid from his bedside table.

"Drink this." He sat down next to me, stinking of boy sweat and beer. That mixed with the taste of something that was *not* orange juice made my stomach flip and I started to cough, acid rising.

"What the hell is this?" I put the glass down and heaved.

"It's vitamin juice- woah!" Mark leant away from me and grabbed a small bin from beside his bed.

Holding it in front of me he actually leaned back in and put his hand on my back, if I didn't think I was about to throw my guts up I would have commented on his chivalry.

A few deep breaths and the sickness passed. When the colour returned to my face I knew what I had to do.

"I left home." I pointed to the bag I'd dropped at my feet. Mark leaned back onto his desk, the towel, thankfully, staying in place. He ran his hand though his hair and frowned at me.

"No shit." He said this to himself, more than me, but I nodded.

"When I got home last night my parents were waiting for me. Long story short; huge argument so I packed my things. Ended up here." I couldn't go through the idea of rehab with him because if he made any attempt to joke about it I might actually break down.

He nodded, thinking about something. Probably trying to remember the night. After a second the thoughtful Mark vanished and was replaced by the real Mark; wiggling his eyebrows and smirking.

"Stop that," I gave him a gentle push. "I actually came here looking for *you*, but you'd passed out and were otherwise unresponsive to my calls of help. So thanks for that."

"Why would you come looking for me?" Mark asked, frowning.

"I don't know," I felt my face blush, we were in unchartered territory. "Because I knew you'd help me and not ask any questions." I didn't say what I actually thought. Because we were friends, apparently.

"I might have been drunk but I think I would have asked why you were showing up in the middle of the night with your whole life packed into a bag - wait, so, that's *all* you own?"

Mark kicked at the bag with his bare foot. I took the moment to actually look at him and saw something unexpected on his face; care. For some reason it knocked me for six.

I frowned letting the moment come and go, following his gaze to the crumpled bag at my feet.

"What? No. I had to stow the other bags in the tree house-"

"And you just happened to stumble into Dean..." He was trying to make this into some sordid story, I glared at him to shut him up.

"Do you want to know what actually happened or are you just going to make jokes?" The exchange was familiar but it was usually with Rob. The figment of my imagination. Were you cured when you finally admitted you were insane?

He waved his hands at me, urging me to continue. I thought he would have lost interest by now but he was uncommonly patient.

"I was trying to get you to let me in, but you were passed out *drunk*. Dean let me in and basically forced me to stay. I slept in the bed, he slept on the floor." I left out the part where I cried myself to sleep in Rob's room.

"And, what are you doing now? Dining and dashing? The walk of shame?" He was enjoying the jokes a little too much for my liking.

"I'm going to pick up the car and get breakfast, actually...if you'd want to join me?"

My mind reeled off a kind of mantra, in hopes I'd somehow discover I had secret powers of influence. Please-say-no-please-say-no-please-say-no.

"Nah, I have to have a shower. You go... can you get me a muffin?" This time it was me who wiggled my eyebrows at him.

"First getting drunk and now processed sugar? It's true what they say, it *is* a slippery slope." I stood up and began pulling jeans and a t-shirt from my bag.

"Whatever... maybe just a granola bar, then." He slapped me on the butt as he walked into the bathroom and closed the door.

As if I'd been holding my breath I felt exhilarated that I'd side stepped further questioning. As long as I got out of here before Dean woke up I'd be fine.

After I dressed I went to the window and opened it wide. I lowered my bag out and dropped it down to the grass. It landed with a soft thud, I just hoped the garden wasn't water logged.

Without the bag I moved onto phase two; get out of the house.

I had made it down the stairs, through the hallway, past the living room door and into the kitchen, thinking I'd almost made it when I ran into Rob's mum.

A depressing thought flitted through my mind so quickly I couldn't stop it; she wasn't Rob's mum anymore. Or, more to the point, Rob wasn't her son anymore.

Florence sat in the kitchen with a cup of tea and a pile of toast, like she'd made too much, expecting company that didn't arrive.

I pulled my shoulders back and walked in like it was normal for me to be here so early. If she was surprised to see me she didn't show it. She smiled up at me and held up a slice of toast as an offering.

"Oh, no, I'm OK, thank you." I said, waving her off.

As I got close to her she raised to give me a hug. I remembered the last time I'd seen her had been at the awful incident at my house. I couldn't tell her what had happened it was too humiliating.

"I just came over to pick up the car keys, I had to leave it parked in town yesterday. Dean took the them because I'd had a drink with some friends..." The excuse came so fast I was impressed with myself, I lied on the spot with such finesse Rob would have applauded me.

The mention of drinks with friends made her face light up, she was visibly happy which made me feel terrible.

"Oh I hope you had fun, it's about time you started getting out again." She smiled softly but her words were sharper than she'd intended.

Despite her cheery face her demeanour was off. She seemed less depressed than she had been but there was still that longing in her eyes. For a moment I thought about telling her about Rob.

"Is Dean up?" She asked, smiling. The moment passed. It wasn't fair to bring Rob back into our lives so vividly when he was finally starting to fade. Well, not him but the pain of the memory. Hearing a sound out in the hallway sped up my escape plan. My ability to remain aloof was starting to waiver.

"No I think he's still asleep, but I ran into Mark and he gave me the keys." I patted my pocket and smiled as normally as I could, hoping it didn't look like a grimace, though it felt like one. "I'd better get going."

I headed for the back door, each step a victory.

"Amelia, you're doing OK, aren't you? You're not, alone? I don't want you to be alone…" Her words stopped me in my tracks but I didn't turn around, her words had slipped into my heart, between my ribs where other words hadn't been able to penetrate.

"I'm not alone, I have you guys! I'll see you later, OK?" I smiled over my shoulder as I left the house, ignoring the fact that Florence's eyes were shining with unshed tears.

It took all my determination to walk past the window without looking back. I knew my face would give me away.

As soon as I'd cleared the zone I ran to grab my bag, pushing the thought of a sad grieving mother, broken brothers, a workaholic father and a dead best friend from my mind. Sadder still; I didn't even have to worry about not thinking about my own family. I'd given up on them the moment I'd closed the front door for the last time.

I aimed to leave the way I came in; grabbing my bags and cut through the back of the garden, over the fence and make it to the road that led into the town. My steps almost faltered when I stole one last look at the house. A ghostly figure stood looking out of the kitchen window. From this far away I couldn't tell who it was but they were definitely looking around for something, or someone.

I pulled myself away, breaking the gravitational pull I'd felt for so many years. If it was Dean looking to see where I'd gone I had to move quickly.

I'd planned on heading through the centre of town to where I'd parked the car but that might be the most obvious route so I deviated. The plan was slap dash at best anyway. Planning was something I loved to do, this flying by the seat of my pants business was more Rob's style but I felt pretty good about it. Cutting through the local high school grounds I made my way to the train station, laden with the few bags that contained everything important in my life.

✿

The sound of the front door opening jolted me from my near hysteria and I looked up to see Mark at the door.

"Are you coming in?" He asked, his voice was gruff, hostile even; his shirt was untucked and tie loosened, his messy dark hair only added to his roughly handsome face, which at the moment could only mirror my inner turmoil.

Frustration and anger crackled in the air around him making him seem unhinged, if not a little bit scary. He'd loved Rob, obviously. He loved having a little brother to push around and now God only knows how he felt, but whatever it was it was hurt and ugly and it didn't like me.

I looked up at him and nodded my response, and he walked away, leaving the door wide.

Luckily not many people had come back to the house, probably out of some respect for the fact that Mrs Wood was a wreck. No one wanted to see it, least of all her friends it seemed.

Word had already gotten out that there would be a party for the wake turned birthday party in a weeks' time so the obligation to attend today was left hanging in the air like a deflating balloon.

In that moment I let myself forget about Rob appearing to me, blaming it on a lapse in my mental state; it was surely normal. I could move on.

Then I saw him poke his head out from the front door.

"Well come on then – let's see what my funeral looks like." He said, like anything about this was normal. When I didn't answer his face softened. "Don't let me go through this alone."

When he vanished back through the door I hesitantly followed, his words cutting deeper than I thought possible.

A ghost? A ghost? Rob was a damn ghost? Surely it was safer to think I was losing the plot... ghosts? I couldn't stop my mind from speeding to a million differ-

ent thoughts and worries at once, so when I walked into the living room I almost ran into Mr Wood.

"Sorry Amelia, please...excuse me." He said, shuffling past me, trying not to touch me, smelling of alcohol.

Part of me didn't blame him, I was half tempted to reach for the bottle myself but I was scared my sanity would plummet to even lower depths.

I navigated the room to sit next to Mrs Wood, keeping my eyes averted from her blotchy face. There was nothing I could do when she wrapped her arm around me and silently cried into my shoulder.

My inability to comfort her tore into my heart, surely another sign I was broken. When my pathetic hand patting became pointless she excused herself and went to lie down, exhausted by the grief. The rest of the day fell apart without the matriarchal guidance Florence usually offered. Eventually Dean and I ushered the few people who'd come back to the house out and I left feeling like I'd been the most useless person in the world. Rob followed me home, trailing behind, not saying a word. His hands deeply thrust into his pockets like he did when he was feeling down or thinking too hard.

We fell into a routine after that. I would go to the house and Rob would wander around, watching his family, watching me and generally making me feel like a crazy person.

If Rob found it difficult to watch he never made it known. He watched with a jaded detachment that scared me. If he was in my mind I wondered if he was a vision of my true emotions.

We became a team; noticing the little things his family did, commenting on them, like we were watching a reality TV show.

His father worked a lot. More than he ever used to, if it was possible. When he didn't work, he drank; lightly though, manageable. He wasn't the type to get wasted, he had more class than that. Plus, I think it would have taken a crate of *vodka to knock him out; he was a burly, like the twins – strong and athletic and generally huge. I could imagine him as some sort of order-barking general in a war.*

It took us a few days to even broach the subject of how Rob was still around, once we'd decided to move away from the 'insane' idea. Rob liked the idea that he was like Patrick Swayze in Ghost; unfinished business or something. It wasn't that I didn't think it was possible but more like I didn't like the idea of him having any more unfinished business than life itself. I kept my mouth shut, it was easier that way and eventually we stopped talking about it.

After five days I went back to work; I needed to get back to normality. Despite everyone thinking it was to distract myself from the pain, it wasn't. How could I be in pain when my best friend was still around, albeit as a ghost that no one else could see. Even if I was crazy it wasn't hurting anyone.

CHAPTER 17

I alternated between a half walk, half run as I made my way to the station with my bags in tow. The fresh air helped me clear my head and keep on my path. With each step I felt the opposing thought slam against the pavement; Go. Stay. Go. Stay.

Using the age old 'he loves me, he loves me not' logic I carried on, relying on fate to decide what my final step would be.

The only plan I had was the one Rob and I had talked about, I had no contingency, nowhere to go if I landed on 'stay'.

A sharp pain in my chest reminded me I was still carrying him around despite his disappearance. No, his death. My heart ached at the memory of his face, his laugh which could get me to smile no matter what.

The fantasy of me and him older, always laughing, living in a house together like a sitcom from TV flitted into my mind. It was how I always thought my life would turn out but now my future was as empty as my bedroom was.

Leaving seemed like the only thing to do and a fresh start looked shiny on the horizon but the memory of the sleeping Dean I'd left behind, with all the mixed confused emotions, made me wonder whether I was making the right decision.

Stay. Go. Stay. Go.

Everyone would be better off without me here right now. My parents didn't want to see me. Fine. The Wood's needed time to get over Rob's death and, as much as they tried to convince me, I didn't think I should be there for that. The constant reminder.

If I couldn't even look in the mirror without deflating inside it was unfair to make them look at me.

I crossed the road and entered the station. It was still early and the place was peacefully quiet. The departures board, the only high tech modern feature in the old fashioned stained glass station, showed a list of trains that shot out all over the country.

I skimmed the list to find the one I needed. London. From London I could get to Paris and from Paris I was free.

I could travel Europe and find somewhere to live, work, get on with things. I'd be fine. Sure it wasn't as far away as I originally planned, but at the end of the day it was far enough away that I could lose myself in another culture. Forget who I was, what had happened; for the time being anyway.

The door to the ticket booth squeaked when I pushed it open, cutting into the undisturbed air.

I was told by a stocky old man with a heavy brush-like moustache that it would cost £89 including tax, to get to London alone. It seemed like a good starting point so, after digging my hand into my backpack to find the envelope of cash, I handed over the money.

"Rob a bank?" He asked, handing the change over along with the ticket. His eyebrows crept in closer to his eyes as he frowned at me, his eyes flicking from my face to the handful of money.

"Birthday money." I lied, quickly. "When's the next train?"

He regarded me for another second, like he was debating whether he should check an old-school fax machine to see if any wanted posters had been sent through. Eventually he pointed to his screen.

"An hour away, on time." He said just before he jerked his head up, eyes glancing past me to someone who'd started to queue behind me.

"Sorry." I said, keeping my eyes to the ground as I shuffled back out onto the platform. The last thing I needed was for someone to recognise me and tip someone off about where I was.

The morning was cool but, after the rain in the night, the day was bright with a fresh breeze. It was welcome on my skin and despite the goose-bumps that rose on my arms when a gust blew down the tracks I felt warm.

I crouched next to my bag and went to put the money back into hiding when a slip of yellow paper caught my eye, sticking out of the top of my passport.

Frowning, I opened the book to find a post-it stuck inside.

My heart raced at the sight of the cursive handwriting I'd recognise anywhere, the way the letters leaned back, slanting to the left with, all the letters the same size.

Don't ever stop living life - R x

My eyes welled as my breathe caught in my throat.

The note hadn't been there when I'd packed my things, I was sure I would have noticed. With a rush of adrenaline I pulled my phone out, watching as the little light on the front blinked white to signify the voicemail.

It wasn't something I'd even considered but at this moment I knew beyond any doubt who's voice I would hear when I dialled the number to listen to the message.

At first the static was overpowering, the crackle and pop of a bad connection buzzed in my ear. Pressing my hand against my other ear I strained to hear the sound beneath the white noise.

"...it's like nothing I've ever seen before Amelia..." Rob's voice pierced through the void like a lightning bolt against a dark sky.

Fumbling I mashed my finger against the screen to re-start the message. When it played again I found I could make out the start much better.

"Something's changed, I don't know how to explain it. I wanted to say goodbye but I think you've gone now," He sounded happy, excited. "I think I understand what I have to do now, you should see it, it's like nothing I've ever seen before Amelia. I hope you get this and you're OK because I'm OK, I know why I kept having to go back. You should see the amount of flowers they planted for me... I'm going back now. I'll always be with you..."

The phone crackled again and I heard other voices, deeper, talking back and forth and then the phone went dead.

My whole body felt light, like I could float away. I listened to the message again and again. The automated voice on the phone told me it had been left less than thirty minutes ago.

Rob's voice rang in my ears, it flowed through me and I felt every cell of my body buzz with a strange new energy. He had sounded alive again but there was something else in his voice; awe.

If he was still here I had to find him.

I carried my bags back into the ticket office and dropped all but my backpack with my money in it.

"Can I leave these here? I'll be right back!" I didn't wait for an answer as I rushed back out of the door.

Outside the wind seemed to urge me onward, the air at my back I was pushed forwards towards where I was certain Rob was. Despite not being athletic in any way I didn't feel any exertion as I pushed myself forwards, running faster than I ever had.

It wasn't until I finally hit the edge of the grass that I realised I'd reached my destination; the cemetery stretched out in front of me, the old fashioned grave stones jutting out of the group at odd angles like they'd fallen from the sky rather than buried in the dirt.

My heart pounded as I traced the steps I'd only let myself take once. Every few rows of graves the scene became slightly different. The names carved into old crumbled stone changed from Edna, Mary and Harold to Sarah, Charlotte and finally Robert; name printed in gold against the shiny marble stone.

As I approached I worried I'd gotten it wrong but he appeared from under the shade of the tree he'd been buried near; translucent at first and more solid the closer he got.

"You're here." He said, as surprised to see me as I was to see him.

"You're here, too." I couldn't keep the tone from my voice. As much as I felt happy to see him he'd hurt me again, he's left me *again.*

"I finally figured it out." He said, stepping towards me. His hands clasped my hands, he was so happy he was practically glowing. I hadn't seen him like this in a long, long time.

"I thought you'd really gone, Rob, where have you been?" I felt like we were standing on the edge of a cliff, the fear of falling sat in the put of my stomach.

"At first I was just angry, I didn't mean to hurt you but I watched you and you were doing OK so I thought it was for the best." He squeezed me hands and stepped away. I missed his touch instantly because with that one step he already felt a million miles away again.

"I missed you." I said, waiting for him to say he missed me too, but it never came.

"I figured out why I kept coming back here." Rob said, bending down to touch the flowers that had been left for him. "I never told you but every night when you slept this is where I went. I just blinked and here I was. It took me ages to walk back to your house every morning." He sighed and looked up towards the brightening sky at something I couldn't see.

"You came here? Every night? Why didn't you say?" A surge of sadness threatened to overwhelm me.

"I dunno," He shrugged and kicked at the ground. "I didn't want to talk about it, I guess. That's what I figured out, I was coming here because I had to face up to it, I realised it when I left you because I finally started seeing how I didn't belong here anymore."

He turned to face me but rather than look sad he looked relieved. I wish I could have felt the same.

"Do you think being with me stopped you from moving on?" I felt sick at the thought, selfishly. Rob didn't respond with his usual sarcasm, he didn't berate me for not seeing the bigger picture, he smiled like he understood everything I didn't. Like when a parent smiles at a child and tells them they'll understand when they're older.

"No, you helped me realise my life wasn't a total disaster." Rob said, leaning against his grave in his still unrumpled suit.

"So what is it you can see here?" I asked, feeling the tears start to well. I felt like we were in a stage play, running lines. Following a path set out for us already, all we had to do was remember our queues.

"Would you believe me if I told you it was a really bright light? Like, brighter than the sun but it doesn't hurt my eyes." He said with a smirk.

Whether he was lying or not wasn't something I even dared to push.

"The last few times I've been here I've felt something *more*. Like this is where I'm supposed to be - with my body in the ground, how sick is that?" He said with a laugh.

I cringed at the image but there was nothing much I could say, he was on a roll.

"Last night when you came to the house I heard what you told Dean and I realised that no matter what you'd be OK because you're so strong. I think if I stay I'll only make your life hell." He looked at me, waiting. Waiting to see what I'd say because I knew what he was trying to say.

"So you know what to do now? You can just leave?" A tear slid down my cheek. It wasn't that I was sad. I'd already mourned him twice, this time it was relief and happiness. Two feelings I never thought I'd feel again, or at least not for a very long time.

"Would you believe Claire Voyant was right? Apparently I *do* have un-finished business, except it's me, not you." He kicked at his headstone and it was light a cloud had passed over. I shivered.

"What do you mean?" I dreaded his words, the unspoken subject, the cause of everything.

"My life wasn't taken from me, Amelia, I took it from myself. I couldn't own up to it before but now I've seen what I've done I can't escape it. I killed myself... I did it." He stopped, letting the words live around us. The words buzzed like flies.

"You were sick, Rob, you were depressed and you didn't tell anyone. You should have told someone." As much as he'd never acknowledged it, neither had I. Not with anyone. When my parents had sent me to a therapist I refused to acknowledge the subject and I eventually stopped going. Pretending was coping.

"I know. I couldn't keep running away forever I guess. I think that's the key, the only way I can move on is to let it go but...I'm worried about you." He said, and I could see the worry in each line on his forever young face.

"You don't need to worry about me, without you I wouldn't have made it this far." I felt the goodbye lingering. The rest of the world melted away and it was just us.

"I've seen how my darkness spilled into you, you have to live life Amelia, you can't hold onto me and what I did. You have to do whatever you can to be happy, even if it means leaving and never coming back-"

He stopped talking and we both looked towards the entrance to the cemetery. Someone was calling my name; loudly and urgently.

"I think this is it now," Rob grabbed me and pulled me into a hug. When he released me he was transparent again like a mirage. "Don't let my mistakes ruin your life."

He smiled and looked over my shoulder at whoever was coming after me. I followed his gaze and saw Mark running through the grave stones fast. As soon as our eyes locked I felt an absence in the air around me.

Rob's touch was there and then gone in an instant. I spun around and searched for him but he was gone. Like he'd never even been here.

When Mark finally reached me I was kneeling at Rob's grave. Tears spilled down my cheeks but I only felt relief. Relief he'd moved on, relief I wasn't crazy. Nothing about this had been in my mind, it was clear by the way I felt. I couldn't have conjured up this kind of thing, Rob had always been right. I didn't have that good an imagination.

"What the hell was that?" Mark said, kneeing beside me. He gently turned me towards him, checking me over like I'd fallen over or something. I shrugged him off as gently as I could.

"What was what? I just came to say goodbye." I swallowed the lump in my throat.

"I was sure I saw a crazy light over here, like a beam of light... I thought I saw..." Mark trailed off quietly, his eyes falling to the grave and the flowers. "I've only been here once since the funeral."

"I've not been here at all. It's actually quite peaceful." I smiled, imagining Rob was still watching.

In an instant Mark's attitude changed. He stood up and pulled me to my feet, towering over me. His face was set to 'mad'.

"What do you think you're doing?" He snapped at me. Before I could stop him he had my backpack from the ground and he pulled out the train ticket.

"A train to London?" He asked. It was the most concerned I'd ever seen him. His initial anger faded to something more caring, which was strange and made me feel awkward.

"And then to Paris." I said. There was no point in lying now. Everything had worked out in a way that felt difficult but *right*. I went with the feeling, waiting for life to carry me forward.

"Paris? Are you mental? You can't even speak French can you? Why are you going to Paris?" He sighed and did something even more unexpected; he wrapped me up in his arms, hugging me tightly.

"I just wanted to get away for a while." I answered as honestly as I could. There was no point telling him I might never come back. When I pulled away from him he looked hurt, his shoulders hunched like Rob's used to when he was feeling low.

"You can't just run away Amelia, we need you here. You won't be OK on your own." He ran his hand through his hair and stepped back sheepishly. I knew he'd just opened up, possibly more than he ever had in his life.

"I'm fine on my own. Why can't I just have some time for myself?" I argued out of habit but the truth was I wasn't sure I actually wanted to leave now. Saying goodbye to Rob had somehow magically put a lot of things to rest for me, things I didn't even know I needed closure on.

"What about us?" Mark jerked his thumb towards the entrance of the cemetery. "Mum and Dad? Dean and me? Dean was furious when he figured out you'd gone, y'know!"

"What? You told him? What the hell?!" My heart dropped to my feet and I felt nausea roll over me like a wave.

Mark bit his lip, looking like he may have regretted either telling Dean or telling me.

Dean never really lost his temper but when he did it wasn't a pretty sight. He was so calm that any deviation from his usual self was a terrifying concept.

"Well, yeah. Mum mentioned you'd gone to get the car but he said he still had the keys... Mum didn't really see any need to panic but Dean, I don't know, I've never seen him like that," he smiled despite his warning. "He took his keys and stormed out, I literally had to run after him."

The thought of him caring that much was enough to make me regret even going to the house last night, he probably felt like it was his responsibility to look after me now.

"Where is he now?" The trees around us rustled, there was a feeling in the wind that felt like Rob was enjoying watching me panic.

"I managed to convince him that he should go to where you left the car just in case, you know, like there was no need to panic coz you might have gone to the car," He rambled a little, maybe feeling more hungover than he liked to admit. "So I said I'd look around for you as well. Figured you might come here."

"So where did Dean go when he realised I wasn't at the car?"

"I don't know, he wasn't really thinking straight. He thought you were leaving because of last night so he might have gone to the station."

I looked away from him, down at my feet. This mess I'd created.

"I don't know what I'm going to do, if Dean finds me he'll never let me leave. I need a fresh start..." At this point I wasn't sure who I was trying to convince.

"And why do *you* get a fresh start?" He asked, being stern again.

"You could go anywhere you want to Mark, no one's stopping you." Maybe we all needed a break.

"You're wrong. I couldn't leave, not now. Definitely not now, I'm not going to run away just because I'm scared of my life. You have to choose to stay with the ones you love when times get hard."

He stopped talking and we stood in silence, the truth of everything, the harsh reality rearing its ugly head.

There was nothing worse than when Mark was right. His face lit up when he realised he'd hit a nerve. Rob was right. I couldn't let the darkness consume me. If I left it couldn't be because I was running away, I would never forgive myself.

"Well are you going to call him or do I have to?" I said, giving in to logic. I'd never live down the fact that Mark had given actual sage advice.

"Yeah, wait a second." He dug his hand into his pocket, unable to hide the smile that spread across his face.

"Thank god you're here!" Dean came running towards us carrying the bags I'd left at the station. He was out of breath and, from the look on his face, worried. Very worried. His face was unnaturally pale.

Mark looked at me, confused.

"Twin link?" He asked, putting his phone back in his pocket.

It wasn't like Rob's grave was a long shot but it still felt spooky that he's arrived just as we were about to call.

As he approached us he stopped in his tracks, staring at the grave. Clearly I wasn't the only one to avoid the place.

"I was literally just about to call-"Mark said, closing the gap between them.

Dean totally ignored him, pushing past and pulling me into a hug that was so tight I felt my air supply slowly being cut off.

"I was so scared you'd done something..." He whispered, clinging to me.

I let him calm down before I pulled away from him, looking up at his face he was still so pale and worried it broke my heart.

"What would I do?" I didn't understand until he looked down at the grave again. "Oh, Dean, no!"

This time I hugged him. Looking over his shoulder I saw Mark wipe something from his eye. That was probably why they'd both been so worried. A scenario I never would have imagined; first my parents thought I was crazy and now Dean and Mark thought I was capable of following in Rob's mistaken footsteps. I saw myself through their eyes and it was horrible. I was horrible.

"I just saw the bags at the station and I thought you'd done something stupid but then the ticket guy said you'd just left them there so I thought you'd *really* done something stupid because why would you leave your things there?" He looked at me, searching my eyes for answers I didn't think I was ready to give.

"I was leaving but I had to say goodbye..." Even without Rob here I felt him. I think the others did too. "How did you find me?" I asked, trying to gloss over the fact that I'd come so close to abandoning everything.

"Twin link!" Mark exclaimed, like it was the best invention in the world, as though he'd managed to send a message telepathically.

Dean shook his head and smiled at his brother, dismissing him with a raised eyebrow.

"Er, no. I found this with your bags and took a chance." Dean reached into his pocket and pulled out a Polaroid picture.

I took the picture from him and stared at the over-exposed image of me and Rob. My eyes were closed, as they often were when Rob surprised me with a flash bulb.

"I remember this..." My finger traced the lopsided smile on Rob's face. Using my thumb I ran it over the message underneath, the ink still wet enough to smudge a little.

'Really, really good looking friends'.

I laughed out loud at his stupid movie reference.

I'd completely forgotten about its existence. I hadn't taken it with me which meant Rob had been playing ghost matchmaker again, lurking behind doors no doubt.

Little memories from last night surfaced; the figure in the window at night and again in the morning when I left; the blonde hair when I woke in his room in the middle of the night.

"Are you leaving, Amelia?" Dean's voice brought me back to reality, his face sombre. The smile that had found my face faltered.

"She's going to Paris, can you believe it? She can't even speak French." Mark said, speaking for me. His eyes crinkled at the edges as his sarcasm returned.

"I *was* going to get away for a while-" I started to explain but I stopped short. Anything I said would be tainted with a lie so I side stepped. "I guess I wasted my money."

Dean smiled like he'd won something. He stepped towards me, close enough that I could smell his deodorant, close enough that when he leant in to kiss me I hardly had to move to kiss him back.

We kissed as if it were natural to us, as if we always did and always would. It was romantic and perfect despite the location and the grossed-out sounds Mark was making, including the dry heaving.

When we broke apart I was breathless.

"Could you two be any grosser? Let's go home." Mark covered his face with his hands and walked up the path, only dropping his hands when he'd passed a few grave stones, out of our sight.

Home. I had nowhere to go. Panic overtook the peace I'd just felt with Dean's kiss.

"Mark! Hold on." Dean called after his brother, shouting into the silence of the cemetery. He turned to me with a look he'd given me that day he'd whisked me away from my house. "How about we don't go home? How about some company?"

It took a few seconds to understand what he was saying; company. I'd always thought my trip away would include Rob but there was no reason for me to go alone if there was another option.

"Oui." I said, as seriously as I could. After a split-second I burst out laughing, the feeling of happiness was overwhelming but in the best kind of way.

"What's going on?" Mark reappeared, looking between the two of us laughing, he frowned and folded his arms. He'd never been good at being on the outside of a joke.

"Me and Amelia are going to Paris." Dean said, his arm found its way around my shoulder and he pulled me into him. My arm slid around his waist, a perfect fit.

"You mean you, me and Amelia are going to Paris?" Mark corrected like it was his plan all along.

The more Mark opened up to me the more I realised how much he and Rob were alike. All these years we'd treated him like the older brother we kind of wished we didn't have but now I felt like I was seeing the real him for the first time and he wasn't that bad.

"What do you think?" Dean picked up my bag and slung it over his other shoulder, passing my train abandoned bags to Mark to carry.

As we walked out of the last place I'd ever see Rob I felt like everything had actually worked out the way it should have. I made a mental note to let Claire know she'd been right all along.

"I guess the more the merrier, but can we make a rule that you can't spend all your time just chasing after girls?" We walked, the three of us, through the cemetery, passing the names of the dead. I wondered how many of them had come before me and Rob; how many had lingered, how many had been deathless like Rob, and how many had found their way like we had.

"Hey, for starters I don't chase girls, they chase me, and if we're talking about ground rules..." Mark grimaced and made a point of shivering dramatically but he couldn't hide his smile.

"The only ground rule is that you two can't go out drinking together ever again." Dean said. He squeezed his arm around me and planted a kiss on my head. "Oh, and I am *not* going to be the one to tell mum and dad."

CHAPTER 18

The willow tree was in full bloom and the tiny leaves of the new under-growth brushed my skin as I lay in its shadow. I remembered the last time I'd sat here and the echoes of sadness panged in my heart. Someone came and sat down behind me, hands squeezing my shoulders. I smiled and leaned back into them, breathing out as I relaxed into the pressure of the massage.

"Are you ready to go?" Dean asked, leaning forward he brushed the hair out of my eyes and kissed the top of my head. I mumbled no and closed my eyes, enjoying the sun too much to go into the house to face his parents.

"Yes... and no." I said, grabbing his hands so his arms encompassed me. We sat there for a few minutes just enjoying the fresh air when I heard Mark approaching.

"Come on, dad says if we don't go now we'll have to get a taxi and I'm not allowed to get in a taxi because the last time I puked." He ran his hand through his hair, and smiled.

Ever since the day at the cemetery he'd been a different person. We'd all found closure in one way or another but for Mark it was more apparent. He'd let go of whatever guilt he'd had for Rob's depression and he was treating me like the sister he'd always wanted. Which was creepy in some ways but I still liked it.

"Once again I'm putting a ban on any drinking of any kind... for both of you." Dean stood up and pulled me with him.

The branches of the tree swayed in the wind, pushing them in towards me so the leaves brushed against my skin. *Goodbye*, they seemed to whisper to me.

Mr and Mrs Wood had actually taken the idea of the three of us going to Paris very well. Florence, in particular, set about planning everything for us immediately and Mr Wood, who I still couldn't bring to call by his first name, told my parents I was staying with them indefinitely. Apparently they didn't put up too much of a fight.

"I'm never drinking again, anyway." I said. We walked up to the house and picked up our bags, squeezing them into the boot of the car.

We'd paid the guy at the ticket office to change the date of my ticket for the week after and Dean and Mark bought a ticket each as well. The ticket man's moustached face seemed glad to see the back of me.

"Do you have everything?" Mrs Wood asked, hugging us all before we left. We were only going for a month but she acted like it was forever. I understood why.

"Yes mum, we'll call when we get there, OK?" Dean hugged her twice to reassure her and then we left.

Coming out of the Gare Du Nord was surreal. The blue sky reflected in the glass windows that decorated the arched entrance; it was magical. I expected the figures that stood atop watching and waiting to wave or smile but they remained stony faced.

It was the end of one journey and the start of another. The three of us crossed the road to take the Metro to our hotel, dodging tourists who were already taking pictures of their surroundings.

As Dean and Mark descended the steps I stopped in my tracks. A tall guy with sandy hair and kind green eyes with a camera in his hands caught my eye standing outside a café with a red awning.

As if he could feel me looking at him he looked up, meeting my eyes. With a smile he lifted his camera and took a photo of me, a lopsided smile crept on his face.

"Hey, are you coming?" Dean grabbed my hand, distracting me, pulling my attention back. He lifted his sunglasses and gave me a look that sent a shiver down my spine.

When I looked back to the café the guy was gone, swept away by the busy flow of people.

"Yeah, let's go." I said, taking his sunglasses from him and putting them on with a laugh, hoping he didn't notice the tears in my eyes.

THE END

ABOUT THE AUTHOR

Frances June is the pen name of author Samantha Cummings.

She spends most of her time in her small flat in Cheshire with her long-term partner Brian and when she's not writing she's either cooking, eating copious amounts of noodles, staring guiltily at her TBR pile, or walking her dog – the vivacious Juno the Beagle.

She is extremely passionate about self-publishing but still dreams of going through the full querying process to publish commercially, saving her given name for that miracle.

Check out more books by Frances June:

The Fantasy Girl Series:
Etta!
Baby Steps

Seven Princes of Hell Saga:
Saul

www.samantha-cummings.com

Printed in Great Britain
by Amazon

20143663R00159